Abc

JACK-KNIFED

JACK-KNIFED

Wonny Lea

To John.

My biggest fan, my biggest critic, and my best mate.

Chapter One

Paula Williams finished doing her make-up, put on her probably-too-high platform heels, and donned the long, lightweight multi-coloured coat she had bought in the January sales. She wore a blue sleeveless top and white linen trousers, and didn't really need to wear a coat at all in the warm spring air, but she'd fallen in love with one of the few designer labels she had in her wardrobe and was determined to wear it as often as she could.

The weather had been scorching over the past week or so. According to Derek the weatherman, temperatures in the city had reached the high 20s, but as Paula was fair-skinned she could justify covering up: even the evening sunshine turned her skin bright red.

She had inherited her colouring from her father, and her mother had often said that Paula's naturally dark chestnut hair and olive-green eyes were the only good things her father had left behind when he'd buggered off and left them. Paula couldn't be considered an outstanding beauty, but she was certainly attractive, and her friendly, outgoing nature drew people to her – as she'd sometimes found to her cost …

She locked the door of her flat in Claude Road carefully, and felt very angry that one of the other residents in the house had once again left the main front door on the latch. There had been a spate of break-ins in the surrounding streets, so many in fact that the local police had made house-to-house visits and posted leaflets in an attempt to get home owners to become more security conscious.

Paula adjusted the lock and slammed the door loudly, hoping that the message would get through to the other tenants, but the mixture of loud, tuneless music and drunken laughter from various parts of the house told her she was wasting her time.

To be fair to her neighbours, she hardly heard a sound from them during the week when, as they were all students, she assumed they were either at one of the colleges or sleeping behind their forever-closed curtains. It was usually around 6 p.m. on a Friday that the house woke up, and stayed awake and rocking until the early hours of Sunday morning.

Still, she would be happy when she could afford to put down a good deposit on a home of her own, and her recent promotion to manager of the travel agency she worked for on Albany Road had brought that day nearer. Paula had been saving every penny she could manage since her acrimonious split with Chris almost nine years ago. Even now, though, simply remembering him caused her to feel anxious, and she realised that she was breathing faster than she had been a few minutes ago.

It wasn't surprising that the thought of Chris Benson was having this effect on her, as for seven months after she had ended their relationship, he had stalked her and did everything he could think of to make her life a total misery.

In the early days of their relationship he had been charm personified, and Paula had to admit that she had been very happy and more than a little swept away. They had moved from meeting to living together at breakneck speed, and then Paula found that more and more it was just the two of them, always, to the exclusion of Paula's friends and relatives.

It had taken her some time to realise that Chris didn't have any friends that she knew of, and he frequently described his relatives as 'a waste of space'. The first sign Paula had of a very different side to Chris's nature was when she had quite innocently suggested that they invite his parents to lunch one Sunday. He had flown into an instant, uncontrollable rage, shouting at Paula and throwing his cup full of steaming black coffee against the kitchen door, smashing the cup and one of the glass panels.

Copious expensive presents and ardent lovemaking followed this incident, as Chris declared his undying love for Paula, and tried to explain that she was the only thing that mattered to him, that all they needed was each other. Happy for the most part, Paula initially went along with this, but she soon began to realise that although Chris constantly told her he loved her, what he really loved was being in control of her. This scared her, and her fear was reinforced when she realised that her friends and family had stopped ringing. By now she was wary enough not to mention this to Chris and instead made her own enquiries.

Everyone she spoke to told her that Chris had been in touch and had explained to them that Paula was depressed and close to a breakdown. He had asked every one of them to ensure that she was left alone to sort herself out. With the benefit of hindsight, Paula remembered many phone calls when Chris had rushed to the phone, telling the caller never to ring again and slamming the phone back into its cradle. His explanation had been that they were getting nuisance calls and that it was best that he dealt with them, being a man and less likely to be intimidated. At the time, Paula was totally unaware that it was in fact her friends and relatives who were being lied to and verbally abused in her name.

The break up was like something out of a psycho film. First of all, the violence, including a blow to Paula's face and the destruction of all the Wedgwood china she had inherited from an aunt. Then the renewed, gratuitous demonstrations of so-called love and affection. Paula moved in with to her friend Suzanne's home just outside Cowbridge, and was completely freaked out the following day when six different florists delivered bouquets to Suzanne's door, starting with a dozen red roses.

The number increased by a further dozen every hour, finishing at 3 p.m. when a bemused young man rang her doorbell and handed over a bunch, almost as big as himself, of seventy-two red roses. Each delivery had arrived with a card hand written by Chris for Paula with the same message: 'You are and will always be mine and no one else will ever love you like I do.'

The words, now as then, sent a chill through Paula, and she shook her head to prevent any further memories of the hell she had endured in the months following that day, the day she received a total of two hundred and fifty-two red roses sent not with love, but with a deep-seated desire to possess, control, and dominate her.

She kept walking.

The Eurovision Song Contest had been broadcast every year since 1956 and was still watched by millions. Paula wondered just how many groups of sad people on Planet Earth were planning a similar evening to her. She was meeting three friends, and every year for the past seven years they had gathered for an evening of listening to bizarre contemporary songs, only made bearable by copious amounts of good food and wine. It had become a cult event for them and she always looked forward to it.

Tonight, everyone was going to Mark's house, and Paula knew that it would be a special occasion. Although Mark was the only male member of the group, he was more of a woman than Paula herself, Anne, or Suzanne, she thought fondly. His house would be aglow with strategically placed candles, and he would have been cooking all day and producing the most delicious Turkish desserts imaginable. Paula felt her taste buds making her mouth water as she looked forward to some *tuluba*, the semolina doughnuts in syrup, and those almond cookies he called *acibadem*. She smiled to herself as she thought of his speciality, *diber dudaği* – a sweet paste soaked in a light syrup and shaped to resemble ladies' lips.

Nothing would ever be further from Mark's mind than real-life ladies' lips, as his only interest in any woman was friendly – and to be fair, no woman could do better than to have Mark as a friend.

Although all his close friends knew that Mark was gay, he

4

gave the outward impression of being a good-looking heterosexual hunk of a man, just over six feet tall with his thirteen-stone build being one of total muscular fitness. Suzanne had often commented that it was a terrible waste no woman would ever enjoy him, and that there would be no little Marks growing up to delight future generations, but they all agreed it was good to have the friendship of a man without the usual jockeying for a position in his bed. Paula turned the corner into Claude Place and headed towards Albany Road, her mind still on Mark and remembering his version of the events that had brought him to Cardiff.

Mark was a bit older than Paula, having been born in August 1968 on the new council estate at Penrhys in the Rhondda valleys. His father was a miner, and Mark had often recalled happy memories of his early childhood being at home with his mother when his two older sisters were at school. Their new home was his mother's pride and joy, with its coal-fired boiler that gave them heating throughout the house and oodles of hot water, which they used constantly because the cost was included in their rent.

Mark had darker memories of the weekends on the estate; of the Friday and Saturday nights that often saw usually placid men turn into bullish, aggressive animals after too much beer, lashing out at each other and at women and even children who deigned to look 'the wrong way' at them.

He was five or six years old when things started to go really wrong. The oil crisis of 1973 had put an enormous strain on his family, as the increased cost of fuel had to be recovered by the council with ever-increasing rents. Many of their neighbours opted to move to other villages in the Rhondda where they were able to take more control of their heating costs.

Gradually, more and more of their new neighbours were families dependent on state benefits, and the men who were unemployed had nothing better to do than hang around the place. The estate quickly deteriorated through lack of maintenance by the council, and the unkempt appearance encouraged the dumping of anything from litter to torched cars.

It didn't take the new, streetwise neighbours long to realise that Mark was not a little boy who enjoyed kicking a rugby ball about, or scrapping, and he became known as 'Mummy's boy', a name that was tame in comparison to what was to be endured as he grew to become a teenager. Mark's father found it hard to cope with the taunts and the innuendoes of his fellow miners, and pushed his son into physical sports in an effort to knock what he called the 'namby-pamby nonsense' out of him.

When recalling these years of his childhood, Mark had told Paula how he remembered his mother soaking him in the bath at night and trying not to hurt him as she dried his cuts and bruises. He believed she felt his hurt and in some way blamed herself for his predicament. After all, the sort of son that he was developing into could have inherited nothing from his beer-swilling, rugby-playing, loud-mouthed father, who was one of the boys in every respect. His relationship with his father deteriorated as the latter took to using his fists to knock some testosterone into his small son, and his mother's defence of Mark made her another target for this angry, disappointed man to land his punches on.

After a particularly brutal Saturday night beating for both Mark and his mother, Mark's eldest sister Sarah intervened, and she got in the way of a vicious punch from her father that sent her reeling and crashing into the edge of the kitchen table. It would seem that her neck was broken on impact, for she never regained consciousness and died in Prince Charles Hospital in Merthyr Tydfil two days later.

The lasting memory Mark had of the event was one of silence. Sarah had been screaming and screaming at her father and then suddenly you could hear a pin drop. He still believed that this accounted for the fact that he was unable to cope with silence and the first thing he did in the morning was switch on the radio. Music or sound of some sort or another had to be with him throughout the day.

Paula could barely begin to imagine the impact of the horror of that night on a vulnerable little boy. He was already damaged by physical and mental abuse and by his own feelings that he was different from the other boys in his class, and now he believed that he was in some way responsible for his sister lying still and so pale on the kitchen floor.

The ambulance crew, the police, and the social workers came and went at different times during that evening, as did a constant stream of nosy neighbours. Most of them had never previously been inside the Wilsons' house but at that time had pretended to be part of a caring community.

Mark had told Paula how he remembered a skinny policeman with lots of eyebrows taking him to his parents' bedroom so that he could say goodbye to his mother and sister and hearing talk of a place of safety and being taken into care. Safety and care were comforting words but all Mark wanted to do was stay with his mother in spite of the fact that she didn't even seem to know he was there, and just stared ahead crying for Sarah and saying that it wasn't Bob's fault.

If his father was not to blame for hurting his sister then Mark thought he must be responsible, and that that was why the policeman was taking him away.

Mark couldn't understand why this had to happen when Amy was staying. He hadn't been aware that his distraught mother had told police and social workers that she couldn't cope with her son and begged them to take him away. It seemed that she was now holding Mark responsible for the anger and hatred he had instilled in his father.

He had screamed and held on to the handle of his mother's bedroom door but she had not got up to help him and Amy, the youngest of his two sisters, just sat on the edge of the bed sucking her thumb. Bizarrely, Mark thought she was lucky that their father had been taken away as he would have shouted at her for sucking her thumb as he had always done, calling her an eight-year-old baby bunting and threatening to tell her friends she still wore nappies.

One of the social workers gently removed Mark's hand from the door handle and held it very firmly, leading him down the stairs and out into a dark and drizzly February night. The rain

7

and the lateness of the hour had not prevented the sightseers and Mark had never seen so many of their neighbours in the same place at the same time, and again he heard that strange sound of silence everywhere.

Paula thought back to Mark's accounts of the next few years of his life. He had told her bit by bit over a long period of time, and usually after a couple of bottles of wine, how he had been passed from one foster home to another. Until he was fifteen Mark had never stayed in one place longer than eight months, although foster parents and social workers were always keen to point out that this was because of exceptional circumstances and not because of any problems with Mark himself.

The best possible luck had come Mark's way in August 1983, just ten days before his fifteenth birthday, when yet again he had packed up his belongings and got into the car of his most recent social worker to be taken to a couple living in Cardiff.

By then Mark was a tall, good-looking boy, but far too thin and not surprisingly lacking in social graces. His churlish attitude served mainly to disguise an underlying shy nature and a decided uncertainty about his place between being a child and a grown-up, and his preference between men and women. The couple he was taken to were Norman and Sandy Harding, and all he knew about them at the time was that they were older than the norm for fostering. They had been a pain in the side of the local authority for some time in their efforts to be considered suitable as long-term foster parents.

Already in their forties, the couple were seen by the authorities as a definite 'no' for caring for young children, but an unusually enlightened official had eventually agreed that they had a lot to offer some of the children who were nearing the end of their childhood placements and were needing support to take them out of foster care and into independent lives.

Regrettably, their first opportunity had been with Sophie, a fourteen-year-old girl who after just three weeks at the Hardings' had invited half the teenage drug scene of Cardiff into her new home, an event culminating in the theft of some of Sandy's jewellery and Norman taking a beating before handing over just £22.50, which was all the cash in his pocket at the time.

Maybe most couples would have turned their back on thoughts of any more fostering, but Norman knew what a difference a good experience could make to a child, as he himself had been fostered in Cardiff at the age of thirteen by a fantastic couple with three children and two dogs of their own, and a home that had had rules and discipline, but only in the context of love and lots of fun.

He had lived with the family even after his eligibility for foster care had ended, and when the Parry family had decided to move to Australia in 1962, Norman had gone with them and become a partner in the very successful company set up by Jim Parry with his two sons and his daughter, Sandy.

The company, SurfitA, was involved in every aspect of surfing that Southern Australia had to offer, with its base close to Boomerang Beach in New South Wales. Local staff were taken on by the company to make surfboards to suit the local conditions, and after a few years the name SurfitA was on all the gear of any serious surfer, not just in Australia but around the world.

What a place to be a man in his late twenties – and little wonder that Norman fell hopelessly in love with Sandy Parry, and proposed to her one evening as they were watching the dolphins surfing around Boomerang's northern headland. Their life together followed the fairly typical pattern of many married couples', with the ups of weddings and births, and the downs of family illnesses and deaths, but their biggest regret was having no children of their own.

It was Sandy who always wanted to return to the real Wales, as she called it, and was on the eve of her forty-second birthday, as they sat reflecting their lives a little distance away from the frenzied celebrations of their relatives and neighbours, that Norman finally agreed and their preparations to return to Cardiff began. They spent hours considering the parts of the capital that they remembered from growing up there, but were amazed by the changes, sometimes forgetting that it was more than twenty years since they were last there and then laughing as they remembered how much they had changed in that time.

The house they chose was just outside the main city, in the village of Whitchurch, chosen because the area seemed relatively unchanged but was not far from the city centre, and the house itself was old and could do with complete modernisation. All of the negotiations for the purchase of the house were done over the phone and the sale went through without them having set foot in their new home. They employed an architect and builders through a brilliant project manager, Elly, so that by the time they set foot in Cardiff the house was just as they wanted it, even having the fridge and freezer well-stocked.

Elly met them at the Cardiff Wales Airport and drove them to the house that turned out to be everything they had hoped for and more. It was as they prepared their first meal in their new house that they decided to share their good fortune and came to the conclusion, as they were unlikely to be considered as viable adoptive parents, already being past the usual child-bearing age, that fostering could be an option. From that moment on, all their efforts went into transforming their new house into a home for whichever children they were fortunate enough to be entrusted with.

It hadn't occurred to either of them that it would take such a long time for the authorities to process their application and indeed for it to be rejected in the first instance as they were definitely considered to be too old to foster younger children. So eventually, after almost three years of being subjected to every form of scrutiny and putting aside their first bad experience, Norman and Sandy welcomed Mark into their home and, as it turned out, into their lives.

From day one, Mark and Norman hit it off, and Sandy was fascinated to see how easily her husband related to the needs of this strangely sensitive young man, whose background could easily have made him aggressive and bitter but instead had taught him to appreciate every bit of good fortune, no matter how trivial. Small wonder that Mark thought all his birthdays had come at once when he was shown his room equipped with a sound system and even a computer, things he had previously only dreamed of or shared with others, but only at their convenience.

The next three years were exceptional by anyone's standard, but to Mark they were beyond his wildest dreams. He finished his education at Whitchurch High, where diversity seemed to be the norm, and where the more out of the ordinary you were the more likely it was that you'd be accepted. For the first time in his life he met other boys of his age who were openly gay and, although he didn't meet anyone he wanted to be with, he felt the shadow of being different lifted from his shoulders, and was at ease with the girls in his class, who knowing where his true feelings lay were happy to accept him as a friend.

He met Paula and Suzanne, and although both were a couple of years younger than him the three formed an instant friendship, and the girls become regular visitors to Mark's home in Whitchurch. Sandy was only too pleased to cook for them and generally make them welcome. She felt so happy that Mark was able to treat their house as the home he had not had since he was a very young child.

At eighteen, Mark went to art college, and it was there he met Anne, who was a couple of years older than him and had joined the class a couple of weeks after the start of the first term. She seemed to make a beeline for Mark, and although her spiked blond hair and body piercings were not to his taste, they soon became partners in all their college activities. On finishing college, both she and Mark got jobs at the same graphic design company on Newport Road in the east of the city. Anne was invited to Mark's home and was accepted as the fourth member of the group. They all shared their secrets of growing up, from relationships to ambitions and from thoughts to downright silly ideas, seemingly safe in the friendship they all thought was solid and unquestioning.

It was now well over twenty years since they had all first met, but the friendship had stood the test of time, and so it was that all three girls were on their way to Mark's house for one of their eat, drink, and gossip sessions. Sandy and Norman, now in their mid-seventies, had made numerous friends and contributed greatly to the life of their chosen community, but their proudest day had been Friday 16th June 2000, when after years of consideration they had finally adopted Mark. Paula knew that they were planning a surprise visit to Australia to celebrate the tenth anniversary of that special occasion. Although still regular visitors to Sandy and Norman in Whitchurch, the girls were now going to Mark's house that was near the top of Penylan Hill in the Roath Park area of Cardiff.

Five years earlier it had been Norman's idea that Mark should get a house of his own and be more independent. His adoptive parents helped him both psychologically and financially to make the break. It was at the time that SurfitA was sold, and Norman and Sandy became not just comfortably off but extremely wealthy. In spite of his protests that he should not be taking their money, Mark was finally persuaded that Norman and Sandy had no one else who needed it and there was no one they would rather give it to than their chosen son.

Mark had gone for a three-bedroom detached property, one of the older style Edwardian houses, in excellent structural condition but with a somewhat dated décor. The garden was well-established, with mature shrubs and trees, and had obviously been created by someone with a love of nature, as throughout the year different flowers emerged and then retreated, to make way for new colours and scents as the seasons changed.

The interior gave Mark a blank canvas on which to stamp his own creativity, and with the help of Norman, Sandy, and the girls, he created a contemporary but warm and inviting home – especially, thought Paula, when the real coal fire was lit. His one big indulgence was his 'doona', a Christmas present he bought for himself in 2009 when the new John Lewis store had opened in Cardiff.

Paula recalled Mark telling her about the pretty young girl in her smart new uniform who had explained that the sofa was called a doona after the Australian word for a duvet, and that's just what it felt like! Mark wasn't sure if it was the Australian link or the understated style and sink-into-it sumptuousness that made him part with £3500 for a pale coffee-coloured sofa, but it had become the centrepiece from which the design for the rest of the room had developed.

Over the years, and usually after more than your average amount of Cabernet Sauvignon, Mark had spoken about his biological family and of the efforts made by a number of social workers in the early days to get them reunited. He had learned that his father was convicted of manslaughter and spent several years in prison, and that the experience had made him a bitter and violent man, but one who was able to say the right things in terms of remorse and contrition to the authorities, and so after seven years he got early release.

It had been arranged for Bob Wilson to stay at a hostel in Pontypridd on his release, but at the first opportunity he had made his way by bus and taxi to what he still believed to be his family home in Penrhys. Bob knew that Joan still lived there, and that following their divorce, which she had secured against his wishes, she had moved in an old drinking mate of his called Barry Evans.

Joan had gone to pieces following the death of her daughter and the scandal of Bob's trial and imprisonment. As time went by she had grown to hate the little boy she had once loved so dearly, and was encouraged by Amy, who had always been jealous of her brother, to have nothing to do with him. She took to drinking as a means of blotting out his memory and sought the company of other men to compensate for the absence of her husband.

Things had not worked out well with Barry, though, and he was proving to be more than handy with his fists. He also had an increasing desire not for Joan, but for her daughter Amy, then aged fifteen. Bob knew about this because during the last year of his sentence Amy had been visiting him in prison. She had been only too willing to fill her father in on all the sordid details of her life, with her mother's casual flings and Barry's drunken and lecherous outbursts.

Amy, with her mousy-coloured curly hair and hangdog expression, was not an attractive teenager, and her life experiences had, not surprisingly, made her morose and difficult, so that she had few friends and lacked any loving relationships in her life.

Bob arrived on the Penrhys Estate that everyone now agreed had been badly designed and built and dogged by problems from the beginning, and which was now regarded as a dumping ground for people who had nowhere else to go. For Bob there was nowhere else he wanted to go, because when brooding in his prison cell for seven years this return visit had been the sole focus of his very existence.

Although Mark was not sure of the exact details, it seemed that his father had arrived at their old family home to find Amy fending off the unwelcome sexual attentions of Barry, while her mother was slumped at that memorable kitchen table drinking herself into oblivion. Years of prison self-preservation and wilfully built-up hatred and anger had overcome Bob and he beat Barry to a pulp, before turning his attentions on Joan, who would have ended up just as dead as Barry if Amy hadn't intervened – it was as if with some small variations history was repeating itself.

Bob fled the scene, and with no exit plan in place was picked up within hours by the police and returned to prison. Joan suffered an even worse fate, as during the violence she had received a serious spinal injury that was potentially life-threatening. Consequentially, after several months in different hospitals, and numerous protracted and difficult surgical interventions Joan was transferred to a specialist spinal injuries unit at Rookwood Hospital, where she died just two weeks later.

Social workers and a psychologist specialising in the behaviour of displaced teenagers from dysfunctional families had spoken to Mark at the time of his mother's death and they had decided there was nothing to be gained by him attending the funeral. It was recorded that this was Mark's decision, but in reality he had by the age of thirteen learned that acquiescing with people in authority meant that they soon went away, he presumed to deal with less compliant people than himself, and that suited him well.

Mark was told that his sister Amy had been taken into care at the time her mother had been attacked, but he had no idea of her whereabouts, and his social workers had always told him she had become psychologically unstable as a result of everything that had happened to her and that meeting up 'would not be a good idea'. On reflection, meetings with his mother and his sister had not been a good idea for as long as he could remember, and he had only seen his sister once since his father had killed Sarah. Meetings had been set up, but Joan would at the last minute ring social services feigning sickness for either her or Amy, and one social worker had told Mark that Amy was a disturbed young lady who seemed to think her little brother Mark was to blame for all the family problems.

When things had improved for Mark, and with the help of Sandy and Norman, he made some attempts to contact his sister, but to no avail, and so finally they agreed that as she had gone to such lengths to conceal herself, she clearly did not want to be found.

In the distance, Paula could see Suzanne walking down the hill towards her, and she waved to her friend and walked a little faster towards Suzanne's familiar smiling face.

'You look like a cross between Joseph and Doctor Who,' laughed Suzanne, eyeing Paula's coat before giving her friend a bear hug that left Paula almost breathless. 'Haven't you heard we're in the middle of a heatwave, and that these sub-tropical conditions could be the beginning and end of our summer for this year?'

'Not like you to walk further than you have to,' retorted Paula, ignoring her friend's comment about her coat. 'Why didn't you go straight to Mark's house instead of walking past the door and down the hill, only to have to turn around and walk back?'

'I did call in but couldn't get an answer. There are the most delicious smells of cooking coming through the letterbox and a pink glow from the little tealights in the hall, but I rang the bell and hammered on the door and no-one came.'

'Mark's probably got his headphones on, you know what he's like about needing constant music when there's no one there to talk to,' said Paula, but what she actually thought was that it was strange not to have Mark standing on the doorstep waiting for them.

Both girls walked a bit faster towards Mark's house, and although neither of them could understand it, they both felt a strange nervousness as they approached the gate leading to the front garden, which exploded with the scent of early summer flowers and a late-blooming variety of bluebells.

Chapter Two

The dark blue wrought-iron gate was slightly open, and Suzanne said it had been like that when she got there and she had probably left it open after failing to get any response from Mark and deciding to go in search of either Paula or Anne. Almost draped over the gate was a small lilac tree, hanging with fragrant white double blooms, and beneath the tree and under the hedges around the whole of the front garden were masses of long-stemmed bluebells. In the warm and still evening air the combination of scents was wonderful and as they walked towards the front door two tubs bursting with lily of the valley continued with a heavier sweet perfume.

Paula remembered that only a couple of days earlier Mark had told her about some legends associated with the lily of the valley, also known as Our Lady's Tears. The story he liked best was that 'Our Lady' referred to the Virgin Mary, and that Mary's tears had turned to lily of the valley when she cried at the crucifixion of Jesus. Typical of Mark that he not only looked after the plants and flowers in his garden, but also learned everything about them, from their botanical names to the folklore and legends linked to them.

They had automatically closed the gate behind them, but now they both jumped as the gate swung open again, and Anne turned into the garden, looking a bit red in the face and slightly out of breath.

'Hi, guys,' she said, and Paula wished she wouldn't call them guys, knowing that it was an expression that particularly annoyed Mark. But she said nothing, just smiled.

'Are you late, too?' continued Anne. 'I thought I was late and you would have all started without me, so why aren't you inside? I can smell the baking even over the scent of the flowers.'

It was then that Paula realised that the smell of the delicacies Mark was preparing for them was no longer making her mouth water, more making her eyes water and her nose wrinkle up at the smell of burning.

'I've been here once already,' said Suzanne. 'I couldn't get an answer and now I'm getting a bad feeling that something could be wrong. It's just not like Mark to keep us hanging around, he usually can't wait to show off his cooking.'

Paula rang the doorbell and a muted orchestral version of 'Waltzing Matilda' echoed in the house, causing Anne to suppress a spontaneous giggle. 'Well, that is one present from his adopted family that Mark *would* like to bin,' she commented, but stopped short of any further opinions as she could see that her two friends were now looking seriously worried.

All three girls began shouting through the letterbox and banging on the door, and it was becoming more obvious that something was wrong as the pink glow of the tealights in the hall was becoming mixed with a haze of pale grey smoke. The smell of burning was becoming more pungent.

Paula went around to the side entrance, but as always the door was locked. She looked through the window that normally enabled a view of the kitchen. The haze in here was thicker, but there was no sign of any fire and Paula assumed that whatever was in the oven was by now burned to a cinder. She wondered why the smoke alarms had not gone off. And, more importantly, where the hell was Mark?

She went back to the front of the house, where Anne and Suzanne were now hammering hell for leather on the door and calling to Mark through the letterbox, but with no luck, and now a neighbour had come through the gate and was asking what all the noise was about. The neighbour, Abdi, a short Turkish man in his mid-fifties, was someone with whom Mark swapped recipes, and whose wife ran an internet café on Albany Road. Quickly assessing the situation, and without hesitation, Abdi ran back to his house, returning within seconds armed with a lump hammer. He told the girls to stand back as he hurled the hammer, with all his weight behind it, at the lock on the front door.

Abdi was no lightweight, and the lock gave way immediately. The wood splintered along the whole length of the door as he kicked it open, and he told the girls to wait as he went inside. The smell of burning was now overwhelming, but fortunately there were still no flames showing, and the first thing Abdi did was to rush to the kitchen to turn the oven off.

His next action was instinctive – but a mistake. As he opened the door of the oven, he was met by a wall of smoke and heat that made him choke and sent him reeling backwards.

The biggest shock was yet to come as Abdi almost tripped over a large object on the kitchen floor and rubbed his watering eyes to see what was lying there. Abdi would never to his dying day forget the horror of what he saw, and his legs almost gave way, causing him to hang on to the side of the kitchen island and knock two dishes to the floor, creating a dramatic crash.

The girls were unable to contain themselves. Covering their mouths and noses, they came towards the kitchen to see what was going on. Somehow Abdi managed to get a grip of the situation and blocked their view turning them around and back towards the front door.

'What's happened? You have to tell us what has happened,' shouted Suzanne. 'Where is Mark and why can't we go in? Has Mark hurt himself or what? For Christ's sake, Abdi, you are really scaring me now, what the hell is it?'

Abdi stood against the wall of the hall, where the wallpaper had been torn off in his assault on the front door, and struggled to get his words out. 'There is terrible accident,' he said. 'Mark … Mark, he is dead and we have to send for police – we must get police.' He looked at the girls and then spoke to himself in his native Turkish, as if this reversion to something familiar and comforting would change the awfulness of what he had witnessed.

Paula felt sick and struggled not to cry, but managed to use her phone and dial 999, asking Abdi if they needed an ambulance, and maybe a doctor to confirm that Mark was actually dead. The look on Abdi's face told Paula that there was no doubt about the fact that Mark was dead, but she was not to know until later the full horror of what Abdi had seen in that smoke-filled hell of Mark's kitchen.

The three girls and Abdi stood in the front garden, all trying to get to grips with what was happening. For some reason she could not rationalise, Suzanne picked an armful of the long-stemmed bluebells and placed them on the front porch, only then realising that they were past their best, with some of the blooms looking befittingly dead.

All Paula could think about was who was going to tell Norman and Sandy about Mark. How would they cope with the loss of Mark who, although not their biological son, was the apple of their eye, and their focus in life for nearly thirty years?

Anne stood at the gate and was the first to see the flashing blue lights, which were confusing at first as they seemed to be coming in more than one direction, but that was because two separate squad cars were approaching the house.

Already people were crossing the road to see what was happening, but the first officer that got out of one of the police cars told two middle-aged women to move on quickly before approaching Abdi who broke away from the girls and walked towards Sergeant John Evans.

Sgt Evans was a man in his late fifties and conveyed an air of experience and calm. Close on his heels was PC Helen Cook-Watts, a twenty-something who looked far too young and attractive to be going into what Abdi knew to be a scene of macabre devastation.

Sgt Evans was not one to rush into any situation. He listened with an increasing sense of disbelief at what Abdi was telling him, and after getting an idea of what they were facing he checked with Helen that she was OK, before stepping into the hall and then moving towards the kitchen. Forewarned is forearmed, apparently, but even with his thirty years of experience Sgt Evans had never witnessed anything like this, and he noticed the colour drain from Helen's face as she too took in the carnage confronting them in that previously well-ordered kitchen.

The two officers who had arrived in the second squad car had not spoken to Abdi, and were expecting something in the nature of a routine domestic disturbance that had got out of hand. They were not prepared for something that was normally the preserve of nightmares and horror movies. Because the first two officers had come to an abrupt halt on entering the kitchen, the others had to move to one side and as the third officer, PC Mike Thomas, slipped forward slightly his eyes went down to the floor and he saw the cause of the problem. The tip of his boot had edged into a pool of slightly congealed blood and the blood had come from an arm. But that was all it was – an arm – not attached to a body. And alongside it was a leg …

The whole kitchen looked like a slaughterhouse, with severed arms and legs lying in no particular order on the grey quarry-tiled floor. A torso with the head still attached was actually on the central island, alongside some lovingly prepared hors d'oeuvres and a bowl of pink punch in which were floating some tiny strawberries.

The atmosphere in the kitchen was something that would have been unpleasantly familiar to Mark as, yet again, the sound of silence was deafening. Sgt Evans was the first to act, and told his colleagues to step back and not touch anything as it was obvious this situation was well outside their remit. The CID would be needed, together with Scene of Crime Officers and the whole entourage that accompanied any investigations into such brutal crimes.

Retreating from the kitchen with the other officers, Mike realised that he had left a small trace of blood on the carpet, which would need to be reported to the SOC team. They had already been alerted by Sgt Evans, who had learned that it would be Detective Chief Inspector Phelps heading up the investigation – a fact he accepted with gratitude. Martin Phelps was not one of the fast-tracked senior CID officers that uniformed staff loved to hate, but an officer who had come up through the ranks, was streetwise, and was personally aware of the difficulties and the frequent sheer drudgery of routine police work.

The officers had been asked to carefully check the rest of the house while waiting for the Scene of Crime specialists, and they did this in pairs, with Constable Thomas and his mate taking the upstairs and Sgt Evans and PC Cook-Watts checking out the lounge. All the officers were geared up for the worst after what they had witnessed in the kitchen, but the devastation observed in the lounge was simply bizarre, and it took the two officers a few minutes to work out the cause of it.

The room resembled one of those glass balls that you shake and cause artificial snow to fall on a scene below, and even as they looked small wisps of 'snow' moved about the room. Of course, it wasn't really snow, and soon it became obvious that the particles floating around the room had come from the sofa. They decided against going into the room, as they could see that the sofa had been slashed over and over, as if someone had gone berserk with a Stanley knife, and what looked like soft coffee-coloured leather was in bits. It didn't seem possible that so many soft, white particles could have been contained in one, albeit large, sofa, and in a strange way it was almost more unbelievable than the gruesome mayhem in the kitchen.

From the doorway they could also see that the coals in the fireplace had recently been lit, and even as they looked the underlying coke and sticks collapsed, causing a thin wisp of smoke to rise but not doing enough to rekindle a flame.

'Not the sort of evening for lighting a fire. Although someone should burn in the fires of hell for the evil done here. On such a beautiful day. And in such an obviously loved home.' That was the first thing a shocked PC Cook-Watts had uttered since entering the house.

Her colleague and self-appointed protector looked at her and not for the first time wondered why someone as bright and

22

attractive as Helen, who was the same age as his daughter Angela could possibly have chosen a career that would soon strip her of any illusions she may have about the human race. Sgt Evans outwardly shuddered at the thought of his Angela being forced to look at the abomination that Helen had witnessed this evening. He remembered some of the horrors that he had seen as a young PC, knowing that each one had the potential of irredeemably changing your personality. He hoped that Helen would not get too hard and embittered, as he had seen others become over the years.

Nothing had been found upstairs, other than three beautifully furnished bedrooms and a bathroom that Constable Thomas said he would 'die for,' before hastily retracting his words as he realised that the owner probably was dead and in pieces in the kitchen. With nothing more to be done in the house the officers made their way back to the front porch and to the garden, where Paula and Suzanne were now openly crying and a hysterical Anne was being consoled by Abdi.

Routine police work kicked in and the officers were surprised at how easily they went about getting the basic details and accounts from those present. Sgt Evans agreed that they should all go to Abdi's house with the other officers while he and PC Cook-Watts waited for the SOC team. There were by now a sizable number of onlookers, and John Evans vented some of his emotions on these ghouls, suggesting they move on sharpish, or move into the back of his police car.

What were these people doing hanging about on a beautiful early summer evening, waiting and seemingly wanting to see what horror human beings, in a so-called civil society, could do to one another? They would have been the cheerleaders in another time, when Christians were put in the arena with the lions or when public hangings were a regular spectacle.

His tone in dealing with the intrusive public left no room for doubt in the minds of the onlookers, and in moments the front of the house was cleared, except for one man on the opposite side of the road who looked suspiciously like a journalist. Surely the press weren't here even before SOC – it was in fact less than ten minutes after any police presence had arrived. He had asked himself many times over the years how they got to know so quickly, and had tonight come up with the same answer as before, wondering not if, but who, it was within his organisation had boosted his or her monthly pay cheque by a quick phone call to a contact in the media.

A familiar large white van turned the corner, and as Sgt Evans raised his arm to indicate his presence and confirm the location of the crime it pulled into the side of the kerb. The nearside wheel drove over a half-empty can of Coke with a surprisingly loud pop and squirted the remains of the sticky brown fluid onto the pavement.

A tall, well-built man in his late thirties got out of the driver's seat, pulling open a plastic packet containing the familiar white suit that was the uniform of his trade and would be mandatory for anyone now entering Mark's home. He handed three similar packets to Sgt Evans, who would make it his responsibility to ensure that no one got past him without first covering their street clothes and so avoiding contamination of the crime scene.

'What have you found for us this time?' questioned Alex Griffiths, his shaven head gleaming in the evening sun. 'Don't you know it's a Saturday night and I was within minutes of heading for a hot date and sampling the swinging, sexy nightlife of this vibrant city? The message we got made us all wish we had chosen another profession – is it really that bad?'

'You wouldn't want to pass this one to anyone else,' replied Sgt Evans. 'I expect you know that DCI Phelps has been appointed to head up the investigation, so it will be what the uniformed staff call the 'A Team,' and heaven knows this case is going to need it.'

Alex Griffiths, one of the most respected Scene of Crime Officers in South Wales, had a reputation for a thorough and systematic approach. This, accompanied by an uncommon insight into criminal behaviour, had in the past been a key factor leading to the prosecution and conviction of some seriously hard felons. What a different animal was Alex

Griffiths when heading up SOC investigations, compared to the flamboyant and party-loving creature known to his friends as 'Brains'. The origin of the nickname was a bit vague and yes, Alex could be described as an intellectual, although he was curiously keen to hide the fact. He had taken to shaving his head long before it had become a fashionable thing to do and so his brains were almost on display. However, the more likely origin of his tag was that the first three letters of his name spelled 'ale,' and given that the famous beer in Cardiff was Brains' bitter, Griffiths had become 'Brains'!

Four other members of the SOC team had got out of the van, three men and one woman all now clad in their space suits. They followed Alex and Sgt Evans towards Mark's front door.

As they walked down the path, Evans told the team that whatever information they had been given, it was unlikely to prepare them for what awaited them in the kitchen. 'Yes, it really is that bad,' he said in response to Alex's earlier question. Sgt Evans explained as they got nearer that the damage to the front door had not been done by a possible intruder, but by a concerned neighbour, and was about to offer more of an explanation when another car pulled up outside and they all turned to see Professor Dafydd Moore getting out of his newly acquired cream-coloured Lexus.

Dafydd Moore was what any person would have sketched if asked to draw a picture of a professor, from his half-moon glasses to his longish, untidy hair and haphazard dress code. He was also a total misery, and Alex Griffiths grimaced at the thought of spending the next few hours, and having to work for the duration of this case, with Cardiff's least-loved (but to be fair, most brilliant) pathologist. The group waited for Prof. Moore, to reach them and after a brief acknowledgement Sgt Evans once again tried to prepare a colleague for what he thought would be a shocking sight.

'Seen it all before, so shall we just get on with the job?' was all the thanks he got from the professor, but the response was typical of him and so came as no surprise to anyone.

Still, it was useful that Alex and Prof. Moore were going to be entering the house together, and would be able to get a fuller picture of the information surrounding the crime, before the arrival of DCI Phelps and his team. Sgt Evans remained at the front door and watched the officers outside securing the crime scene with the familiar blue and white police tape, ensuring that no one would now get past him unless they were germane to the investigation.

No matter how many years of experience police officers may have, there still has to be an innate revulsion when seeing a fellow human being not just recently killed, but brutally slaughtered in his own home. Alex remembered that one of his old trainers had once said that any officer who is not affected by a scene of unspeakable violence had better look to drawing his or her pension and getting out of the service immediately. Years of training had taught Alex to stand back and use his eyes first, and to make contemporaneous notes, jotting down thoughts, no matter how trivial, that might at some later point help with piecing together what was in essence a complex jigsaw.

There was no requirement for Prof. Moore to confirm that Mark was dead and he set about using his expertise to affirm the time of death, recognising that on this occasion the condition of the titbits in the oven would be as good an indicator as anything he had to offer. After the first visual assessment of the scene both men stood to one side and made room for the SOC team of photographers and forensic evidence gathers to get on with the their unenviable jobs.

Alex made some initial suggestions and continued to make notes, and after a while it was almost as if the team was no longer seeing Mark's dismembered body but was hell-bent on finding out the hows and whys of what had happened – and, most importantly, who had perpetrated the disgusting act.

The scene in the lounge particularly caught the attention of Alex and he made speculative notes about the possible reason for the destruction of the sofa and wondered if it was in the lounge that the horror had started. There was no sign of a struggle, not an ornament broken, not a piece of furniture out of place, and there was certainly no sign of blood anywhere.

Alex knew that he would be working closely with Martin Phelps, and that his thoughts and ideas would be welcomed by Martin at all stages of the investigation. Alex knew that, with the skills of his experienced and thorough team, there would be within a few days a clear picture of exactly what had happened in Mark's home before, during, and after his murder.

He walked around the sofa, examining its ruin, and judged there to be around twenty cuts in the leather. Most of them were short, as if the holder of the knife had just stabbed and stabbed, but with a couple of very long slashes into the seats from where most of the filling had escaped. It didn't appear as if anyone had put up a fight to stop this destruction, as the sofa was the only item in the beautifully furnished lounge to be damaged, and there were other free-standing ornaments and pieces of furniture that would certainly have been casualties in any struggle.

There was no further movement from the fireplace, but Alex could see that the fire had only just burned out. Looking closer, it was clear that a lot of the coals had never even begun to burn. There were signs of some quite large folds of paper which had mostly burned; perhaps the whole purpose of the fire being lit was just to destroy some sort of documents – after all, it was far too warm to justify a fire, even if it did add to the ambience of what was still a beautiful room. Alex called one of the photographers to capture the state of the debris, but refrained from moving and bagging anything, as he knew Martin would want to see it in situ, before it was disturbed.

Back in the kitchen, Alex puzzled over the pieces of what looked like two broken white porcelain plates. These, and numerous lovingly created hors d'oeuvres scattered over the floor and on top of the body parts, and were the only signs anywhere of a potential struggle.

Surfaces were being dusted for fingerprints, and samples of blood, hair, and fibres were taken as flash after flash lit up the now-darkening rooms. From every conceivable angle, Mark's body parts and their surroundings were photographed, measured, and documented. Screens had now been erected outside and arc-lamps positioned, as officers prepared to work through the night both inside and outside the house.

'Could someone switch on the lights?' grunted Prof. Moore. 'There's not much more I can do here so I will be packing up and expect to have the body and limbs available for me to do a full post-mortem examination in the morning.'

'I expect DCI Phelps would like to speak to you before you leave,' suggested Alex. 'I rather thought he would have been here by now, although he does prefer us to get as much of the preliminary work done ahead of his team arriving.'

'Well, I've got better things to do than to wait around for people who think they are more important than the rest of us,' muttered the professor, as he put a thermometer back into the Gladstone bag that was one of the relics he had kept from the time when he was a proper doctor.

'Oh, come on, Prof, that's hardly fair', said Alex. 'Martin Phelps is the least likely of us all to take advantage of his position, and no one works harder than he does, especially when it comes to catching the likes of whatever bastard did this.'

'OK, point taken, no offence meant,' grunted Prof. Moore. 'Maybe I'm just getting too old for this level of human depravity. I just need to get out of here. Permanently.'

Alex looked at the professor and realised that he had never really thought about his age. He couldn't remember a time when Prof. Moore had looked any different to now, but at a guess Alex would put him in his late sixties. He had years of experience and, although an acquired taste, he was without doubt one of the country's leading criminal pathologists. Alex thought what a tremendous loss Moore would be to the business of investigating serious crime in the whole country, let alone the county, when he finally retired. So, thought Alex, the lowlife responsible for the murder and mutilation of Mark Wilson may also have to take some blame for the loss, to his profession, of such a brilliant mind as Prof. Moore. Although Alex had enormous sympathy for Mark and his family, he felt that in some ways the loss of the Prof. would be the greatest crime.

Chapter Three

The interview was taking much longer than expected, but Detective Chief Inspector Martin Phelps believed he owed it to the widow of a very brave member of the public to let her give vent to some of the anger she felt regarding her husband's death.

He knew something was going on with his team. He had seen his sergeant pacing the corridor outside his office, and he was anxious to know what had come in but careful not to show any signs of being distracted from Elaine Philips. Her husband had been what the press seemed to delight in calling a 'have-a-go hero', and although the family had no reason to hold the police responsible for the death of Daniel Philips, there was no doubt that Mrs Philips, and in particular her eldest daughter Karen, did hold them responsible for their failure to find and prosecute the killer.

The incident had happened more than six months ago, when Mr Philips had called into his local tobacconist's in Ely, an area to the west of Cardiff city centre and considered by some to be one of the city's less desirable localities. Many people still remembered the so-called 'Ely Petrol Riots' of 1991, when angry gangs had burned down a number of shops and houses, and Mrs Philips had told DCI Phelps that it would have been better if they had moved away at that time. But their family home was there, and for the most part the family had always considered themselves to be a firm part of a diverse but usually well-knit community.

So it had been a sickening blow to the family when, in the middle of a quiet Thursday afternoon, the tobacconist's shop door had been kicked open by a man brandishing a long-bladed knife. The shop owner had said it was an attempted robbery, and that he had been prepared to hand over what was in the till, but a customer – Daniel Philips – intervened, and the robber had lashed out and stabbed him. It was a superficial wound, and according to forensic evidence it would not have been fatal. In spite of stabbing him, it seemed as if the intruder barely noted the presence of the customer as he focused on the shopkeeper, and presumably the contents of his till.

But Mr Philips did not leave it there, and apparently shouted, causing the man to turn, as Mr Philips ran straight at him and heavily into the path of the now forward-facing knife. Instantly Mr Philips had crumpled to the ground; with the robbery not going according to plan, the would-be robber retrieved his knife and left the shop.

There was apparently hardly anything that Mr Addula the shop owner could remember, as he said he had been terrified and unable to move while the attack was actually happening.

He recalled afterwards that because there was relatively little blood, he thought that Mr Philips had just fainted. He'd waited for a while before approaching the collapsed man, in case the man with the knife returned.

It was in fact another member of the public, coming into the shop for a newspaper, who first went to the aid of Mr Philips, but it was already too late. The post-mortem report described how the knife had gone between two ribs and made a direct entry into the heart just below the aorta. DCI Phelps could not remember another case in his career where there was so little evidence pertinent to bringing a killer to justice.

As a first-hand witness, Ali Addula was worse than useless, and each time he related his account of the incident there were differences in the sequence of events. He apparently had no idea whatsoever what the attacker had looked like. In one account he was over six feet tall and had dark hair, but this was in contrast to a different recollection of the killer wearing a black hoodie and Mr Philips, who was just five feet nine inches, towering over him. There was a CCTV camera, but no tapes, and the crime scene being a shop meant that there were countless footprints and fingerprints – none of which had matched up with any known criminal.

Even though the shop was normally busy with lots of passing trade, no one saw anything. The knife was never found, and in spite of radio and television appeals there were no genuine leads. For now, at least, it looked as if there was little or no progress to be made.

Martin had been, and in fact still was, the senior officer for the investigation, and he had agreed to meet with Elaine Philips on a regular basis to tell her what was happening. He knew he was getting to the position when he would have to tell her that their regular meetings were becoming pointless, and he looked at her sadly as she got up from her chair and held out her hand towards him.

She looked pale and tired, but as always she had a quiet dignity and in many ways it was this acceptance of what she considered to be the inevitable that made Martin so desperate to find her husband's killer.

'As always you have been kind and respectful,' Mrs Philips said. 'For the past six months I have thanked God that you were assigned to this case, Mr Phelps, but I sense that there's nothing more that can be done at the moment. I know you will not give up, but it will probably be better if you just let me know if there are any developments in the future, rather than you having to meet me just to say "sorry, no progress". That can't be easy for you.'

Martin drew in a quick breath as he got up to shake her hand, and marvelled at the fact that she was concerned about making things easy for him, and that she had been the one with the courage to bring their regular meetings – and the hope they represented – to an end.

He replied. 'I have your number and I will of course be in contact if anything at all turns up. And yes, you can be one hundred per cent sure that I will not give up. Please look after yourself, Mrs Philips, and if there is anything you or your family and friends think of, please do let me know.'

'Goodbye, Chief Inspector Phelps.'

'Goodbye for now, Mrs Philips.'

Martin watched her walk down the corridor and then closed his office door, hoping he would have a few minutes to gather his thoughts before encountering the eager face of Detective Sergeant Pryor and the prospect of a new case. Surely it would not be one as hopeless as the Philips murder.

Looking up at the ceiling in his office, Martin marvelled, as he always did, at the Victorian beauty of the room. He particularly loved the stuccoed ceiling with the centre rose featuring a sunburst motif surrounded by swirling bunches of grapes and bold flowers.

The Victorian building known as Goleudy, in which his office was housed, was an enormous block of six floors that had been built near the docks in Cardiff at a time of frantic activity, with endless industry and coal exports to countries all around the world. The building had been erected in 1878, and it was the heart of the business for one of the major coal companies working out of Cardiff Docks until the late twenties.

At that time there was global competition from cheaper German coal, and many companies went bust, including the Evans brothers' operating company which owned Goleudy. Martin remembered hearing the history of the building, long ago, but he hadn't really absorbed all the details, and now he could only recall that the place had been abandoned for many years, before becoming the centre of a major family dispute and a court case over property rights.

The upshot was that somewhere along the line the property had been bequeathed to the South Wales Police Force, but with so many caveats that it had barely been used until 1998, when the decision was made to transform it into a state-of-the-art centre to house all the agencies involved with crime detection and prevention in South Wales. Critics of the scheme had favoured a new building, but detailed cost analysis of the requirements revealed that all this was possible in Goleudy, without needing to purchase land – land that was now at a premium, with the Cardiff Bay redevelopment being so successful.

And so in 2005, quite soon after the first appointment of a woman Chief Constable to a Welsh police force, that this amazing facility was opened for business. The planners had been sensitive in the modernisation process, keeping the red-brick façade and changing the grand entrance hall into a fit-for-purpose reception area.

It made sense to accommodate a traditional-style police station as the 'front of house' facility, and this was how the general public came to see Goleudy. The reality was that each of the floors was given over to specialist fields of criminal detection or crime prevention. The ground floor behind the reception area contained the usual array of interview rooms and offices, and the vitally important cafeteria, where some officers felt more at home than in their own kitchens. In the basement was a set of eleven holding cells complete with the latest surveillance monitoring, and a security door at the side of the building allowed access from the large car park.

Martin's office was on the floor above the reception area, and he could look out on to the pavement outside the building, and down the road towards the Cardiff Bay area, although the Bay itself was obscured by other buildings. It did however mean that he was within walking distance of Mermaid Quay, and he was known to walk around the area when he was particularly puzzled by a case. The Philips case had seen him circle the whole Bay on more than one occasion.

His phone rang and he noticed that the call was from Shelley Edwards, who was a civilian appointed to the training department on the third floor. Shelley's auburn hair and deep green eyes had been a key factor in the last year's exemplary attendance record for what had previously been the least-enjoyed topic on the compulsory training programme. Shelley covered health and safety law and had her own views on why the British were compliant in more areas of this complex legislation than the rest of the EU combined. She brought a potentially dry subject to life, and her special take on risk assessment left her course attendees with examples that would remain with them for a long time.

Shelley and Martin had a comfortable relationship, and had shared the occasional lunch in the staff dining room and the odd couple of drinks on the way home. Martin sensed that Shelley would be more than willing to take their friendship to a different level, but he already had an ex-wife and a number of failed relationships behind him, and had become wary of anything serious because of the demands it would bring and the almost inevitable conflict with his job.

Because Shelley was one of the few people working in Goleudy with whom Martin did not come into contact with directly concerning his cases, he was able to talk to her about other things. This had provided him with some precious intervals that he was not at present prepared to compromise.

'Hello, Shelley, you're not someone I would have expected to be ringing from her office at this time on a Saturday night,' laughed Martin into the receiver. 'Everything OK?'

'I hope so,' Shelley said. 'It's just that we have the first of the all-Wales courses starting on Monday, and I wanted to make sure that the equipment's working properly and that the seating arrangements suit the programme. I understand I should be honoured by the fact that the Chief Constable has agreed to give an opening address, and so I thought it best to check everything is ship-shape. I can't do any more now, so I wondered if you felt like a drink? Always supposing you are about ready to pack it in for today.'

'Nothing I would like better, but,' replied Martin, who was somewhat surprised to realise that he was genuinely disappointed, 'I have just finished a quite tricky meeting, and my sergeant is pacing the corridor excitably, so I suspect something has come in that is going to send my Saturday evening in a very different direction.'

'Not to worry,' returned Shelley. 'We can do it another time. And let's hope that DS Pryor brings you less trouble than you imagine.'

'That would be a one-off, but still, fingers crossed and good luck for next week – not that you need it!' That was the last that Martin was able to say, before DS Pryor could contain himself no longer and propelled himself into his boss's office.

Anyone not knowing Matthew Pryor, Matt to his friends, could be excused for being alarmed at the sight of his cut and swollen left eye and bruised right cheek. They could have been the result of a run in with some criminal ne'er-do-wells! Those who did know him were more likely to ask if it had been a good game, as Matt was one of the prop forwards for the South Wales Police rugby team.

He certainly fitted the image of a prop: he was strong and heavy, and well-suited to winning rucks and mauls and drive the game forward with what some said was too fearless a determination. He would possibly have made it as a professional rugby player in past decades, but he lacked the commitment to the level of training required for the modern game – and he also had serious ambitions to succeed as a detective.

'Better get your skates on, guv, there's been a particularly brutal murder in Penylan and you're heading up the team. And before you tell me not to jump to conclusions, just consider how likely is it that someone would have committed suicide by chopping off all their own arms and legs.'

'If that's a joke, it's in pretty poor taste, even for you,' said Martin, looking at his sergeant and trying to guess what level of exaggeration he was currently registering at.

'No joke at all, guv – it's obviously shaken up poor Sgt Evans and he was only willing to give a brief outline of the situation over the phone, but he did say that the SOC lot are there, as is old Prof. Moore, who wants to push off but he's been persuaded by Brains to wait until you get there.'

Reaching for his jacket and pocketing his iPhone, Martin followed DS Pryor, who'd finally paused for breath, to the car park. He indicated that they would use his car, and zapped the lock of his five-year-old metallic blue Alfa Romeo 156jts. Martin was one of the least car-mad members of the South

Wales police force, but when his favourite Aunt Pat had died back in 2003, she'd left him her end-of-terrace cottage in Llantwit Major, together with the £26,472 in her bank account. A couple of years later he had bought the car, and he knew that his aunt would have been delighted to see it standing on the drive of her home.

Although Martin could not be considered a malicious person, he remembered feeling relieved at the time that his divorce had gone through before he got his inheritance, otherwise Bethan's slick solicitor would have got his hands on half the money. Though Bethan could not be blamed for the breakdown of their marriage, as Martin readily agreed that the original problem had been his job – very few women would have survived the crazy hours, spoiled meals, and endless time alone that Bethan had been exposed to.

Being eight years younger than Martin, Bethan had thought that marriage would mean a few years of fun with their friends before settling down to make a family of their own, but that just wasn't how it worked out. The job had come first with Martin since the day he joined the force, and through the course of his career he had been used to working with women who were independent and unlikely to wait for a man to mend a fuse or, unlike in Bethan's case, change a lightbulb.

It was her blonde hair and amazing pale blue eyes that had drawn him to her in the first place, and to begin with he found that her uncanny reliance on him flattered his male ego.

Because she wanted, and indeed needed, to be dependent upon him, she was disproportionately distressed whenever his phone rang and immediately took him away from her prettily prepared dinner table to answer the call of duty against some of the lowlifes of South Wales.

Her job prior to their marriage had been as a receptionist with the Cathays Medical Practice and when it had merged with a larger group she had been only too willing to opt for the small redundancy package that was on offer. She told Martin that it was kismet as it meant more time for her to look after him and prepare for babies, and on the money front Daddy would always give them anything they needed.

Martin remembered his sheer relief a few minutes after that suffocating proposition, at the sound of the demanding ring of his mobile, and the need for his immediate presence at the scene of a potential arson attack in the middle of City Road. Although the fire investigation didn't take long, it was way past midnight when he had returned home, and not before he was seriously drunk and his head was swimming as he crashed out in the living room.

He had made a mistake, he knew that then, and the next two years in a stifling, cloying relationship were to prove that fact over and over. He had never blamed his wife, knowing that it was he who had accepted her servility and adulation and mistaken it for love, whereas he now knew that for him lasting love would have to be free and uncompromising.

Martin had recently learned, through a mutual acquaintance, that Bethan was set to marry a quiet, unassuming middle-aged man who managed a small group of charity shops in and around the Roath area of Cardiff. That sounded like an ideal setup for Bethan, and Martin sincerely hoped she would find happiness and that they would be blessed with at least one child to take some of the pressure of constant devotion off her new husband. A smile tugged at the corner of Martin's mouth as he envisaged the couple formally sitting down to an elegantly prepared dinner, and Bethan comparing their idyllic relationship with her former marriage from hell.

Starting the car and moving out into the busy city traffic Martin reflected, as he had often done before, on whether or not it was possible to drive more than 50 yards without encountering a set of traffic lights. It was probably the same in all city centres, but he thought his own capital city seemed to be blessed with more than her fair share. Strange, he thought, how one's mind is able to focus on the mundane aspects of life while encountering the awful side of it – such as driving to what he now had reason to suspect was a gruesome and horrendous affront on human life – but that was how he and others like him held on to their own sanity.

As they drove, Matt Pryor filled him in on the little he knew about the crime. With the few pieces of information available to them, both men began to speculate on the possible motive for such a gross murder.

'Hardly a chance robbery that got out of hand, and from what I have gathered from the team it's more like a ritualistic planned assault. It looks like some kind of hate or vengeance attack, and certainly planned – but then this type of killing is unlikely to be just opportunistic, is it?' enquired Matt.

'Wouldn't have thought so,' replied Martin. 'What do we know about the victim?'

'Assuming the victim is the home owner, the checks I did while waiting for you to finish with Mrs Philips show the house as belonging to a Mark Wilson. I tried matching his name with police records and got nothing, but I did get a hit on the name with our shared Social Services records. If it's the same Mark Wilson he's the son of Bob Wilson, currently inside for the savage murder of a neighbour some years ago on the Penrhys estate. But that wasn't his first, as that murder was committed when he was out on licence after serving time for the manslaughter of his daughter.'

'If he comes from that illustrious background, it's a wonder he hasn't accumulated a thick police file of his own. But you say we have nothing on him?' asked Martin.

'No, he drops out of the Social Services records at sixteen, and so far I've been unable to fill in the gap between then and the purchase of this house in 2005. Our computer whiz-kids have identified that the house was bought for cash, so no mortgage, and it's quite an expensive address. If it is the same Mark Wilson, it makes you wonder how someone with his start in life could come to be living in such relative luxury. My sister was looking to buy a house in Penylan last year, but she couldn't find anything anywhere near the level of mortgage she could manage, even with a sizeable deposit.'

Martin didn't ask which sister Matt was talking about, as he knew that there were four of them, all older than Matt. Each had three daughters, whose birthdays covered every month of the year – so Uncle Matt was constantly buying birthday presents, or getting one of his girl friends to buy girly stuff, for his twelve nieces.

Both men became demonstrably focused as Martin turned his car into the road that was obviously the location of the crime, even from some distance away. Alongside the police tape there were television cameras, journalists, and reporters waving microphones. There were also a number of noxious members of the public, who had nothing better to do with their lives than gawp at the misery of others.

Sgt Evans moved the cones he had put in place to allow Martin to park his car, and then lifted the blue and white tape to give the two men access to the house. Microphones were thrust in Martin's face as he set foot on the pavement. He recognised a few local media personalities in the pack that was already baying for news, and would continue to do so until something else took their attention.

'As you can see, I have only just arrived on the scene, and there is nothing I can tell you at this moment,' were words that Martin had heard himself speak on many previous occasions. 'When there is anything to tell the public, you will be the first to know, but for now please just back off and let us get on with the investigation.'

Hoping to get a bit more information, one of the reporters shouted. 'The neighbours say that this house belongs to Mark Wilson and that he is gay – has Mark been murdered and is it a homophobic killing? Surely you can tell us that much?'

The careless remarks angered Martin, and he turned to the journalist in question and told him that whereas some people could speculate and be creative with the facts, it was his job to ascertain at least a modicum of actual information before labelling a crime or motive. He decided against using some of the choice expletives that came to mind to emphasise his point.

Over the years, and particularly since he had become a senior officer, Martin had developed a good working relationship with the media, especially some of the local hacks. Heaven knew he had been obliged to attend enough media training courses, and to be fair he knew that most of them were just doing a frequently difficult job. Still, there was always one who managed to raise his blood pressure by asking bloody stupid questions at inappropriate times, and by trying to put words into his mouth.

Now was not the time to be irritated, though, and Martin quickly turned his mind back to the task in hand. He followed Sgt Evans towards the house and into a scene that he had been trained to handle – a scene that would call on all the skills of detection he had learned together with his own congenital skills of intuition and judgement. Everything else could wait until tomorrow.

Chapter Four

The first to speak to Martin as he passed the damaged front door was Prof. Moore, who offered a brief acknowledgement before giving Martin a synopsis of the situation, concentrating only on that for which he was able to give an expert opinion.

'Many of the facts speak for themselves, and things like temperature, state of muscle contraction, and the fresh and only partly congealed blood, all demonstrate that we were called to this scene within a very short time of the crime being committed. Ludicrously, this is supported by the condition of the cake-type things that had been put in the oven, and would probably have only taken about half an hour to cook before starting to burn. When we found them they were still warm, completely frazzled but not so much that we couldn't tell roughly what they were.'

Martin nodded as he realised that the smell that still pervaded the house was a mixture of baking and burning – not a common feature at the scene of a murder, at least not one he had ever previously encountered.

'You will see that the body has been dismembered and that brings me to the most significant factor, as far as my part of the investigation here tonight is concerned.'

Prof. Moore looked directly at Martin as he knew that the information he was about to convey would shock the DCI – the discovery had certainly stunned the professor.

'Each of the limbs has been removed from the torso by the use of a different weapon, so instead of your usual 'murder weapon', on this occasion you will be looking for multiple weapons, and by that I mean four different types of cutting, sawing, or axing tools. I will be able to give you a more complete picture of the implements that were used and the order in which the limbs were removed when I have completed a full post-mortem, which is booked for eight o'clock tomorrow morning.'

Instantly Martin's brain tried to picture a murder where four different weapons were used. It flashed up the idea of four killers, and considered this to be unlikely.

He returned his attention to Prof. Moore, who was now making his way towards the front door and who could obviously not wait to get out into the fresh evening air. Martin could see that the Prof. was shaken by his findings, in spite of his many years of witnessing some of the worst crimes in the country. It was probably the sheer calculated brutality that had caused this level of disgust. Martin knew that they would be looking for some strong motives of hatred towards the victim, as this was certainly no random butchering, but something much deeper and complex.

Making his way to see, first-hand, the atrocity in the kitchen, Martin tried to get his head around what sort of person – or persons – would mutilate another human being like this? For a start, was it one person or two, or maybe there were four of them, taking a limb each ... Was the victim alive or dead when the massacre began? What could the victim possibly have done to deserve an ending of such unimaginable horror?

In many respects it would be better if there were a number of people involved, making it more likely someone would have noticed that level of activity in and around the house. If so, he thought, someone may come forward tomorrow, when the appeal for witnesses would be made. That appeal could produce information that may be key to the solving of this crime, though Martin knew from experience that it was also likely to produce numerous false leads, sending his precious resources off on wild goose chases.

Now standing at the entrance to the kitchen, Martin took in

the surreal sight of a body, complete with head, lying in a central position on the grey granite worktop, with an arm and a leg on each side, at random angles on the floor. The imprint this scene made on his mind was less of an affront than it had been for those who had seen it before him, as the room now contained men and women in white scene-of-crime clothing, and this somehow made the spectacle more clinical than real. He had recognised, at previous grim crime scenes, that this white clothing not only protected the evidence from contamination, but also seemed to protect the wearers, in that it separated them from the monsters.

Thinking of the original stark horror that Sgt Evans and his colleagues must have witnessed, Martin gave himself a silent reminder to check that the uniformed staff were coping, and to offer any help if required.

Matt Pryor was now at his side and let rip a few sentences that on any self-respecting daytime television programme would have had more bleeps than words – but this was one occasion when Martin shared his sentiments, and had no problem with the use of language Matt usually kept for the rugby field. He related to Matt, and loud enough for all members of the SOC team to hear, the information Prof. Moore had given him about the possible use of multiple weapons, and asked if anything had yet been found.

Alex Griffiths, who had been supervising his team's work in the lounge, came into the hall, greeted Martin, and offered to summarise the findings and so save him a bit of time.

'The kitchen, as you can see, is where the crime was committed, or at least where the arms and legs were severed. It looks unlikely that the victim, who is Mark Wilson, the owner of this property, was killed elsewhere and mutilated here, because that scenario doesn't fit with the prof's findings. There is no evidence of a struggle, and the broken china and pieces of food strewn across one arm and leg are as the result of a neighbour knocking them off the edge when he witnessed the leg on the floor. Nothing else in the kitchen is damaged, and there's no sign of a weapon, certainly not the multiple weapons that we are now looking for.'

'My team have photographed everything and dusted the whole place for fingerprints, and unless the killer, or killers, wore gloves, we may be lucky on that front, because the victim was certainly house-proud and generally there are few prints around on these clean surfaces. When you have seen all you need to in the kitchen, the guys will bag up the evidence including the body-parts and get it all down to Goleudy, where Incident Room One has been allocated for this investigation.'

Martin could see that Alex and his team had done their usual intensive scrutiny of the whole area, and he indicated to them that they were free to get on with the next part of the task, getting everything to the labs and making use of the innovative crime detection facilities back at base. He knew from past experience that by the time he and his team arrived in Incident Room One the following morning, there would be ready-developed pictures of everything relevant, along with fingerprint analysis and much more.

Once again Martin inwardly thanked the foresight of his predecessors in setting up Goleudy where the post-mortem would be carried out and where all the agencies involved with the detection of this execrable crime could share information as quickly as each party discovered it. It was a far cry from the days of setting up incident rooms in local halls and waiting for outside agencies to do your lab work at a time convenient to them.

Alex directed Martin to the lounge and explained the white blizzard effect, commenting that the sofa had once been an impressively expensive piece of furniture, hard to believe now it sagged with the absence of most of its filling, which had landed on practically every surface in the room.

'It's a bit like the kitchen, in that there seems to be only one thing that has been attacked, and whereas there it was the victim, in here it's the sofa. Again, everything else is in place and there's no sign of a struggle, and at first I thought it looked as if someone had gone crazy with a knife but it's more deliberate than that.'

Alex continued. 'If you look at it closely, you will see that there are four clear sets of four deep cuts into the soft leather. Each one is at least a foot long, with one set on each of the two seat cushions, another set on the front, and the fourth on the back. I guess the filling would have been tightly packed initially, but it's very soft and would have just flown out freely with each slash of the knife or whatever was used.'

'Bloody mental,' remarked Matt, and nobody disagreed.

'It's going to be a hell of a job, but we have to assume that whoever did this had to walk over pieces of the filling to get out of the room, so each piece will have to be examined – but a piece that was trodden on may not still be on the floor – it could have subsequently floated on to the windowsill, or anywhere else. Don't really know if we will be able to find anything, but we will make every effort.'

Matt had wandered over to the fireplace, and Alex followed him, suggesting that the detectives look at the contents of the grate, which were now cold and would soon be gathered as evidence to be looked at under a microscope. Martin, with gloved hands, picked up an ornate metal poker lying in the hearth and gently prodded the coals and lifted some fragments of burned paper.

'Careful, boss,' warned Alex. 'Looks like those documents are close to disintegrating. The more of them that we can keep together the more likely we are to get a fix on what they are.'

'Sorry, Brains. It looks like there are a few thicker folds of paper on the edge of the coals, and I get the feeling that at least one document is a long piece of paper, maybe something like a birth certificate. Your people can take it all away whenever they're ready, and I look forward to having them tell me what exactly was being destroyed here.'

Matt Pryor commented that if the contents of the grate were papers that the killer wanted destroyed, this was one part of the crime that had been botched up, so maybe they were just papers that the victim had wanted to burn. Martin was sceptical.

'If you had papers you wanted to burn, would you chose to do it on a warm early summer evening, and one on which you were expecting to entertain friends? Anyway, doesn't everyone just shred stuff? No, everything else in this house is meticulously prepared for the expected guests, and it will be the possibly uninvited and unexpected visitors that started this little blaze and may have left us some clue as to the reason for it all.'

'There are no signs of a forced entry either at the back or front, and no broken windows,' said Matt, who had gained some facts from Sgt Evans. 'It would appear that the expected visitors, who are three women, got anxious when they could smell burning in the house and were unable to get any response from their friend Mark, who they assumed was inside. The front door was smashed open by a neighbour, and he and the victim's friends are next door having their initial statements taken by uniform, and probably trying to get over the shock of it all.'

Martin continued to stare into the coals and ashes, praying silently that these remains really would turn a key in this investigation, for other than this possible mistake it looked like a well-organised and well-executed plan. The killer, or killers, seemed to have done only what was intended, and Martin speculated that the sequence of events started in the lounge – maybe with Mark being forced to witness the burning of some personal documents and the seemingly ritualistic destruction of his sofa, before the horror of being sacrificed in the kitchen.

Nowhere was there any sign of a struggle, and Martin mentally pinpointed three areas where intensive work would have to be carried out. There was the area immediately on and around the kitchen island, the fireplace, and the sofa. He checked with Alex that they were on the same wavelength, getting the confirmation that his experience had led him to expect.

'What the hell went on here, guv?' quizzed Matt. 'Considering the level of the massacre in the kitchen, you would expect the whole house to be a bloody mess. The only blood smears are in the hall and have apparently come from the boot of PC Mike Thomas, who stepped unknowingly into some blood on the kitchen floor on first entry. This couldn't have been just one killer, could it? And why didn't the victim put up a fight?'

Martin ignored the somewhat rhetorical questions from his sergeant, as he had no answers to give and knew that, at this stage, no answers were expected. He made his way into the hall and up the stairs. All the doors were open, and he made a note to check with Sgt Evans whether his colleagues had found them open or closed. It would probably be of no consequence, but experience had taught Martin that the devil was in the detail when it came to solving such tortuous crimes, and it was his intention to allow no detail to be overlooked.

Two doors led to rooms at the front of the house. One room, which was the master bedroom, was decorated with pale green designer wallpaper. The curtains and bedspread didn't match it, but were deliberately chosen as a contrast, being a deep burgundy colour. The en-suite was dressed with the same deep burgundy tiles and Martin tried to figure the cost of this level of interior design. He had no real idea, knowing only that Matt's youngest sister had recently installed a top-of-the-range B&Q bathroom that had cost just over £3000 and wasn't even in the same league as this.

The second room was similarly decorated with style and flair, this time in shades of light blue, navy blue, and silver, and a corner of the room was established as a home office. Martin noted the difference between his 'office' at the cottage, with its ungainly trailing wires and extension sockets, and this wireless affair with all the latest technology and clean lines. He called to Matt.

'Get Alex to pack up this lot and get it back to Goleudy for the IT boys to get a good look at it. I want to know every key that has ever been pressed and get an in-depth picture of any social networking, or membership to any particular organisations. Building up a profile of Mark Wilson's character and any strong affiliations may be helpful and we can only hope he has left us some clues somewhere.'

Matt shouted down the stairs and they heard Alex leave the house and go to the van to collect some boxes for transporting the computer, running the gauntlet of increasingly impatient newsmen and women. When he came back he reminded Martin that the IT *boys* would not be looking at this box of tricks, but that he would be putting it into the capable hands of Charlie Walsh, and when he had last looked there was nothing boyish about her.

Charlie, or, more formally Charlotte, Walsh was an Irish colleen with black hair and green eyes and a shapely upper half that she frequently and shamelessly flaunted as she manoeuvred her motorised wheelchair with the same dexterity she demonstrated on the keyboard. Still only in her early thirties, Charlie had forgotten more about computer technology than Martin and his team would ever know, and he knew they were lucky to have her as she had been headhunted on more than one occasion by the Met.

Her response to their repeated and quite lucrative invitations had always been the same, as she claimed the importance of her Irish roots, and a feeling of being more at home with her fellow Celts in Wales, meant more than what was arguably a more exciting job in London.

Martin was relieved to hear Alex coming up with just a bit of his old banter, as this would take the edge off the horror that every member of the team had so far experienced. It was a coping mechanism, and if by the time they all left there was a healthy bit of swearing and black humour it would, he knew, be the difference between screaming nightmares and mere vile dreams for most of the group.

'Yes, I'll give the whole set-up to Charlie, but her team will have to make a start on it, as I happen to know she is in Ireland this weekend for her sister's wedding, with a promise to be in on Monday morning, with the best or worst ever hangover – pre-warning us all to keep out of her way.'

Alex always seemed to know what was happening in Charlie's life, but there were no rumours of any relationship, and in a place like Goleudy, where it was possible for a flirty wink to be translated into a full-blown affair, it would be the best-kept secret ever.

The final bedroom was a bit out of character with the rest of the house, being more floral and feminine, and although the furniture and décor was every bit as expensive as elsewhere, there was something a bit tacky about the overall effect. It flashed through Martin's mind that this could have been planned with a particular person, probably a girl or a woman, in mind, but there was no sign of that person or anyone else ever having used the room.

The drawers were empty, and in the wardrobe there were just six pink, silk-padded clothes hangers similar to those he had noticed hanging in his aunt's bedroom when he had moved into her cottage. He half expected to be able to smell mothballs, as the room, although recently decorated and furnished, was giving him the illusion of belonging to a different era, and for some reason he felt a degree of unease that didn't make a lot of sense.

The bathroom was straight out of a top-quality magazine but for Martin's taste more in keeping with the Hilton than a private home, and it was so clean as to appear unused. Martin felt the dark grey sponge and suspected through his gloved hands that it was damp and called to Alex.

'Looks as if someone took a shower earlier on so you may be able to pick up some samples for DNA examination – it will probably only match up with the victim, but we need to pick up on anyone who has been in this house lately, and ideally someone known to the police and on our DNA database! Well, I can dream, can't I, and as I am never likely to have the good fortune of a killer standing over his victim with a smoking gun, it's back to our usual round of solicitous searching and the everlasting examination of whatever facts we can muster.'

Sgt Evans had come to the foot of the stairs, to confirm that initial statements had been taken from the four people so far involved with the investigation, and was asking if they could be allowed to go – or did DCI Phelps want to interview them tonight?

Martin overheard the question and moved to the top of the stairs. 'I will see them all briefly and individually, but only to get a feel of their initial reactions. After that they can go and I will take home their draft statements and look at them later prior to the formal interviews that you can arrange for first thing tomorrow morning.'

'OK, guv,' replied Sgt Evans and he walked off to make his colleagues aware of the DCI's intentions.

Having come down the stairs, and now standing in the hallway between the kitchen and the lounge, Martin took a final look at the setting of one of the most brutal murders he had ever known. The scene had already changed as the body and its parts had been removed and taken to the incident van, together with what already amounted to hundreds of carefully labelled samples from all corners of the house. Not for the first time, Martin admired the dedication of the SOC team, and called out in a voice that was controlled and strong and deliberately hid some of his own demons.

'What we have all witnessed here is beyond the wildest belief of most people, and once again I want to express my thanks for the amazing way in which you get down to the job and make the life of my lot so much easier. The whole thing is a team effort and together we will get to the bottom of this murder and bring the evil bastards to justice. Thank you.'

Alex nodded towards Martin as he left the house and was grateful to his colleague for acknowledging the work of the SOC investigators, for although Alex himself was not slow to praise their efforts, there was always something more substantial at being recognised from outside the team.

Following Sgt Evans to where the witnesses were waiting, Martin had barely got a foot on the pavement outside Mark's house before microphones were thrust under his nose, as reporters leant over the police tape and bombarded him with questions.

'They brought out more than one body bag, so is it a multiple murder?'

'Are any of the people who are waiting next door going to be arrested for murder?'

'Come on, Chief Inspector! Tell us how the victim was killed – was it a fight?'

More questions followed and Martin held up his hands in an attempt to get some semblance of order in to what was little more than an unruly mob, but he knew it was no use fobbing them off and so turned to face the cameras.

'A little quiet, if you please. I will make just one statement and then you may as well all go home, as there is nothing else you will hear officially tonight. Earlier today there was a murder at this house, and all I can say at this time is that the victim is male, but until the next of kin are notified we will not be giving out any further details. We have no reason to suspect that any of the people who were visiting this evening, or the neighbours we will necessarily be questioning, had any part to play in the crime, and for the moment they are simply helping us with our investigations.'

'Check with your offices in the morning and you will be made aware of any press statements and the likelihood of any press conferences or public appeals. That is all for now, and I mean that is all, so don't push your luck.'

Martin turned away and walked quickly towards the house next door but not without hearing still more questions shouted at his back. There was no sign of the pack retreating. What part of 'that is all for now' didn't they understand?

The questions that really worried him related to Mark's sexuality. Even if this had nothing to do with the crime, Martin knew that the newspapers were likely to turn it into an issue in some way or another.

What a difference between two houses. The house into which Martin and Matt now walked had hardly been changed since the day it was built, and that was probably more than a hundred years ago. True it now had electricity, the telephone, and a television, but otherwise it was like stepping back in time, although the house was certainly not unloved.

Complementing the Victorian style of the interior were large pieces of furniture that possibly dated back to the nineteenth century, when there was an international taste for all things Asian when it came to furniture and other objects for decoration in the home. The pieces here were certainly of Turkish origin,

51

and the mellow wood shone out a welcome that had been encouraged by years of careful and dedicated polishing. Sgt Evans led the two men to the back of the house where in the kitchen, at a banquet-sized table surrounded by numerous high-backed chairs, were three clearly upset women, and a man who literally bounced out of his chair when the kitchen door opened.

'Thank goodness you come, this is terrible night, I tell the policeman but I not tell the ladies, it is too bad … it is too bad.'

Abdi paced along one side of the kitchen and continued muttering. 'Too bad, too bad,' he said constantly, until his wife put her arms around him and pulled his face into the safety of her more-than-ample bosom, and he sobbed like a baby.

'That's been on the verge of happening for some time,' murmured PC Cook-Watts, who had been helping with the constant supply of coffee, having completed the initial round of witness statements. 'He really needs to talk to you, but maybe it would be better if his wife, Aella, helps him to compose himself and you speak to the ladies first.'

Martin looked across at the couple and agreed that he was unlikely to get any coherent information from Abdi in his current state. Although he felt some sympathy for the man, he reminded himself that at this stage even these witnesses were potential suspects, and he needed to get on with his job.

'We have been using Aella's sewing room to take the statements, and the ladies know that you will not be going over everything again with them but will just want a few minutes tonight before the formal interviews tomorrow.' Helen Cook-Watts spoke as she showed the DCI and his sergeant into a surprisingly large room just off the kitchen. They accepted her offer of coffee, and sat down at a table, where all the paraphernalia needed for various types of needlecraft had been moved to one side to make room for the officers.

Paula Williams was the first to come back into the makeshift interview room. She sat down opposite the two men who noticed her red, swollen eyelids and blotchy face.

'I understand Mark was a good friend of yours, and I am sorry you have lost him under such dreadful circumstances. I am Detective Chief Inspector Phelps and this is Detective Sgt Pryor, and we are aware that the uniformed officers have taken full statements of your movements this evening and how you came to be here. For now, I am keen to know more about Mark, and in particular your initial thoughts on why this should have happened.'

Paula did not rush into responding, and seemed to be mentally trawling through the years of knowing Mark, before answering in a voice that was close to a whisper as she fought back her tears.

'I've known Mark since we were pupils at Whitchurch High School, although he didn't come to the school until quite late on. I know that at the time he was in foster care and until then he hadn't had a good experience of the social care system. Sandy and Norman were different to other foster carers he'd had, they looked after him properly and then they adopted him later on.'

At the thought of Sandy and Norman, tears welled up in Paula's eyes and spilled over her cheeks. 'Do they know what has happened to Mark? Oh, please, someone must tell them! But they will be devastated …'

Martin assured Paula that he would personally be going to see Mark's adoptive parents within the hour, and Matt Pryor took the address and telephone number from Paula, who knew them off by heart, as the Hardings' house was a place she frequently visited and was always made welcome in.

Would she still be welcome there – or would Sandy and Norman think she could have saved Mark if she had taken the trouble to go earlier and help him with the preparations for the evening? Logically, she knew that it was her own conscience that was nagging at that thought – and how earnestly she wished it had nagged her earlier.

Composing herself to make the rest of her statement, Paula went on to explain how she had remained close friends with Mark when they had left school. And, yes, she knew that Mark was gay, although it was a side of his life about which she knew very little.

'It never was an issue from my point of view, and I didn't get to meet any of his gay friends. It was as if he kept that aspect of his person separate and that's the way he wanted it. I do know there had never been anyone serious and that all his relationships – and there weren't that many – had been casual things, with no heartbreak or regrets when they were over. So I wouldn't imagine that what has happened here tonight has got anything to do with Mark's sexuality, although I guess some psychopathic, homophobic maniac could be responsible.'

The last few words were spat out and Martin rose from his chair, suggesting that it was time for Paula to go home, where perhaps she could talk things through with someone and try to get some rest.

'I live on my own and my flat is within walking distance, so perhaps the fresh air will do me some good.'

'Not a sensible idea,' said DS Pryor. 'You will undoubtedly be pestered by the media, and we really would suggest that you are not on your own tonight, as it's been a massive shock, and one you are likely to relive throughout the night.'

When Paula had left the room, Matt Pryor turned to Martin and commented that Paula seemed more than usually shaken over the death of a friend, even taking account of the circumstances, but Martin disagreed.

'The trouble with this job is that we look for villains in the most innocent of people, and to be honest all I see is a really decent woman, who has lost a kindred spirit and who therefore harbours some pretty evil thoughts towards whoever is responsible. However I could of course be wrong, and by the end of the investigation I could be eating my words.'

The interviews with Anne Davies and Suzanne Shepherd went along the same lines as the one with Paula had, and when they were all back in the kitchen it was decided that Suzanne would go back to Paula's house for the night, but that Anne would go back to her own home.

'I won't be on my own, my boyfriend will be there,' explained Anne when her friends tried to change her mind. 'I've sent him a text, and he's organised a taxi to pick me up. It should be here any minute now.'

Arrangements were made for an officer to take Suzanne and Paula back to Paula's house, and the taxi arrived as expected to take Anne home. Within a few minutes the women had left and Martin was sitting in the kitchen ready to speak to Abdi.

'Aella must not hear me tell you about Mark, for she will shock,' he pleaded.

It seemed as if half the Turkish population of Cardiff had arrived at the home of Abdi and Aella Nicanor, and Aella readily went and joined her friends and relatives in the central living room.

Martin learned that Abdi had lived in Cardiff for more than forty years, but noted that he still had only a fundamental knowledge of the English language. He could easily get by with day-to-day conversation, but his grammar was all over the place and he frequently used words in the most inappropriate contexts.

He explained that he knew Mark was expecting company that evening but had been surprised to hear the women shouting and banging on the door when he was returning with his wife from visiting friends. The women were all frightened that Mark could have had an accident and so could not get to answer the door, and were especially worried about the smell of burning.

'We should have called fire engines but I was quicker with my hammering,' said Abdi, puffing out his chest and now getting some fulfilment as he realised the importance of his evidence to the police.

Martin allowed Abdi to tell the whole story, which he did slowly and deliberately, taking the two detectives through every detail of how he had entered the house, turned off the oven, and found the body parts on the floor.

'I know this is difficult for you, but can you describe everything you saw in the kitchen?' asked Martin.

'I have shock when I see leg and I bump into that table thing. Two dishes fall on floor. I have more shock when I see him on that table but then I must get the ladies out 'cause they was coming in.' Abdi gave a demonstration of how he had ushered the women from the kitchen before they could look at the outrage he had witnessed.

'Can you positively identify the person you saw as Mark Wilson?' asked DS Pryor. 'It is very important that there is no mistake on this.'

'Yes Mark, yes Mark, dreadful, dreadful, yes Mark.'

Martin wound up this first of what would probably be many sessions with Abdi Nicanor and, as with all the others, he wondered if, in the final analysis, this seemingly distraught and upset man would be as innocent as he now seemed.

Walking back to Mark's house, Martin noticed that now there were even more journalists hanging around the area, but he ignored their questions and, after briefly checking with Alex Griffiths and Sgt Evans that everything was under control, he made his way to his car. DS Pryor followed, but Martin stopped him getting into the car, suggesting it would be better for him to stay at the scene and clear up any loose ends.

'I'll take PC Cook-Watts with me, as I suspect it may prove to be an advantage if there is a woman present when I break this news to Mark's parents. And on the subject of parents, can you get our people looking into his biological family?'

'Will do,' replied Matt Pryor, as he opened the door for Helen Cook-Watts to get into Martin's car and then watched his boss switch on his headlights in the fading light and drive off. Having worked with Martin for nearly three years, Matt knew that his 'guv'nor' was now en route to do the job he most hated, but one he always did with remarkable sensitivity, seeming to have an inbuilt awareness of the right words to use on these occasions.

Just as Martin Phelps began his drive from Penylan, Sandy and Norman Harding had just come in from tidying up the part of the garden they had replanted that evening. They joked about the need to tell Mark exactly what plants to get for the far edge. The plants were to be Sandy's birthday present, but they knew that if they left Mark to his own devices he would be over-generous and could well turn up with ten times the number they actually needed.

Their life was happy but even as they expressed their feelings of gratitude for the good fortune life had brought them, a car was travelling across Cardiff towards their home, destined to turn their world upside down in the cruellest way imaginable ...

Chapter Five

Martin pointed the car away from the city centre and took a left turn into one of the side roads. He knew this area of Cardiff well, and definitely better than the back of his hand. What a strange expression that was, he thought, as he imagined that most people would be hard pushed to describe the back of their hands. He looked down at his own, placed at ten to two on the steering wheel. Their only distinctive features were his longer-than-average fingers, but otherwise they presented a picture remarkably similar to those of most men of his age.

His forensic colleagues would undoubtedly be pleased to enlighten him on how far this was removed from the truth – but then they were the clever sods and only too pleased to demonstrate to the likes of Martin how the amazing developments in all the sciences impacted on his job and were often the key to solving crime. And, in all fairness, they were right.

Helen Cook-Watts sat quietly in the passenger seat and recognised that DCI Phelps was psyching himself up for the moment they would be breaking the most terrible news to two as-yet-totally unsuspecting people. This would be the first time she had been at the sharp end of such a meeting, and her mind raced through the training seminars on 'breaking bad news' she had attended. She wished there had been more.

This whole journey was likely to take less than twenty minutes, and she was not sure whether to ask for some advice from the DCI or to just leave him to his own thoughts. At least this first experience of the thing that all her colleagues found so difficult was for her going to be in the company of a senior officer known for his supportive attitude towards less experienced staff.

As they turned into Manor Way and were three-quarters of the way to their destination, Martin appeared to have completed his internal deliberations. Glancing at Helen, he began to reassure her, and prepare her for her role in the proceedings.

'It is likely to be a difficult session, and I gather from the victim's friend Paula that these are his adoptive parents – in their seventies, but fit and very active members of the local community. Just take your lead from me and I will tell them as much as I feel they can take initially about their son's murder, but they are likely to ask lots of searching questions and I will have to consider as we go along just how much detail to divulge.'

'Just don't want to let you down guv,' replied Helen. 'My one real fear is that if the mother breaks down and cries, as is likely, then I will be crying with her.'

Martin took another glance at this young PC, appreciating her honesty and respecting her sensitivity. 'That wouldn't be the end of the world, provided you stay in control of yourself. The days of professionals having to keep a stiff upper lip have gone, thank God, and it's now perfectly OK for us to demonstrate some natural emotion when dealing with the victims of crime.

'Many criminal psychologists believe that officers who show a human face when breaking bad news can make a difference to the subsequent coping for relatives and friends. I am not suggesting that you blubber all over the place, but I am not expecting completely dry eyes, Helen.'

The last sentence produced a wry smile, and Helen felt she was now as ready as she could be for whatever the rest of this bloody awful day could bring. She refrained from closing her eyes to collect her thoughts, as that instantly flashed an image of Mark's limbless body and she wondered how long it would be before that dire picture would fade.

A couple of turnings off Manor Way took Martin into Park Road and then, following Paula's instructions, into Ty Parc Road, which was one of the smallest side streets, with no through road and leading to just three mature detached houses. The Hardings' home was the second on the left, and Martin pulled the car into the kerb just outside it, ignoring the fact that the drive had ample space for at least two more cars. He wanted to walk the length of the drive and get a feel of the place.

In estate agents' jargon the property would be described as 'a luxurious detached residence located in a select area of Whitchurch', and 'accompanied by just two similarly prestigious properties within a quiet cul-de-sac'. Way out of the league of most would-be home purchasers, Martin guessed the value at three-quarters of a million pounds, possibly more. He liked the look of it – solid and in no way ostentatious.

There were no gates to the drive itself, and halfway up a pathway branched off to the right and led directly to a porch, almost completely covered with wisteria that had shed most of its fragrant blossom. The flowers had settled up to several inches deep around the front door. Out of the corner of his eye Martin saw movement through one of the downstairs windows and so was not surprised when the door was opened even before the bell had stopped ringing.

Norman Harding stood in the doorway, and his eyes went past Martin and rested on the uniform of the police officer behind him, knowing instantly that a visit so late on a Saturday evening would have nothing to do with routine community policing and could only mean bad news.

Before Norman had a chance to speak, Martin held up his warrant card and, as required, made the formal introductions.

'Good evening, sir, I am Detective Chief Inspector Phelps and this is Police Constable Cook-Watts. We are looking for Mr and Mrs Harding, and if we have the right house may we come in, please?'

Norman stood aside and gestured towards the first door that led into the lounge and as he passed the foot of the stairs he called up to his wife.

'Sandy, would you come downstairs please?'

Sandy had already heard the doorbell and was aware that Norman had let someone into the house, and so she came quickly down the stairs, following almost immediately behind them into the lounge.

Her face turned pale as her eyes also took in the uniform of the police force and in the time it took Martin to re-introduce himself she had made her way to her husband's side and was gripping his hand tightly.

Martin spoke quietly. 'There is no easy way to break this news, but it would be better if you both sat down, as what I have to tell you will be a terrible shock.'

Mr and Mrs Harding moved to a nearby two-seater settee and sat closely together, both their minds now in total turmoil and somehow knowing that something had happened to their son.

'Has Mark had an accident – is he badly hurt?' asked Sandy quietly but with a voice that shook a little and a face that anticipated the worst.

Martin looked at Sandy and Norman and could barely guess at the misery his news would bring them.

'I'm afraid it's something more than that, Mrs Harding. I am sorry to say but the dreadful news is that your son is dead, but it was no accident and we believe Mark was deliberately killed.'

Two faces crumpled, and it was as if in ten seconds a cruel ten years of age had settled on them as they clung to one another and sobbed piteously. Nothing else was said by anyone in the room for the longest ten minutes that DCI Phelps could ever remember and the only movement was when he indicated to Helen Cook-Watts to stand back and not approach the couple, as in these terrible moments all they wanted was one another.

It was Sandy Harding who first raised her head, and she cupped her husband's face in her hands and gently kissed both his closed eyelids, before tightly gripping both his hands in an effort to stop him shaking.

The sight of this total love and consideration of one person towards another was the thing that totally took away for Helen's composure, and she stared down deliberately at her sensible uniform shoes, in an effort to focus on something mundane as she fought back her own tears.

Sandy's voice was thick and her eyes were swollen as she looked up and asked the inevitable questions – the ones Martin had been mentally gearing himself up to answer.

'What happened, how did he die? Was it a car accident, or a mugging? It must have been a random thing – or you must have got it wrong – no one would want to deliberately kill Mark.'

The questions tumbled out and at the end of the short outburst she stumbled over the use of Mark's name and a fresh flow of tears streamed down her face.

Now it was Norman's turn to hold on to his wife, and they stayed together and completely apart from their unwanted visitors for a further five minutes, before turning to face Martin and waiting to hear the answers to Sandy's questions.

'We know it happened earlier this evening at Mark's home in Penylan, but as yet we haven't been able to get a clear picture of exactly how Mark died. There is no doubt that we are looking at murder and we will be doing everything possible to find and arrest the killer as soon as we can.'

Martin knew that he would have to answer any questions from the couple honestly, but he hoped they would not be asking for too much detail at this stage. It was surely more than enough to know your son had been killed without having to know how he had been carved up, in his own home, by one or more potential psychopaths.

Sandy was now sitting on the edge of her seat with her arms wrapped around her knees and staring at something no one else could see but then suddenly she got to her feet.

'I need a drink, maybe a cup of tea to begin with but then something very much stronger.' Sandy moved surprisingly quickly towards the door and headed for the kitchen followed immediately by PC Cook-Watts whose offer to make the drinks was turned down politely but firmly.

'I can cope with things better when I'm busy,' insisted

Sandy. 'Will you ask the Chief Inspector if he would like tea or coffee while I put the kettle on?'

Helen looked at Sandy, who was bustling around her kitchen as if she were just making drinks for friends. Belying that image, the mugs clattered one against the other when she set them down on the central oak table and tried desperately to stop her hands from shaking. Sandy was doing something so routine and so familiar to her that it was helping her from completely breaking down, and it would be these everyday jobs that would help her along the long path to mending, though never completely healing, her broken heart.

Returning to the lounge Helen found the DCI sitting next to Norman. Martin indicated that he would have a strong black coffee but Norman said nothing and just kept shaking his head.

'I'm sorry, but I can't remember your name,' said Sandy as Helen came back into the kitchen. 'I can remember the Chief Inspector is Mr Phelps because we once had a neighbour called that, but what did he say your name is?'

'Well, officially I am Police Constable Cook-Watts, but please call me Helen, and please do tell me if there's anything you want me to help with. Do you need to make any phone calls to relatives or anything?'

'Nothing that can't wait – I'm struggling to take it in and just now I am hoping that maybe it's a nightmare and I will wake up in a minute. Did Norman say if he wanted tea or coffee?'

'He didn't say anything' replied Helen. 'The DCI likes his coffee black and very strong, and if it's OK I'll just have a glass of water, please.'

Sandy started to lift the tray with the drinks, including a mug of hot, strong tea for Norman 'whether he wants it or not', but her hold was unsteady and Helen took it gently from her, and followed her back to where the two men were now in deep conversation.

In the short time the two women had been in the kitchen, Norman had made a considerable effort to compose himself,

64

and was telling DCI Phelps about the way in which Mark had come into their lives. At the Chief Inspector's request was relating what he knew about Mark's biological family.

'He was nearly fifteen when he came to us, initially to be placed for foster care, and I'm not sure but I think that would have ended when he became sixteen or maybe eighteen – but in any event we all got on really well and he stayed with us on a permanent basis.

'Although Mark was never critical of Social Services, he did over time tell us of some of the disastrous placements he had endured during the years of being in care, starting from when he was just about five or six years old.

'His own family history is the stuff of nightmares and I think his real father is currently in prison, possibly in Bristol. We always encouraged Mark to talk about his family, but we could understand why he was reluctant to do so.

'He had only just started going to school when his father, under the influence of drink, lashed out at him, but his older sister intervened and was sadly killed. The father, a man called Bob Wilson, was convicted of her manslaughter and Mark was taken into care, but his other sister Amy stayed with their mother.'

Norman gave a huge sigh and looked as if he was going to lose it again, when Sandy put his hands around his mug of tea and sat on a footstool next to him, taking up the saga of the Wilson family history.

'It would seem that after getting his sentence shortened for his apparent remorse and good behaviour, he returned to the family home, where Mark's mother still lived, and he beat up the man she was living with. The man died, and Mark's mother was so badly injured that a short time afterwards she also died, and it was Amy's turn to be taken into care.

'There is no doubt that for all the years he was in care Mark blamed himself for his eldest sister's death and for the repercussions of that event, because in his mind everything stemmed from his father's disappointment of Mark's femininity when he was young.

'The truth in my mind is that Bob Wilson is a despicable, homophobic, evil man. He made Mark's young life a total misery by trying to change him, and possibly blaming Mark's mother for not producing what he would call "a real man". We tried many times to tell Mark that he could not be held responsible for his father's actions, but his feelings of guilt weren't helped when he learned that his sister Amy had gone completely off the rails with drugs and mental health problems.'

'We tried making contact with his sister over the years, but we got nowhere, and at the time we formally adopted Mark ten years ago he resolved only ever to think of his new family and leave the past in the past.'

Sandy obviously had a sudden thought. 'Do you think his father has killed him too? Could he have escaped from prison?' The thoughts clearly scared her.

Martin responded. 'Mark's friend Paula told us a bit about his family background, and the facts you have given us may well be helpful in our enquiries, but it's very unlikely that Bob Wilson has escaped as it's the sort of thing we're likely to have heard about.

'However, the family history could certainly be relevant, and I'm grateful to you for your courage in sharing this information. I would urge you to make a note of anything you may remember in the next few days.'

'I have to ask you – how was he killed? Was he shot? Did he suffer?' Sandy choked on the words but the DCI had anticipated the questions.

Martin did not want to tell them anything that would subsequently be proved untrue, but remembering the gory details of the killing he could not bring himself to tell them everything at this stage.

'He wasn't shot and he wasn't beaten up. At this stage, we are looking for weapons such as knives that could have been used. I would like to tell you he didn't suffer, but the truth is I don't really know. But from my experience of such killings, death is usually rapid, so please take some comfort from that.'

He inwardly willed them not to ask any more questions, and

thankfully it looked as if they had no further appetite for knowledge of the circumstances, and were just sitting together, locked in their individual and shared grief.

Martin explained that he would be back to see them at some time tomorrow, and told them a family liaison officer would be appointed to ensure they were kept informed of progress, hopefully before reading about it in the press.

'Please, may we have Helen?' requested Sandy. 'We've met her and would feel more comfortable contacting her than having to start again with a complete stranger.'

Martin explained that he was not directly responsible for PC Cook-Watts, but nevertheless said he would speak to her sergeant to see if the request could be granted. He put his own business card down in the centre of a small hall table. 'In any event, if there's anything you want to know, or if you remember anything you think may help, no matter how trivial, you can contact me directly.'

Helen suddenly took it upon herself to hug Sandy as Norman opened the front door to let them out, and this spontaneous action seemed to trigger a release valve that caused Sandy to give vent to her emotions and she rushed, sobbing, but also swearing angrily, back into the lounge. Norman rushed after her, and DCI Phelps indicated to the flustered PC that they should take their leave. He stepped aside for her to pass before ensuring that the front door was properly closed.

Nothing was said and neither officer looked back towards the house as they walked down the drive and Martin fished into his pocket to retrieve his remote and clicked open the car doors. Turning in the semi-circle just past the house, it was Martin who from the driver's side got the best view as they exited the road. Externally there was no change to this striking property, but inside were two people whose lives would never be the same, as the foundation for their very being had just been wickedly destroyed.

Helen buried her head in her hands. 'I messed up, didn't, I at the end there? It would have been better if I had just shaken her hand but no, I had to get all physical.'

'No, no, and no again,' was Martin's response. 'You did nothing wrong. Sandy is just one step ahead of Norman, in that she has moved quite quickly from sorrow to anger, but it won't take long before the air is blue in that house. I suspect they didn't spend years in Australia without learning a few choice Aussie expletives. You have probably helped her more than you know, but there will be many more stages of grieving for them to battle with before getting through this ordeal, always supposing that they do – eventually'.

Nothing else was said as they drove back towards Cardiff Bay and observed the nightlife of the city. It was now well past midnight, and the usual weekend revelry was at its peak, with taxis moving clubbers from one venue to another and groups of party-seekers at various stages of intoxication.

Helen had said that she needed to return to Goleudy as her handbag with her house keys was there, as was her car, and as they drew into the rear car park she summoned up the courage to ask about the possibility of her being the Harding family's liaison officer.

'I haven't done all the courses yet, but I did shadow one of the FLOs a few months ago so I know the rules I and think I could do it,' she suggested.

'I'm sure you could, but as you know it's not my call. However, I will speak to Sgt Evans in the morning. There'll be a full team meeting at around lunchtime and you need to be available for that. I'm not sure exactly what time it will be but after Prof. Moore has completed the autopsy and after I have formally interviewed the people who were at the scene, so one o'clock at the earliest I should think.'

Helen shut the car door and made her way up the back steps, then through a side door leading to the staff rooms to collect her bag. She knew that there would be little sleep for her tonight, as her mind was already trawling through everything that had happened since she had arrived with Sgt Evans at the murder scene.

Yes, the whole thing was gruesome, but it was also a day she would always remember as the day on which she had decided on the direction of her future career. She had the greatest of respect for Sgt Evans, who had chosen to remain in uniform, and recognised most of her fellow officers as hard-working men and women of average intelligence content to persevere with the routine nature of the job – but for her it was now CID that beckoned.

Martin had within a few minutes left the city limits and was heading for home, feeling confounded by the fact that even on an evening such as this the thought of heading for his aunt's cottage was comforting. He wondered how long it would be before he stopped referring to his home as his aunt's cottage, but maybe he didn't want to.

His aunt had been his mother's sister, and as his mother had died from of pancreatic cancer when Martin was just eight years old, he was never sure if he remembered his mother or if over the years her face had merged with his Aunt Pat's. She had had no children of her own, and her job had always fascinated Martin as it brought her into contact with exciting people through the media of film and television.

As a teenager, Martin spent many days in the school holidays on various production sets where Pat worked as a costume standby. It was her job to ensure the quality and continuity of the actors' and actresses' costumes and any props used at all stages of the production. She had to be there watching everything intently, and she often got Martin to watch with her, developing in him a keen eye for detail and the ability to pick out anything that was not as it should be.

'Thanks for that, Aunt Pat,' whispered Martin to himself, as he turned off the A4050 and onto the quiet B roads leading to the coastal village of Llantwit Major.

The roads were now virtually deserted, and despite the sustained adrenaline rush of the latter part of the day Martin was beginning to feel tired – and not just tired but, to his surprise, actually sleepy. He just hoped that when his head hit the pillow he would be able to smother the thoughts that would attempt to invade his mind, reminding him to consider every detail of his latest and most gruesome crime scene.

The cottage was on the end of a terrace made up of just four houses, and had a driveway along the whole of one side, but Martin stopped the car just before the set of cottages and switching off his headlights pulled up at the side of the road.

Although she never complained, Martin was aware that his neighbour, a lifelong friend of his aunt, was a light sleeper, and the erratic hours that Martin's job demanded often meant comings and goings at all hours of the night. He tried to be as considerate as possible, which was appreciated, and in return she looked after his garden and cared for the plants so carefully chosen by his aunt, and about which he knew almost nothing. He couldn't be bothered making himself a hot drink, but poured himself a glass of orange juice and took it straight upstairs, setting it down on the bedside table as he set his alarm for 7 a.m. He wasn't expecting to get what would now be just under five hours' kip, but he stripped off and lie on top of the bed, anticipating hours of endless struggles with sleep and its opponents.

To begin with, all the detail of the crime scene started to invade his thoughts and he mentally began a journey through Mark's hall and into the kitchen. His mind then jerked quickly into the extraordinary appearance of the lounge – there was certainly a story to tell here – but, suddenly, he was asleep. Not a dream interrupted him, to say nothing of nightmares, and he slept deeply, his glass of juice not even touched. It was his mobile phone ringing out the 7 a.m. alarm that woke Martin, and he opened his eyes, only to close them again quickly in an attempt to erase the memory of Mark's staring out of his cold, dead torso.

Chapter Six

At seven o'clock on Sunday morning Goleudy was a hive of activity, as the case had been all night. The SOC team, under the direction of Alex Griffiths, had set up three picture galleries to rival even the most bizarre exhibitions sometimes on show in the modern art sections of the National Galleries. The first was gruesome and showed the kitchen scene from every possible angle, with strategically placed labels indicating distances of the limbs from the torso and patterns of blood spillage and splatter.

It was Alex's job to configure every possible way in which this murder could have been executed, and he was impatiently waiting for Prof. Moore to carry out the post-mortem and to give the SOCOs some more information regarding the type of weapons they were looking for. Throughout the night members of his team, together with uniformed officers, had searched the garden and the immediate area around the house, but nothing had been found.

With the welcome return of daylight and the support of additional officers, a wider and more exhaustive search had already begun, but Alex had a gut feeling that the killer or killers were unlikely to have left the tools of this treacherous act around to be found and forensically examined.

It would be interesting to see how Martin viewed the crime but it was Alex's belief that it had been well planned and consequently tracks would have been carefully covered. Thankfully, in his experience, criminals rarely covered all their tracks and with criminal detection technology improving almost daily, the smallest mistake could lead to a major breakthrough.

The most frustrating part of this process was that the discovery of that crucial criminal error, and the subsequent collection of lawyer-proof evidence, could take days, weeks, months, and even years. In that time, a sick and possibly still dangerous monster was shopping in the local Spar, or taking an open-top bus tour around the city.

Alex prayed for an early clue, but knew it was more likely that what lay ahead would be round-the-clock microscopic examination of every detail of the crime scene for his team, endless interviews for the detectives and house-to-house searches for countless police officers and special constables.

The second set of images showed the living room and focused on the sofa with pictures of the four definite sets of four deep slashes into the beautiful, expensive leather. The pictures that were highly magnified made it easy to see that the cuts had all been made with the same knife and that it had been a sharp, fairly long blade with no serrations.

Alex knew that this sort of information would help to focus the minds of his detective colleagues later in the day. He checked the rest of the setup before standing his team down, indicating that they should all get some rest before the initial Mark Wilson murder team meeting, which he guessed would be early that afternoon.

The final set of visuals showed six pictures of the fireplace in Mark's living room and showed the virtually destroyed papers exactly as they had been found, with close-ups focusing on what appeared to be two separate documents. A quick glance at four of the images would leave most people just seeing heavily charred paper and partly incinerated coals, but the last two had been computer-enhanced and enlarged so that it was just possible to see what had been set alight. Alex was especially pleased with these findings and hoped that they would help Martin begin to piece together a possible motive for this killing.

Suddenly feeling very hungry, Alex made his way to the staff dining room and after eating bacon, egg, and toast he was aware of another feeling – overwhelming tiredness. Because his home was on the outskirts of Swansea it took Alex about an hour to get from work to home and it was not a journey his sleepy eyes would enable him to consider now. So what was new? he thought.

He made his way to the fifth floor and to one of the small rooms set aside for such times, and punched his ID number into the keypad on the wall outside. The rooms were always clean and the tiny en-suite facility in each was supplied with a pile of fresh towels and basic toiletries. He instantly stripped off and had a cool, refreshing shower.

Afterwards, wrapped in a towel that barely covered him, he gingerly opened the door and stepped back into the corridor, where he was confronted by a bank of eight small lockers, five of which had names inserted in the slots on the doors. His six-digit ID gained him access to the locker labelled Alex Griffiths, and he pulled out the emergency set of clothes he kept there and the all-important toothbrush. He took a cursory look at the other four names and fleetingly wondered what the two women would keep in their lockers, but decided, best not to go there …

Before blanking out into a deep but mind-churning sleep, Alex picked up the phone at the side of the bed and let the front desk know he was crashing out for a few hours.

Recognising the voice at the end of the line, Alex asked PC Thomas to give him a shout if he had not surfaced by midday but Alex barely heard the reply because nature was taking over and there was nothing he could do to stop his eyes closing.

Martin reflected on the time when a drive at 8 a.m. on a Sunday morning would have meant passing just a few cars, but over the past ten years or so the peace of Sunday had been well and truly shattered, and now he considered it was probably one of the busiest days in and around the city.

His drive from home to the office was just long enough to provide a comfortable distance between these two parts of his life, and when a case was fresh he used the time to plan out the day, knowing it would be the only part of it where he would have real personal thinking time. He had already spoken to his

DS, and Matt had confirmed that interviews were already set up, and that Alex's team had done a first-class job in their appraisal of the crime scene. So Martin knew that the ball was now well and truly in his court.

Matt was already in Incident Room One when Martin arrived. He was deep in conversation with one of the IT bods, who was explaining how the technology worked and how the various images could be linked in all manner of ways to get a perfect three-dimensional view of any of the three investigation spots. It looked impressive, and Martin could see that Charlie's team had pulled out all the stops. He knew that she would be the first to acknowledge their efforts on her return from the Emerald Isle.

Although the images from Mark's house were fresh in Martin's mind he was, as in the past, surprised when looking at the photographs to find how now, in a more dispassionate setting, he was noticing small details that could be important. The kitchen was large, and a person could easily lie on top of the central island with arms and legs not even protruding from the sides of it, and Martin speculated that somehow Mark had been put in that position prior to death – though surely not of his own free will.

Had he been drugged? Toxicology findings would reveal that.

Had he been tied up? Martin moved to the photographs of the severed limbs and could see no obvious evidence of restraint marks on the wrists or ankles, but he would take a look at the actual body parts in the post-mortem suite later.

The arms on the floor were bare, and the top half of the body wore a designer-label black sleeveless vest. There was a similar one hanging in Martin's wardrobe back at the cottage, bought for him by his ex-wife as a birthday present. She had jokingly told him it had cost her an arm and a leg. Cost an arm and a leg – losing both arms and legs – life threw up some strange links. This particular link determined that the lovingly bought present would soon be on its way to the nearest charity shop, as he would never be able to wear it again without the image of it being stuck to Mark's body by its owner's own blood.

The legs were covered with what were once grey lightweight cropped trousers, and an unusual multi-coloured leather open-back sandal was still on one of the feet. Methodically, Martin looked at the other leg, and saw that the sandal was covering the arch of the foot with the sole facing upwards – could have happened during a struggle?

Martin quickly dismissed that theory, as taking in the complete images of the kitchen he knew that there had been no struggle and the sandal would simply have been displaced when the leg fell to the floor. How could Mark have been persuaded to lie on what was virtually a kitchen table seemingly of his own free will? It was more likely he was under threat and probably terrified.

Questions and random answers raced through Martin's mind and he was moving over to the pictures of the lounge, when Matt Pryor walked towards him, reeling off a string of messages.

'Just heard that all but one of the people for interview have arrived, and Prof. Moore has made a start on the post-mortem, requesting we leave him to get on with it and he will let us know when he is ready to answer questions. He's got his most miserable face on this morning but if he gets interested in the findings of the PM his mood will improve, so staying out of his way for now is best for all concerned.'

'I totally agree,' said Martin. 'In any event, it's the way I planned to work, and although I am not hopeful of getting anything new from the interviews we have the advantage of the preliminary statements. And at least we can look out for any anomalies.'

Matt looked intently at his boss. 'Don't think any of them could have done this, do you? It would take some bottle to butcher your friend or neighbour and then turn up on his doorstep probably within the hour pretending to expect an evening of wine and song.'

'No, I don't think any of the women killed Mark, and what possible motive would his Turkish neighbours have? No, I guess these interviews will just serve to give us a better picture of the victim, and with any luck they'll give us some new avenues to explore. Later today I also need to get back to Whitchurch as there are a few more things I would like to talk through with Mark's adoptive parents.'

'I spoke to Helen Cook-Watts just now and she told me about your visit to the Hardings' home. It's obviously made a lasting impression on her and she's keen to stay involved with them, if it's possible for her to be allocated as their liaison officer. She's good. I see a bright future for that young lady.'

Martin laughed. 'Is that purely a professional opinion, Detective Sergeant Pryor, or do I detect a more personal interest?'

'I normally respect and admire your skills of detection, guv, but on this one you are way off,' Matt said. 'Have to admit though, there aren't many female officers capable of turning their institutional uniform into such a shapely outline …'

Both men walked in companionable silence towards the interview rooms and put on the professional faces required for what was going to be hours of painstaking interrogation.

Abdi Nicanor was sitting adjacent to a police constable in the first of a block of four interview rooms and at first the two detectives were hard pushed to recognise him. Gone was the unruly, flyaway grey hair – that was now flattened with some sort of gel and was sleek and shiny. The floral open-necked shirt had been replaced – Abdi now wore a cream turtle-neck cotton sweater and brown trousers. Martin had a mental image of Mrs Nicanor determining what she considered to be a suitable image for her husband to portray during his meeting with the police, but it was clear that Abdi did not feel comfortable with her choice.

He shifted nervously in his chair and for all the world gave the appearance of a guilty man, but experience told Martin that although at this stage he was a suspect, it was more likely that his nervousness stemmed from a lifetime of carefully avoiding any contact with officialdom. Martin knew very little of the ways of the police force in Turkey, but one of the secretaries who worked in Goleudy had been arrested in Ankara about ten years ago and told horror stories of the eleven nights she spent in a shared cell. She had been completely innocent – in her case it was mistaken identity – but that had not stopped her being locked up, and it was only with the intervention of the British Embassy that she had been released.

Perhaps Abdi thought he was about to be locked up, and Martin, remembering the 'innocent until proved guilty' code, did his best to make Abdi feel more at ease in a situation that by necessity had to be formal.

The police constable rose and moved to the back of the room as Matt sat down and adjusted the recording equipment, explaining to Abdi that there would need to be a record of the interview.

'I didn't be doing nothing wrong.' Abdi's voice was wobbly. 'My wife, she says I should not have broken down Mark's door and gone in his house, but how I know what was there?'

Martin interrupted what he suspected could be Abdi's lengthy protestation of innocence and justification for his actions of the previous evening.

'No one is suggesting that you did anything wrong, Mr Nicanor, and indeed on the face of it your actions in entering Mark's house are likely to have prevented a fire and the possible destruction of vital evidence, so please try and relax and just take us step by step from the time you became aware that something was wrong next door.'

These comments obviously hit the spot, and in seconds and in his own mind Abdi went from being the stupid old man that his wife now considered him to be, to a potential local hero, and he visually relaxed and even plumped up his chest a little.

After switching on the tape and going through the usual spiel of date, time, and names of people present, Matt nodded to his DCI and Martin took up the questioning.

'What first prompted you to think something was wrong at Mark's house?'

'I hear girls screaming, shouting "Mark, Mark," lots of times, and they bang on the door a lot and it very loud, they not loud before, always quiet.'

'At what time was that?' asked Martin.

'We leave home of my wife sister at eight o'clock and walk is only about twenty minutes but I not very sure of proper time,' replied Abdi.

'Were you in your house when you heard the girls?'

'No, I hear them when we walk up hill and I tell Mrs Nicanor go in house and I will see if any trouble and girls tell me Mark not answering door and they still shout and shout.'

'What happened then?' prompted Matt. 'What made you break the door down?'

'Paula, she is the one I see the most, and she looked through letterbox and say she see smoke so the house could be on fire and Mark still inside. So I get hammer from my house and hit the lock. It break the door more than I thought, but I see smoke so I go inside. I am inside Mark's house before so I know where kitchen is and smoke was from kitchen so I went there.'

It was obvious from Abdi's expression that he was now reliving the horror of what he had seen and everyone waited patiently for him to regain his composure.

'In your own time,' encouraged Martin. 'Just tell us exactly what you did next.'

'Smoke was coming from cooker and I turn it off and open oven door but hot smoke come straight to my face and I go backwards and bump into Mark's leg on the floor.' Abdi struggled and only just managed to continue. 'But … but Mark, he was not on the floor, he on the table, and I feel very sick it was so … so terrible. What happened to him, it is so terrible?'

'That's what we are trying to find out,' responded Martin. 'Anything you can tell us, no matter how small, will help us put the pieces together.' Martin cursed inwardly at his inadvertent pun, and he was suddenly glad of Abdi's inexpert grasp of English.

'I clumsy and bash into table thing and break two dishes and spoil Mark's cakes.' Suddenly Abdi took control of himself and almost shouted. 'You not be able put Mark's pieces back together, but you catch evil swine who did this to my neighbour – to my friend.'

The look on Abdi's face and the venom with which he spat out that last sentence caused both Martin and Matt to take a fresh look at him. Up to now they had been aware of a neighbour who had attempted to come to the rescue of a friend. But he had used brute force to enter the house, and in doing so had provided just cause for his foot- and fingerprints being on the surfaces in the kitchen.

It was certainly not unheard of for a killer to cover his tracks with that type of pre-arranged action, but was this man clever enough to have thought that one through? And, in any event, what possible motive could Abdi have for murdering the man next door? Well, if there was a motive, it would come out in the enquiries, but for now Martin put this possibility on the back burner and asked Abdi to complete his version of events.

'When I know Mark is dead I be sure that ladies not see him and they come down the hall and I shout to make them go not in the kitchen – I shoo them out and say we tell police Mark is dead. Paula she wants to send ambulance but I say no, send police and we stay outside for police and they come soon.'

'Did you see anyone else around the house while you and the girls were standing outside?' asked Matt. 'Did you notice anyone taking a particular interest in what was going on?'

Abdi said he had not noticed anyone in particular, although lots of people had crossed the road to look and some asked what all the fuss was about. He commented that after the police had arrived, lots more people had gathered outside, and added that this morning there was a large group of people mainly from newspapers and television standing around the house.

Realising that there was nothing more to be gained from questioning Abdi about recent events, Martin went on to ask about the relationship between the two men and learned that when Mark moved in about five years ago it had been Abdi's wife who, apparently in accordance with Turkish custom, had knocked on his door and offered him cake and honey. The neighbours shared a common interest in cooking, but that was as far as it went and when asked to recall Abdi thought that he had probably only been in Mark's house a handful of times, and Mark had visited them just three or four times.

He knew that Mark had adoptive parents who lived in Whitchurch and visited quite often, but all he knew about Mark's real family was that he had one sister but was not in touch with her.

He could think of no one who would want to kill Mark, and with no further questions Matt switched off the tape, with the usual formalities, before thanking Abdi for his cooperation and allowing him to leave.

Matt showed Abdi to the front desk and then returned to find Martin still sitting in the interview room staring at a blank wall. He deposited two cardboard cups of coffee on the table, suggesting they both needed a caffeine boost.

'What did you make of that?' asked Martin still staring at possibly an image that was invisible to anyone but him.

'Well, they say it's the quiet ones we need to watch and my initial opinion of Mr Nicanor was that he was a quiet, unassuming sort of man, but he nearly hit a boiling point back there and I for one wouldn't like to be around if he really erupted.'

'Yes, I got the impression that there is more to Abdi Nicanor than meets the eye, but I keep asking myself what possible motive could he have for killing Mark. There doesn't seem to be one, and there is no doubt in my mind that this killer was making some sort of statement – but what, and why, I just don't know yet.'

For a few moments both men drank their coffee and gathered their thoughts and then Martin asked Matt to run through any possibilities, no matter how off the wall.

'Let's assume for a moment that Abdi killed Mark. He would have had no problem in gaining access as Mark knew him and would have let him in – probably even welcomed him if the neighbourly friendship thing is to be believed.'

'The destruction in the lounge must have been done first, as apparently there's no blood anywhere, and a clean knife was used to slit the sofa. But why didn't Mark stop him? Or maybe he was already dead and his body lying on the kitchen table, awaiting the final acts of mutilation?'

Martin wanted to ask a question but set it aside and allowed his DS to continue speculating.

'Then there are the papers that were in the fireplace, and although there's little left of them, Alex and his lot have identified Mark's birth certificate and are working on the remnants of one other official-looking document. With what little we know so far I can't link those up to Mr Nicanor, but who knows?'

'Nicanor is no youngster, but he is sturdily built and I would imagine quite strong. But I would reckon Mark to have been at least as tall as I am, and not far off my weight, and I certainly wouldn't be easily lifted on to that kitchen worktop.'

At this point Martin did interrupt. 'I can't see one man lifting Mark into that position, and there are two things that come to my mind. Either the killer had help, or Mark was forced to get himself into that position, possibly at knifepoint as knives seem to feature throughout this case.'

'Give us a chance, boss, I was about to say exactly that. And then did he kill Mark first, or did he set about methodically chopping off limbs at random?'

'If it was Abdi, it would have taken some sick guts to then leave this massacre and return a short while later as a potential rescuer and good Samaritan. However that would have covered his tracks, as I am sure you have already considered.'

'Wouldn't he have been covered in blood? And, anyway, wasn't he supposed to be at some relatives' house with his wife and family?'

Matt's analysis of possibilities was now becoming just a series of ad hoc questions and Martin stored them away with his own knowing that some of them would be answered over the next few hours through the process of interviews, SOC analysis, and the post-mortem findings.

An early lead would be essential, and Martin prayed for this, not wanting to have Sandy and Norman Harding going through the same hell with their son's killing as Elaine Philips was still enduring as a result of her husband's unsolved murder.

'I don't expect the next few interviews to give us much more regarding the events of last night, but the three women may be able to fill in some background about Mark's lifestyle – relationships, work, money, and all of that – and then I want you to check on the four of them and interview any witnesses who can prove they were where they say they were before arriving at Mark's house.' Martin was ticking off the small details that needed to be checked out, knowing that to take anything at face value could be to miss the vital clue to unlocking this crime – he was not going to let that happen.

As expected, the interviews with Suzanne and Anne had added little to the accounts given by Paula and Abdi Nicanor, but did confirm the exact sequence of events prior to his arrival on the scene.

Suzanne explained how she had been the first to arrive having been dropped off by her seventeen-year old daughter, who was on her way to visit friends and yes, Carla would be able to confirm that she and her mother had been together shopping since about two o'clock that afternoon.

As they had shopped and eaten in their local village, it was certain that any number of people would be able to supply them with an alibi for the hours preceding Mark's murder, and although this would need to be checked out Martin was content that at least one person could be crossed off the list of potential killers.

When she had been dropped off, Suzanne had crossed the road to Mark's house and told the detectives that she remembered being surprised to see the gate open but assumed that Anne had arrived before her and hadn't closed it.

'I knew it wouldn't have been Mark or Paula as they are both a bit fussy when it comes to security, but Anne doesn't tend to think much about that sort of thing, so I guessed she must have got there before me.'

Suzanne went on to say that she had carefully closed the gate and then rang the doorbell but had got no reply and finally she had called through the letterbox, but still nothing.

'At first I thought I'd got the date wrong, but I had heard someone in the café earlier talking about the Eurovision Song Contest so I knew it was the right night – and anyway when I looked through the letterbox I got the most delicious smell of baking, so I knew Mark must be there. I checked my watch and I can tell you that it was exactly two minutes to eight and so I knew that I was right on both the time and the date – not a date I will ever forget.'

At this point of her interview Suzanne almost broke down and she asked a question that had obviously been troubling her. 'If I had been able to get in then, would I have prevented Mark from being killed? It was at least ten minutes after I went to find the others and before Abdi was able to break the door down.'

Martin was quick to reassure her. 'We estimate that by then Mark had been dead for a while, possibly as much as an hour – there would have been nothing you could have done for your friend so please don't torture yourself on that account. What happened next?'

'I got a feeling that something was not right and I used my phone to call Mark's mobile, but when I listened at the door I couldn't hear it ringing inside so I decided to go and find Paula – I know she lives within walking distance and would be on her way. As it happens as soon as I went back out through the gate I looked down the hill and could see Paula in the distance so I walked down to meet her.'

At this point Suzanne and Paula's recollection was exactly the same, as they both remembered walking back up the hill together and causing a bit of a rumpus by hammering on Mark's door and calling out in an attempt to get his attention.

'When did Anne arrive?' asked Matt.

Suzanne thought for a moment and then replied that it must have been almost immediately and she thought it was even before they had started banging and shouting, so yes, she must have come in straight behind them.

When Anne was questioned she concurred that she had arrived just a few moments behind Suzanne and Paula, as when she had crossed the road she had seen her two friends going through the gate.

All versions of the events that followed matched in every detail and after the interviews had been completed DS Pryor ensured that the tapes were numbered and took them to Incident Room One for safekeeping.

On his way back he collected the usual two cups of coffee and this time balanced on top of one cup was a paper plate holding two extra-large, sugar-coated doughnuts.

'Thought you might like a sugar rush,' said Matt, putting one of the offerings in front of his boss. 'I managed to grab some semblance of sleep last night and chose an extra half hour this morning at the expense of anything to eat and I just realised I am starving.'

Martin grinned – his DS was always starving, and it was well-known that food, rugby, and women were his three main loves, and that his indulgence in all three was well above average. 'Thanks. I grabbed a couple of bananas before leaving the cottage, but a sticky jam doughnut will fill the gap nicely and we can get something more substantial from the staff canteen before the first team brief. Hopefully that should start between one and half past and with the results of the PM and the SOC conclusions we should be able to get some idea of what we are looking at.'

'That stuff we got from Paula about Mark's real family was something else – what a family! Obviously rows and beatings were commonplace, but to have your sister killed as a result of a domestic, and then years later for your father, just released from jail, to fatally injure your mother and kill her lover. It's more like something out of a crime novel than real life.' Matt hesitated. 'I presume the father is still inside?'

Having finished his snack, Martin licked his sticky fingers, got up and walked to the door. 'We need to check it out, it's been twenty-odd years but I suspect he's in for most of his life, and anyway I can't put the father at the centre of this killing – sounds as if his victims were as the result of an uncontrolled temper in someone who has come to accept violence as a means to an end. This killer is ruthless, but totally in control, and we didn't see a sign of random rage, nor the aftermath of someone who had hit out at everything with his fists, as was the M.O. for Mark's father.

'Anyway, Matt, you can organise the check-ups on the witness statements and dig up whatever you can on Mark's generic family background. Also, get the latest on any progress regarding the search for the murder weapons and house to house enquiries. We need all that by one o'clock – any problems I'll be in my office trying to plan out the initial meeting before I get the inevitable call to go to the PM rooms to witness the macabre wonders of Prof. Moore's handiwork.'

Checking his watch, Martin saw that it was already 11.40. Matt left, closing the office door behind him, and Martin pulled out a large sheet of paper from his drawer and began scribbling down names and facts as they occurred to him. This was his own particular way of brainstorming, and experience had taught him to avoid any kind of order but just to write down anything that popped into his head. Within minutes the sheet was filled with ad hoc details of the case, and he marvelled at how much was already known, but how little sense could be made of the facts.

He then took out a second sheet of paper and drew three vertical columns. He gave each of the columns a heading and in the first one labelled 'Absolute facts' he wrote down the details such as date, place, name of victim, and anything that was beyond dispute. He trawled his scribble page for every known detail and hoped that this column would have grown considerably by the end of the day. Then he would be able to concentrate on his second column, 'Facts to be checked', and finally his favourite, entitled 'What if'

His desk phone rang and Martin immediately recognised the voice of one of the PM technicians, Mrs Williams, a middle-aged motherly sort of woman whom most people would have identified as, perhaps, a primary school teacher, or even a woman vicar. Few would have envisaged that she spent most of her working life handling body parts and clearing up the mess left behind after post-mortem examinations on bodies that were often the result of horrific criminal activity.

She was always respectful of status, and addressed Martin as Detective Chief Inspector Phelps when she gave him the message, which was that Prof. Moore was at the point where he would like to demonstrate some of his findings. 'Thank you, Mrs Williams,' said Martin. 'I will come straight up.' As he put the phone down, he realised that he didn't even know her first name, and had never heard anyone call her anything other than 'Mrs Williams'.

Martin climbed the stairs to the fourth floor and was greeted by the distinctive smell that he always associated with the laboratories and post-mortem rooms. It was not unpleasant exactly but it always had the same effect of turning his stomach over a bit, with that slightly sick feeling you got when going into an exam or an interview.

He walked along the main corridor, passing lab rooms where technicians were working flat out on what had already been delivered to them by Mrs Williams, finally getting to the room that served as a changing area for the two adjacent post-mortem rooms. The routine was familiar to Martin, and he put on a disposable gown and hat and covered his own shoes with plastic over-shoes before pushing open the door to PM Room 2, the one favoured by Prof. Moore.

On hearing the door open, the professor looked up from the table and indicated to Martin to come over to where he was working.

'It's just as I thought last night – each of the limbs has been severed with a different tool, so we are definitely looking for four weapons. The right arm was, to put it crudely, chopped off, with something like a hatchet – the sort of thing you would use for chopping relatively small pieces of wood, say for a domestic wood burner.'

'The killer didn't quite detach the arm with the first swipe, as you will see from the fact that there are two slightly different angles involved, and with what I have ascertained from blood coagulation this was the first limb to be severed.'

'For some God-forsaken reason, the killer then chose a

machete-type knife for the left arm and must have taken a powerful swing to bring the blade down, as apart from some bone splinters the knife has virtually gone through everything like it was butter. It would also indicate to me that the killer was quite tall, and very strong, not to mention a complete psychopath.'

Prof. Moore waited for Martin to look at some of the areas he had indicated, expecting the usual barrage of questions, but Martin just said 'And the legs?' and so Prof. Moore continued.

'To have the sort of weapons readily available to complete this savage carnage suggests considerable planning, and I think when you can come up with a motive for the killing you will be very near to the killer.

'The left leg was amputated using a blade with a curved edge something like a garden scythe used to cut the grass, not that anyone does that any more. Because of the curve and the fact that the leg was on a flat surface the tip of the blade at the first stroke struck the surface of the work top. The SOC team took some pictures of that.

'I can't really figure out what happened next as the same blade was not used to finish the job, it's almost as if the weapon was turned over and the outer arch used, but I have never seen a curved blade sharpened on both sides – have you?'

Martin shook his head but still said nothing while his brain took in the sheer brutality and complexity of the crime he was faced with and expected to solve. One thing he knew for certain was that the Prof's thoughts about motive mirrored his own and gave him some hope as it was looking more and more likely that Mark had known his killer.

'The order I have taken you through with the limbs is in my view and backed by initial analysis the order in which the killer worked and the right leg was the final limb to be attacked. I am at a loss to give you an exact picture of any weapon that could have been used other than to say it had a serrated edge and could have been a small saw but that doesn't fit into the method used for removing the other limbs.

'A saw means you have to look at what you are doing and it

takes some time to saw through bone whereas the other leg and the arms were removed by very sharp blades and using extreme brute force. Having said that, this was no run-of-the-mill saw and I would put it somewhere between a saw and blade, so it's possible the teeth were very sharp and very close together.'

'What about the torso?' Martin asked. 'Has that been mutilated in any way?'

'Not a mark on it.'

'Was he drugged?'

'Can't say yet, but all sorts of tests have been requested so in the next couple of days we'll know more about Mark Wilson than he ever knew about himself.'

'What about restraint marks? Anything on the arms and legs to suggest he was tied up?'

'Nothing at all, this is one of the most perfect bodies I have ever had on this table, and before this happened he was in very good shape – obviously not a smoker or a heavy drinker. And he looked after himself. We know he was gay, although there are no signs of recent sexual activity, but that's not to rule out any sexual or even homophobic motive for his killing, and I'm pleased to say that's for you, not me, to consider.'

'Thank you,' said Martin. 'I would really appreciate your input at our meeting, and if you could push some photographs through to the computer staff, we could use them to compare with the ones SOC have provided.'

'Mrs Williams has already taken a flash drive downstairs and yes of course I will be at the meeting – wouldn't miss the opportunity of showing off the skills of the Pathology Department.'

Martin managed a smile as he left the room and discarded his protective clothing. He washed his hands before heading to the food his stomach was calling for. A few years ago he wouldn't have eaten for days after a visit to the PM rooms but he had learned to separate his own needs from the sights and sounds of the job and this had led to a much more comfortable relationship with his stomach.

Matt Pryor was already tucking into sausage, mash, and

baked beans, and Alex Griffiths had obviously recently joined him and chosen bacon, eggs, and toast, treating this middle of the day meal as his second breakfast, having just woken up.

Martin picked up a plate of lasagne with salad and a chunk of garlic bread, but then changed the bread for a non-garlic version as a mark of respect for the company he would be keeping later. A message had come through that Sandy and Norman Harding would like to see Mark's body. Martin would make himself available for that viewing if required.

He joined his two colleagues and, unusually for them, nothing was said until they had finished eating and Alex had got them all cups of coffee.

'Ready for the first briefing, guv?' asked Matt. 'Brains has a mass of information to bring from his team, and as you requested a press conference has been arranged. It's starting at 3 o'clock. The PR lot upstairs want to put a stop to the rumours that are already being printed.'

'Well, the press won't get much from me at this stage,' said Martin. 'Heaven knows we're going to need to keep them on board with this one, so I'll just make it short, but certainly not sweet. Let's get the show on the road – with the team we have I know we can bring this evil bastard – or bastards – to justice.'

Chapter Seven

Incident Room One was the largest of the purpose-built rooms at Goleudy, and at ten past one on the Sunday afternoon it was full of technical staff, uniformed officers, and members of the CID team. There was a high level of noise as groups around the room speculated and argued about who could have done this and why. Martin welcomed this scenario as it was often the throwaway remarks at these sessions that led to new lines of enquiry and he was in the business of listening to any ideas and clues – however cryptic!

It would be wrong to suggest that an immediate hush fell over the room when DCI Phelps entered – no one has that level of respect for authority in this day and age – but a definite sense of purpose arrived and the disparate groups moved to sit with members of their own particular discipline.

As agreed, Sgt Evans and PC Cook-Watts sat at a front table with the other two officers who had been the first to arrive on the scene, and Alex went over to join a group of nine SOCOs at the adjoining table.

At that point Prof. Moore arrived and he and DS Pryor sat on the two chairs at the front of the room facing the rows of about thirty uniformed staff. No one had put out a seat for Martin – he was a natural pacer and would spend the next hour or so on his feet and moving between the material that was on display and the large whiteboard that would soon mirror the sheet of paper he had in his desk drawer but he hoped it would also have lots of new information.

One of the IT staff came to the front to adjust the screen alongside the whiteboard, and indicated to Martin that they were all set up to show whatever detail was needed from the SOC investigation, and from Prof. Moore's examination.

'This murder is the stuff of our worst nightmares, and I am duty bound to remind all of you that the force has in place expert counselling and support services to help any of us, including me, if there are issues we find difficult to cope with. There's no shame in seeking help, so please remember that.' Martin looked around the room as he spoke these words, and took in the huge range of ages of the men and women present – he was reminded of the old adage that one must be getting old when policemen look so young – and in his not-that-old eyes some of these looked young enough to still be in school.

'I plan to go through everything as it happened and to encourage everyone to put forward any ideas, no matter whether they seem insignificant, and basically if a question of any sort pops into your mind then ask it, OK?'

Sgt Evans responded to a nod from DCI Phelps and got to his feet. He gave out the details of the time the call first came through and the order in which the two squad cars signalled their acceptance to attend the 999 call.

Martin had already headed the whiteboard with the date of the crime and now entered the documented time of the 999 call and the times that each squad car arrived at the house. As Sgt Evans continued Martin was able to add the names of the people who were at the house, and to note some details such as the damage to the front door.

The room fell deathly quiet as Sgt Evans went on to describe the scene inside the house, and in particular the bloodbath in the kitchen. Most eyes in the room looked towards the images on the first board set up by SOCO.

Holding up his hand Martin stopped Sgt Evans and asked if there were any questions or points to be raised.

'Were the three women and the man together when you arrived?' A PC directed her question at Sgt Evans.

'More or less, but to be exact the first person we saw was

Anne Davies, who was standing at the gate, but she said nothing and just pointed to Paula and Mark's neighbour, Mr Nicanor, who were standing in the porch. The other woman, Suzanne, was actually standing in the garden and had a few flowers in her hand – she had already picked some and placed them in the porch.'

There was a general discussion about the rationale behind picking flowers under these circumstances, but the agreement was that people sometimes did strange things and no one could think of any sinister reason for this action.

'Why did you ask the question?' prompted Martin.

'Just wondering about the relationship between these people, nothing more and probably not relevant,' replied PC Mullen. 'Also wondered if the four people have got alibis for the hours before the murder?'

Matt answered that question, as it had been on the list of tasks Martin had asked him to complete prior to the meeting. 'They have all provided us with alibis and we are in the process of checking them out – not all the people required to verify the alibis have been contacted yet but we are working on that.'

'Was there any sign of blood on any of them?' asked another PC, and in response Sgt Evans explained that the only blood had been on one of the shoes of the Turkish neighbour, and that could be explained as he had already been inside the kitchen.

Sgt Evans went on to describe the actions of himself and the other three officers prior to the arrival of the SOC team, Prof. Moore, and DCI Phelps.

The top half of Martin's whiteboard was now covered in black pen, and he once again asked for questions or comments and for a few moments it seemed the whole room was having difficulty in unscrambling the information. But then a series of randomly ordered thoughts and questions flooded towards DCI Phelps.

'The sofa thing is bizarre, isn't it?'

'Why is there no evidence of a fight or even a struggle – not even a broken ornament?'

'I think the killer must have known the victim and Mark

must have let him in.'

'If the killer wanted the documents in the fireplace, why not just take them with him?'

'I don't get the bit about the body lying on top of that island thing in the kitchen. How did he get there? He wasn't a lightweight, and lifting him up there would have been difficult – but surely to God he wouldn't have agreed to lie there and be massacred?'

The room was now getting noisy as Martin allowed everyone to prod one another into question after question, and that was leading to some pretty big what ifs.

He listened carefully and added a few comments to his board, before drawing a horizontal line across the board and dividing the bottom half into the three columns he now hoped to fill. As before, he wrote out the headings 'Absolute facts', 'Facts to be checked', and 'What ifs'.

Martin called the meeting to order and invited Alex to give the findings of his team. Instantly, all eyes were fixed on the screen, where images were now being shown of the damage to Mark's front door.

'I will take you through everything in much the same way that Sgt Evans has already done, but with the benefit of the coordinating skills of our IT colleagues, who have basically made it possible for us to view the pictures we took from every conceivable angle. This first shot shows how entry was gained to the house by Mr Nicanor, who used a lump hammer to break the lock, and as you can see the force that was used was considerable, splitting the door frame and completely destroying the latch and chain.'

'When we examined all the locking mechanisms of the door it became obvious that the victim was more security-conscious than most of us, as apart from a state-of-the-art lock there was a security chain and a bolt on the inside, and the lock was wired up to a fairly sophisticated alarm system. The security chain was intact – we can assume that it wasn't fastened as if it had been Mr Nicanor would have broken it. We are checking for prints, hoping that Mark would have secured the chain automatically when he let his killer in, and that the killer had to release it on the way out.'

'I can also confirm that the alarm system was de-activated and there wasn't a single fingerprint to be found on the operating system, not even Mark's prints, indicating that it was switched off by the person or persons involved in this crime and wiped clean of any incriminating evidence.'

Alex pressed the remote control he was holding. Now frozen on the screen was a bird's eye view of the kitchen, showing the handiwork of the murderer in full colour and in all its gruesome detail.

There was a sharp intake of breath from many of the audience who although having been told the details of the crime, were now seeing for the first time the real horror of what had happened and Alex deliberately waited a few moments for everyone to take it all in.

'I have spoken to Prof. Moore, and we are in agreement about the way in which the murder and mutilation was carried out, but he may have more to tell us following the PM that was completed earlier, so I am going to leave that to him. Unfortunately from our point of view, there is little in the way of evidence for us to examine – nothing in the kitchen was disturbed, there's hardly anything in the way of fingerprints, and no dirty cups or glasses. Either Mark didn't offer his visitor a drink, or it became obvious quite soon that this was not a social call.'

Alex was aware that his team was not going to be much help with the analysis of the actual murder scene and to the relief of many present he pressed the button to reveal the next scene. He pointed out that the white flecks all over the image were not faults with the photography but very light pieces of the white fibre that had been firmly packed into the sofa.

'This is the lounge,' he explained. 'Here again there is no sign of a struggle and apart from the obvious damage to the sofa there is nothing out of place and, yet again, we aren't blessed with much in the way of fingerprints to examine.'

Alex pressed another button on the remote. The system

zoomed in on the sofa and he let it settle first of all on the seating area.

'Although the destruction is absolute, we don't think that the sofa was destroyed in a wild or random way, but in a methodical, predetermined fashion, with four deep cuts in each seat and four similar cuts across the back. All cuts have been made with a very sharp knife. At first we thought the blade would be long, but on further examination it seems the sofa was so firmly packed that any sharp knife would have done the job, and the super-soft filling would have initially come out with some force. That's why it covers so many areas of the room, and whoever wielded this knife would inevitably have been covered with the fibres.

'There's no sign of blood anywhere in the lounge, which leads us to believe that the sofa was the first thing to be attacked, but it begs the question: why is there no evidence of the sofa filling in the kitchen if the killer moved into the kitchen from the lounge?'

Martin interrupted Alex for the first time and shared what he was increasingly ready to believe. 'There is every possibility we are looking for more than one criminal, and that the lounge and the kitchen witnessed two very separate crimes – the works of two separate criminals, although why is beyond me at this point in time.'

He indicated to Alex that he could continue, and noted that now on the screen were examples of the sort of knives that could have been used on the sofa. Another button was pressed, and a close up of the fireplace in the lounge came into focus. Here Alex was pleased to say that his team had experienced some real success and were able to identify the documents that were seemingly burned.

'In essence what we have found are two birth certificates. One is the original birth certificate of Mark Wilson, with the names of his biological parents, and the other is Mark's adoption certificate, showing the date of adoption by Norman and Sandy Harding –'

'Well done,' interrupted Martin. 'From the state of those

documents I didn't think you would be able to identify anything, so that's fantastic news and it may lead us to finding out a reason for this crime. I am more and more convinced that this has something to do with Mark's biological family, so that's an urgent line of enquiry.'

Some general discussion erupted in the lull after Alex sat down, but quietened the instant Prof. Moore got to his feet and accepted the remote control from Alex. The professor loved an audience, especially one as captive as this, and he knew they would hang on to his every word. And they knew he would not disappoint.

The professor flashed image after image on to the screen, with the first set of photos being those he had taken at the scene of the crime and the second those he had taken at various stages of the post-mortem examination. As he did so, he meticulously explained how he had reached the conclusion that the limbs had been removed in the order of left arm, right arm, left leg, and finally right leg. Although he did not use all the scientific language of his trade, he was not condescending, and treated his audience to a fascinating lesson in blood analysis and tissue examination.

The individual images of each limb taken in the post-mortem rooms were accompanied by photographs of the type of knives that could have been used for their severance, and after he had shown the fourth of the limb sets he looked towards Martin, giving him the opportunity to comment on how the team could best use this information.

'Normally we would be looking for one weapon, but here it is obvious that not only were four weapons used, but that each one is of a different type. I don't believe for one moment we are going to find these knives dumped anywhere – they are significant and in the way that some murderers take trophies from their victims, it occurs to me that these knives may be his trophies. If that is the case, they will still be with him.

'I say "him" as it is unlikely, given the sheer brute strength required to amputate limbs, that the killer could have been a woman, but whether it was one man or two, or even more, is not clear. There is almost certainly a fifth knife, as the blade used on the sofa does not match any of the weapons used in the kitchen.'

He nodded towards Prof. Moore, who completed his part of the meeting by confirming that the usual array of tests had been done to determine Mark's blood group and rhesus type, his DNA, analysis of his stomach contents, and blood tests to cover all eventualities, including whether or not the victim had been drugged, the results of which would be available shortly.

Martin looked at his watch, remembering that the time for the press conference was getting close. He wanted to consider which facts to give out at this stage, and in particular the best way to get an early appeal to the public for help. He shouted over the increasingly animated discussion. 'OK, let's see what we can make of what we have, and what the next steps should be.'

Martin turned to his whiteboard and looked at the copious notes he had made while his colleagues were talking. He used some of the words he had underlined to focus his mind.

'Sgt Evans, you and your team will link up with the SOC officers to complete a search of the house and gardens, and with CID officers to make house-to-house enquiries in the area. As the garden of the Nicanor family is adjacent to the victim's property I suggest we also make that part of the search, but I emphasise that this is merely routine, as we have no evidence that links Mr Nicanor to the crime, as yet. I suggest you get started right away and let me know immediately if anything turns up.'

A group of uniformed officers and some plain-clothes staff were already on their way to the door when Martin remembered something, and hastily called to let everyone know that PC Cook-Watts had been appointed as the family liaison officer for Mark's adoptive parents, and so any contact with them should be through her.

Helen had been leaving with the others but then came back into the room, a little unsure of what she should be doing. Martin indicated that she should join the four men who were left, and who had now settled around the front table.

'It will probably be useful for you to hear this discussion so that you are up to speed with what we are doing, and unless I say anything to the contrary, Helen, you are free to keep Mr and Mrs Harding fully informed of the efforts that are being made to find Mark's killer.'

'Just to let you know, a request has come through to my office – the Hardings want to see Mark's body, and the professor has confirmed that he will ensure the body is ready for them to view at 4 p.m. I suggest you get out to them beforehand and bring them in via the Visitors' Room. I thank God that at least their son's face isn't disfigured; from what I saw in the PM rooms earlier he looks amazingly peaceful, so hopefully they will take some comfort from that.'

'You will remember from the meeting earlier that we will not be releasing the actual details of the killing to the press and so, like the rest of the public, the only thing Mr and Mrs Harding can know at this time is that the murder weapon was a knife, and that there are no suggestions of sexual interference. If they ask questions that you find too difficult, please speak to me, but I'm sure you will be fine, so go and pick them up as soon as we are finished here.'

Prof. Moore said he had nothing further to add, and that he would like to get back to the lab if that was OK? Martin nodded and thanked him before getting up and walking to the whiteboard to get his and his colleagues' minds focused on the next few hours.

'Look at what we have,' said Martin. 'We can only assume that there was no evidence of forced entry before the door was broken down – the women had been in the porch for some time and would have gone in if the door had been tampered with. So either Mark knew the person at the door, or it was the sort of person one would let in for whatever reason – like whom?'

Between them they reeled off possibilities including meter readers, charity collectors, Jehovah's Witnesses, salesmen for Sky packages, and double glazing firms' representatives.

Matt added one of his own. 'Then of course there's our lot,

unless you're a criminal you would probably let in anyone in a police uniform.'

Alex continued. 'My money is on the victim knowing whoever it was that rang his doorbell, but even if gloves were not worn we can forget finding any relevant finger prints there as every one of Mark's friends rang that bell over and over.'

'So Mark let in someone he knew, possibly more than one person, and it would have been at the time he was preparing food for the evening he was planning to have with his friends.' Martin paused. 'He would probably have been in the kitchen when the doorbell rang.'

'The main groups of people we all know are family, friends, neighbours, and work colleagues,' suggested Matt. 'Although Mark wasn't a loner, there don't appear to be too many names on his list, so we should get round to seeing most of them by the end of tomorrow. We checked out his father, Bob Wilson, and he's detained at Her Majesty's pleasure in Bristol's Cambridge Road prison. Mark has never visited, and in fact the only family member to ever request a visitor's permit is Mark's one surviving sister, Amy.'

'Have we got an address for her?' asked Martin.

'There was a fancy visitors' book on the hall table at the victim's house, but her name isn't in it,' said Alex. 'In fact, it looks as if the book may have been a Christmas present, as the names and dates only go back to January of this year. It may give us some help regarding recent visitors, but it's more likely that names and addresses of any significance will be on Mark's laptop and our computer experts are going through that at the moment. Surprise, surprise, all his passwords are neatly written out on a piece of card in his wallet together with what is probably a list of PINs and internet banking details – when will people learn?'

'Yes, but it's not easy. We're told to use different numbers for everything, but most of us have trouble remembering our phone numbers, so it's almost inevitable we need to write these things down somewhere – but in this case the ease at which theft would have been possible makes it simple for us to rule it out.' Matt thought and then went on. 'Absolutely nothing appears to have been taken, and there was plenty to tempt your regular burglar, from the latest wall-mounted big screen television to a wallet, a watch, and even a jar full of pound coins all ready for the taking.'

Martin agreed. 'Let's be grateful for the things we can rule out, and I agree theft is one of them. The only things the killer seemed to want from Mark were the two documents that together seem to demonstrate his life – that is to say, they provide evidence that he was born in the first place, and was then given the opportunity of a new life with his adoption. Although the only reason those documents were needed was to facilitate their destruction. So who would want to enter Mark's home, burn the legal evidence that he lived, make some sort of statement on his sofa, and then cut him to pieces in the kitchen?'

'It's definitely someone he knew and someone with an almighty big reason to hate him. Matt, we need to get our lot working on any known contacts and for them to supply us with alibis regarding where they were between 5 p.m. and 7 p.m. yesterday afternoon. Anyone who is unable to provide witnesses to their whereabouts you can bring in for questioning – I don't care who they are.'

Turning to Helen Cook-Watts, Martin added. 'That includes Norman and Sandy Harding. If they have no one other than one another to verify where they were, we will need to put the same questions to them as we do to any of the others.'

Helen looked visibly shocked. 'You can't possibly believe that devastated couple had anything to do with Mark's murder! They looked like they'd lost the will to live themselves when we gave them the news. I just can't imagine them being involved – and anyway, surely they wouldn't have had the physical strength, would they?'

'You're probably right, Helen, and on the face of it they completely adored Mark. However, none of us know what goes on behind closed doors, especially with complex family set-ups, and so we mustn't let our hearts rule our heads. For now, let's consider that everyone who knew Mark could be the killer or could have arranged the killing. Mistakes have been made in the past, so we'll rule everyone in and only when we are completely satisfied with their alibis will we rule them out.'

Matt and Alex nodded. They had both been here before and could easily remember cases when 'butter-wouldn't-melt-in-the-mouth' little old ladies and middle-aged 'pillars of the community', had turned out to be ruthless killers, and time had been wasted because they had been considered too unlikely to have been questioned properly.

'Alex, I would be grateful if you could return to Mark's house and let me know of any developments there. Matt, when you have got everyone working on the contacts, come and join me for the press conference.' Martin turned to Helen and said, 'I will be around when you bring Mr and Mrs Harding in to view the body, so if they need to speak to me, or if you feel it would be better if I was there, then give me a ring.'

They all got up and moved quickly off in three different directions, leaving Martin to have one final look at his whiteboard and draw a thick black line around the section that included the names of the two remaining members of Mark's genetic family. There was no evidence to support his gut feeling, but all his instincts, and perhaps his past experiences, were leading him in that direction.

Martin hated press conferences in spite of the fact he had probably now been party to hundreds – maybe that was partly why, he thought. He'd attended numerous media awareness courses and recognised that in a case such as this a simple press release would satisfy no one. He also had to admit that, although public appeals via the media inevitably led to false leads and wasted manpower, there was always the chance that just one genuine response could prove really useful.

Matt joined him as he walked down the back stairs, then headed to the front of the building. He went into the room adjacent to the reception that was used for all public meetings and permanently set up to accommodate the press and all its paraphernalia. He used the side door that took him straight to the front of the room so avoiding the leads, microphones, and cameras that were everywhere as the various media types elbowed their way to prime positions.

The table at which the detectives sat was on a slightly elevated platform, and microphones were placed in front of the two chairs on which DS Pryor and DCI Phelps now sat facing a sea of impatient men and women with deadlines to meet.

Martin tapped his microphone and the room became relatively quiet as he first of all read out the statement he had carefully prepared.

'Yesterday, Saturday 29th May, the police were called to the home of Mr Mark Wilson in Penylan after a neighbour had discovered a body in the house. The body has been identified as the homeowner, and we have no doubt that Mr Wilson was brutally murdered at some time between 5 p.m. and 7 p.m. last evening. We would like to take this opportunity to ask any members of the public who were in the area during that period of time to come forward, as they may have seen something that will be of assistance to the enquiry.'

The room erupted, and Martin had to stand and practically bellow into his microphone to get some semblance of order.

'I will take questions but only if I can hear myself speak.' Martin sat back down and nodded towards a journalist whom he knew worked for one of the evening newspapers, and who quickly took the opportunity to ask not just one but three consecutive questions.

'Is it true his head was chopped off? Was he one of the big boys in the drugs trafficking around here? Do you have anyone in the frame for the killing?'

Martin stared in disbelief at the grossly overweight reporter who looked as if he had a season ticket to McDonalds and whose only form of exercise was lifting cheeseburgers from his plate to his mouth. Where did these people get their information? At least he had chosen to ask about the only part of Mark's body that had not been 'chopped off', as he had so crudely put it, and so Martin was able to answer truthfully.

'I can assure you that Mr Wilson was not decapitated, and

we have no reason to link him to drugs in any way, shape, or form, or indeed to any other type of criminal activity. As yet we have been unable to make any arrests, but there has been a lot of evidence gathered from the crime scene that will undoubtedly take us in that direction in the very near future.'

Martin had been advised some years ago to use those sorts of words, as in most cases the murderer would actually be listening with macabre curiosity to radio and television accounts of his handiwork, and even buying up newspapers exposing his notoriety. It had been known to rattle some criminals on hearing that they may have left evidence behind – a longshot, but Martin was hardly going to admit that not only was there no one sitting in the cells, but that there wasn't any likelihood of that any time soon, not without some sort of a break.

Again the room became noisy and Martin simply waited until there was reasonable calm before taking a two-part question from a woman he recognised as Laura Cummings, one of the local television crime reporters.

'Is it true that Mark Wilson's real father is in jail for the manslaughter of his daughter and the subsequent murder of his wife and her lover on the Penrhys Estate in the Rhondda some years ago?'

So, someone had done their homework, but clearly not everyone, as the majority of the reporters were hearing this information for the first time, leading to a flurry of texting and emailing from a variety of mobile phones.

She continued. 'What was it you said? – "no links to criminal activity in any way shape or form" – with a family like that it's hardly the case, is it Detective Chief Inspector Phelps – what else is there you are not telling us?'

It was the norm for reporters to give police officers their full title when they believed they had caught them out and were in the act of exposing some sort of cover up and the inevitability of it amused Martin.

'The question I responded to related to Mr Mark Wilson, and not to his birth parents. And as far as we are able to tell our victim was not in contact with any members of the family since he was a small boy.'

'He was gay!' shouted a short, pimply-faced youth from the back of the room. 'Is that anything to do with his death?'

Prepared for this question, Martin responded. 'It is no secret that Mark was homosexual, and even did some campaigning for the rights of gays and lesbians. But there is nothing to indicate his killing was linked to his sexuality and he was not sexually abused around the time of his murder.'

'Was he shot, knifed, strangled, or what?' The same half-pint reporter was making up for his physical size by using a strangely powerful voice.

'We are looking for a knife, or possibly knives, but none have as yet been found at the scene.' Matt answered this question as previously agreed.

'So how many unsolved murders have you got on your books now, Detective Chief Inspector Phelps?' Laura Cummings' interruption was more of an accusation than a question, and Martin could easily have risen to the bait. Instead he looked straight at her and reminded her that they were there to work together on this case and not to score cheap points on the seeming lack of progress in other cases.

'It seems as if there are no further questions regarding the murder of Mark Wilson, but before ending this press conference I would like to make one final appeal to the public. Please come forward if you can give us any information. There must have been some unusual activity around Mr Wilson's house between the hours of five and eight p.m. last evening. Someone must have seen something.'

The room was quickly emptying as reporters rushed off to meet their seemingly endless deadlines, which Martin suspected were for the most part self-imposed and created to make them seem more important. He did not, however, underestimate the importance of the media, and he was aware that some of the cameras were still pointed in his direction as he and Matt left the room – it would, as always, be interesting to see what he said in print, and even more interesting to see what he didn't say in print.

He was sure that the phones would start ringing in Goleudy as soon as this particular item was read out on the evening news stations and hoped that at least one person out of the inevitable timewasters would be able to bring something of relevance to the investigation.

Instead of going back to his office, Martin returned to Incident Room One and spent the next twenty minutes without saying a word but revisiting every photograph and flicking through the computer images, going over and over the scenes from Mark's kitchen and lounge. He was adding a few comments to the whiteboard when DS Pryor arrived, eager to give Martin the information he had gained about Mark's family.

Paula had already given them some facts, but now they knew for certain the dates and circumstances of the death of Sarah Wilson in 1974, and the subsequent conviction of Bob Wilson for her manslaughter. Matt said that the administration at HM Bristol Prison had been most helpful, and the records of Bob Wilson while serving his first prison sentence seemed to show a prisoner who deeply regretted his crime. One particular psychiatric report described a domestic incident that had gone terribly wrong, and almost depicted Bob Wilson as a victim rather than a criminal.

The reports and an exemplary prison record had led to the early release of Bob Wilson, who within hours of that release had brutally murdered his wife's lover and inflicted an injury on his wife that had resulted in her death some months later.

Bristol had described a very different Bob Wilson when he was returned to prison and he freely admitted to having waited out his previous time in the knowledge that as soon as possible he would kill his wife for bearing their son. Recent psychiatric reports described him as a self-confessed homophobic, and Wilson in turn described his son as 'the bloody little queer' who 'ruined all their lives'.

Martin shook his head in disbelief, calculating that Mark must have been just a small boy when this opinion of him had been formed by his father. Over the years, his father had built up more and more hatred towards his son, in spite of having never actually seen him as a teenager or a man.

The record went on to describe how when Bob Wilson was released, he was within hours back at what he still considered to be his family home. On arrival, he found that a former drinking mate, Barry Evans, was now his wife's bedmate; more than that, he was forcing Bob's teenage daughter Amy to accept his unwelcome sexual advances.

After years of planning to kill his wife, Wilson's attention was turned on his wife's lover. According to the coroner's report, he kicked and punched his victim to death, and even after death continued raining down blows that so disfigured Barry Evans's face as to make identification by his family impossible.

The only statement on record from Amy Wilson was one that said her father had only attacked Barry Evans to stop him groping her, and that he wouldn't have touched her mother if she had stayed out of it – not another word was spoken by the girl and the rest of the incident is described graphically by Bob Wilson himself.

In all his years in prison, toeing the institutional line but plotting his wife's demise, he had never really considered an exit plan. He told the officers who found him, blood-soaked and manic in a nearby bus shelter, that he had done his job. At that stage it appears that he believed the blows he had inflicted on his wife would have been enough to finish her off, but had reckoned without the intervention of their daughter Amy.

Matt concluded by saying that most of the prison officers regarded Wilson as 'a complete nutcase' and to add to this, he had become 'friendly' with some of the most evil elements of the prison population.

'However, for Mark's murder, he has the safest of alibis,' said Matt, 'as just the day before he was the instigator of a punch-up in the prison corridor, and spent the day of the murder in solitary, down there in Bristol.

'I never really had him in the frame for Mark's murder,' said Martin. 'We would almost certainly have heard of any high-profile escapes, and release would not be an option – I can see from this report that he's been turned down for parole three times already. No – the only thing possible could be his involvement in an arranged killing, but that usually involves a ton of money, and he isn't likely to have accumulated that through the modern-day equivalent of stitching mailbags. What about the daughter, Amy?'

'Good news there,' reported Matt. 'It appears she visits her father regularly, and the prison service is looking into any information they have on file and will give me a ring later today.'

'Well, we'll have to take a trip to Bristol and interview Bob Wilson, because although he could not have personally killed his son I am firmly convinced that there's a family connection. We also definitely need to interview the sister, Amy, so let's get those two set up as soon as possible.

'Of course we mustn't forget Mark's new family – so far we have only met Sandy and Norman Harding, who appear to have been devoted to Mark and lavished him with love and all the worldly goods he could possibly need, but was that at the expense of someone else? The couple told us that they had adopted Mark as they couldn't have any children of their own, but do either of them have a brother or a sister, or any other family member who would have benefited from their generosity if it hadn't been heaped on Mark? It's a long shot, but jealousy can be an evil thing, and is the root of many wicked deeds.'

'It can't be far off the time for them to view Mark's body,' Matt said. 'Depending on how they cope with that, I'll dig a bit further into their family background.'

The two men left the room and turned into the corridor, where right on cue they saw Helen Cook-Watts guiding two people whose faces were expressionless and whose hands were tightly clasped, one with the other. She directed them towards the viewing room set up for the purpose with a simple wooden table and a small bunch of white flowers to break up the severity of the setting.

Realising that Helen had the situation well under control, the detectives held back and watched as she faced Sandy and Norman and asked them if they were ready.

Their eyes were on the long rectangular table not quite in the centre of the room, but with enough space for people to stand on either side. The couple stood together on one side and Helen moved to the other side, before carefully removing the upper part of the sheet to reveal Mark's still-handsome face.

There was no immediate reaction, as the couple simply stared at their son's face, and then as if a tap had been turned on Sandy's face was soaking wet – covered with tears that once released she seemed incapable of stopping. Norman held Sandy tightly, indicated to Helen that she should put the sheet back over Mark's face, and then turned to help his wife out of the room.

Helen had been prepared for a long session, and was a bit fazed by the speed at which it was all over. She followed them into the corridor and attempted to get them to sit in a nearby waiting room.

'We just want to get home, thank you,' was all Norman could manage, but Sandy looked at Helen and squeezed her hand, whispering, 'We are so grateful he still looks like Mark, and it was only that brief final look we wanted – the rest of our goodbyes will be said at home. That's where we knew Mark – not here.'

Martin Phelps watched as the group moved towards the back of the building and the car park. His questions could wait until tomorrow; this wasn't the time to intrude on these people's grief.

Life could be so cruel – but was it life that was cruel, or just that some evil people contaminated other people's lives just for the sheer hell of it?

Chapter Eight

Amy Wilson got out of a taxi and handed over a ten-pound note for a fare that was just a little more than five pounds. She laughed loudly at the look of amazement on the driver's face as she waved off his offer of the change, suggesting that he have a drink on her and boasting that there was plenty more where that came from.

Palash had been a cab driver in Newport for the past four years and, although he didn't think the people of the area were mean, his tips were usually in the nature of the fare being rounded to the nearest pound. He couldn't think of another occasion when a passenger had given him a tip that was virtually the same value as the original cost.

Staring at the woman as she walked off towards the station he played the game of 'guess the background', as he often did with the people who used his cab. He figured that in spite of her Goth image, she was no youngster; possibly over forty, but with all that make-up and way-out hair style it was difficult to say.

She wore extremely tight black jeans and high boots with clumpy heels, and Palash thought that she must have felt very warm in all that gear. He then noticed that her arms were bare of clothes, but well-covered with black and purple tattoos. Her face was pale, but Palash, who was no expert when it came to the ways of women, couldn't make up his mind if this washed-out look was as a result of life treating her roughly or an image that she, for some reason, wanted to create.

She was lost to him now, as she had turned the corner to the train station, and he had to admit to himself that here was one fare he could not second-guess. She looked as if she was hiding behind some image of her past, and he remembered that loud, almost forced, laugh as she had handed over that ten-pound note – and he wished that for him there really were plenty more where that came from.

Amy knew she had shocked the taxi driver, and smiled to herself as she collected her ticket, a single to Bristol Temple Meads, and played the same game with the young man selling the tickets. She told him to keep the change, but going red in the face he explained that they were not allowed to take tips, and he pushed her change towards her twice before she finally took it and swore at him loudly.

The woman behind her in the ticket queue threw her a look of disgust, and as Amy walked away with her ticket she heard the woman commiserating with the young man, and describing Amy as 'some weirdo who looked old enough to know better'.

Being called a weirdo was a way of life for Amy, but that word 'old' hit her hard and she went off into one of her moods of deep depression, wondering how long she would be able to hang on to her latest man – he was at least fifteen years younger than her and the source of her new-found financial freedom. Amy had no idea where Jack got his money from, but she was sufficiently streetwise to know that it wasn't the usual nine-to-five office job and as far as she was aware he wasn't employed by anyone anyway.

No, it had to be drugs, and he had to be dealing. She knew for sure that he was not a user, as having been a heroin addict herself for several years she knew all the signs. Still supported by a daily, but legal, supply of methadone, Amy wondered if she stayed with Jack how long would it be before she gave into the temptation of returning to the real thing and ditching the substitute. After all, her reason for giving up in the first place had nothing to do with the damage it was doing to her body, but through necessity as they wouldn't let her near the good stuff in prison. But now there was freedom and Jack's money too, and so maybe …

Amy was on a journey she had made countless times over the past few years, and she knew as she sat down on one of the platform benches that she had about five minutes to wait before the train for Bristol pulled in. It amused her to see people walking up to the bench but then deciding against sitting next to her – didn't they know that looking different was not a disease and that they wouldn't catch it? Maybe they thought they would wake up the next morning pale-faced and with black-rimmed eyes. They're the real saddos, she thought, and most of them have never done anything more exciting than a quick fumble in a darkened room, whereas she had allowed her body to be transported to places these people could not even imagine.

The electronic message board flashed up the news that the 12.44 to Bristol Temple Meads was arriving on time, and two minutes later she was sitting on the train and trying to settle down for the ride of about thirty-five minutes. Settling down to anything was not really an option and her mind jumped backwards and forwards over the events of the past few months, starting from when, at the end of a similar journey to today, she had first met Jack. They had both arrived at the entrance to the prison at the same time, but she by means of the number 70 bus while he had parked his black BMW in one of the side streets off Cambridge Road.

His immediate thought had been that she would look good sitting next to him in the front seat of his car, and he had lost no time in chatting her up. He was mentally inside her knickers even before they had been through the usual security checks and allowed in for their respective visits. She remembered that first meeting, and during her visit she had looked around the room and noticed him sitting next to a man who looked exactly as Jack would look in twenty years, so was not surprised to learn later that Jack was also visiting his father.

Bob Wilson had noticed his daughter looking around and caught his breath sharply when he realised the subject of her attention, asking her quietly if she knew Leo Thompson's son. Amy explained to her father that they had met briefly coming into the prison and had been surprised to hear him warn her off having anything to do with that lot. Bob obviously knew they were linked to drugs, and was aware that his daughter still craved the poison that had so nearly led to her death when she was just sixteen.

'What's his father in for?' she had asked, and been told that it was likely he had killed two men who had attempted to double-cross him. It had been proven beyond doubt that he had beaten his mother-in-law to death. Her father had gone on to say that he and his fellow prisoners were all keen to stay on the right side of Leo, as he was well-connected with the criminal fraternity on the outside.

On the way out from that visit, Amy was not surprised to feel a hand behind her, one that deliberately fondled her bottom. But instead of pushing it away, she moved towards it and offered obvious encouragement. Amy didn't catch her usual train home that day, as the journey from the prison to the station was in Jack's BMW, and their stops at lay-bys had meant that the back seat was in use more than the front ones.

For a few weeks they had co-ordinated their prison visits, and a regular pattern emerged. But like in most relationships, there was a need to move on to the next step. Jack wanted Amy to stay in Bristol, but she was not at that stage. She constantly reminded herself of the age gap between them, and had convinced herself that Jack would soon tire of her.

The reality was, however, quite different, as it was in fact Jack who had become completely besotted with Amy, and thought about her every minute of his waking hours. He showered her with presents and gave her a wad of notes every time they met. On one occasion she had sat on the train returning from Bristol to Cardiff and counted his latest bundle, which had amounted to £835. It seemed he would do anything for her.

Today, though, there was something else causing Amy to move about in her seat, and she once again unrolled the newspaper she held and revealed the headline, 'Brutal Murder of Gay Man'. She knew the man in question was her brother

Mark and was taking the newspaper to the prison for her father. Not that he would need to be informed, as in her experience her father and the other prisoners seemed to know more about what was happening outside the walls than most other people who were free to find out did.

The train pulled into Temple Meads Station, and walking outside she almost immediately spotted Jack's car. She walked towards it, thrusting the newspaper into his hands as she closed her door.

'I've already seen it, and it was on the radio and telly, and so now you and your father will never have to think about your disgusting freak of a brother ever again. Good riddance to bad rubbish is what I think, and your old man will be well pleased.'

Amy watched Jack as he slowly drove the car from the front of the station and took the now-familiar route towards the prison. At first she had been surprised at how carefully Jack drove but now knew that it had nothing to do with road safety but everything to do with him not wanting any unwelcome contact with the law.

Although he wanted her to move to Bristol, she had not as yet been to his house, but she knew that he lived with his worn-out mother, who washed, cleaned, and cooked for him in the same way she had done for his father before him. Even today, she would not be going to the house, but neither would she be returning to Newport as her ticket today was a one-way option, and she questioned Jack now about the arrangements for later.

'You'll find out soon enough, girl, but glad to see you didn't bring any luggage, as you and me is going on a shopping trip before getting the plane – all you need is your passport – got that?'

Amy pretended to have forgotten her passport but her joke did not have the desired effect of raising a laugh. Instead, Jack slammed on the brakes and grabbed hold of her arm roughly, calling her a fucking stupid cow, but letting her go quickly as she held up her passport for him to see.

'Sorry,' he mumbled, and went on to tell Amy that he was in no mood for jokes, before lightening the tense atmosphere by telling her to look in the glove compartment. She pulled out a paper wallet containing flight tickets, and her stomach did a somersault as she read that they were booked on an EasyJet flight out of Bristol airport at 18.45, and that they were going to Malaga. Childlike, Amy asked Jack how long it would take to get there, and was he scared of flying?

'You telling me you never been on a plane, and you nearly old enough to be my mother?' he said, and laughed as he felt her embarrassment. He was getting his own back at Amy's attempt to tease him about her passport, but his reference to the difference in their ages made her wince and she fell silent.

Her mind reflected on not only their age difference but the fact that here she was, years older than him, and she had never been on a plane, whereas it was difficult to mention a country that he hadn't visited – who said crime didn't pay?

Jack had told Amy that he and his dad used to travel to wherever they fancied whenever a particular business deal had gone well, and had found it particularly funny that their old woman had on several occasions kept their dinners warm for hours, not knowing they were in Spain or Mexico or wherever. Amy generally found herself laughing when people allowed themselves to be made a fool, of but she had more of a feeling of pity when Jack ridiculed his mother.

Most of her life she too had been surrounded by men who were only too willing to take advantage of her – it had happened constantly during her years of moving from one foster home to another.

It would wipe the smile off the face of many a smug semi-detached housewife if she told them how their husbands amused themselves with their ward while they were doing the weekly shop. Some of them had forced their attentions upon her, but there were others that she had deliberately led on so that she could get extra favours. It wasn't just the husbands, but some of the sons and even the daughters who were either sexually or physically abusive towards her, and so it was little wonder that she had turned her back on society and now did only what she wanted to do.

But, even now, wasn't she the one being manipulated? The trip to Malaga wasn't something she wanted. It was Jack who had suggested that they disappear for a few weeks and get to know one another better. She had noticed that her ticket was one-way, but Jack's was a return, booked for Wednesday, so in just two days' time she would be on her own in a foreign country. Normally, she would have questioned him about this, but his earlier display of bad temper made her wary and so she decided to ask him later as he would be in a much better mood when they were shopping. Amy had never in her life met a man who liked shopping as much as Jack, and it mattered little what he was buying just as long as he was flashing the cash and impressing giggly young checkout girls.

Jack parked the car as usual in one of the side roads near the prison and they walked to the entrance, went through the usual security checks, and in less than ten minutes Amy was sitting opposite her father who was indeed looking well pleased, as Jack had predicted.

Amy handed over the newspaper, and although it had already been checked at the gate, one of the prison staff walked over and took it off Bob and carefully flicked through each page before handing it back.

'It's only Leo who knows how this killing relates to me and that's the way I want it. I haven't recognised that piece of filth as my son since he started fucking up all our lives, and as far as any of the blokes here know, you are my only child.'

Bob read the front-page story and then pretended to take a great interest in an article on the second page relating to the changing nature of pubs in the valleys of South Wales. He raised his voice so that other inmates and visitors would hear him condemning the way in which the ordinary working man was being driven out of their traditional watering holes by yuppies and fast food chains. A few of the other prisoners, including Leo Thompson, joined in a chorus of mutterings on the subject before the senior prison officer shouted for quiet and suggested they all get on with their individual visits.

Amy looked around her and realised that for the majority of

the men being visited, it wouldn't matter a damn what happened to the pubs where they used to live, as the nature of their crimes meant that for many years to come the only eating and drinking they would be doing would be at Her Majesty's pleasure.

She looked back at her father, who was pleased that he had achieved his diversion and would now take the newspaper back to his cell and leave it open to display the controversial pub annihilation page. When alone, he would revel in reading and re-reading the front-page story of his son's death, with not one paternal feeling getting in the way of the pleasure that the news brought him.

He caught sight of Amy, who was staring across the room, and followed her gaze to where Leo and his son Jack were deep in conversation. He knew that they would both like to know what was being said. Bob knew that Leo was an evil bastard who liked inflicting pain, and had good reason to believe that the son followed faithfully in the footsteps of his father.

'What's the setup with you and Leo's boy – you need to be careful there, you know that, don't you?'

''Course I do, I'm not stupid, but Jack will look after me. It's in his best interests, because he's crazy about me and we're going to live together, so there's nothing to worry about, is there? First of all we're going on holiday and I'm going to fly for the first time, or at least for the first time in an aeroplane.' Amy laughed at her own joke, but her father wasn't amused; his worst nightmare for years had been that his daughter would be found dead following one of her drug-induced 'flights'.

'Where are you going, and how long will you be away?'

'Oh … Spain. I don't have a return ticket, but Jack does, and my guess is that he will be flying back every couple of days, probably to sort out his business deals.'

'Can you manage without your prescription?' asked Bob quietly.

'Don't be stupid, Dad,' Amy said. 'Jack will see me OK – there are always people ready to trade their substitute as part-payment for the real thing, so no worries on that score.'

'Keep your voice down! What about getting through

Customs? They could pick you up if Jack is carrying drugs,' said Bob.

Amy looked panic-stricken, as she had not even considered dealing with Customs, and as a first-time air traveller obviously had no experience of the process. She turned to her father for help, but in vain.

'You're asking the wrong one, kid, no good asking someone who's only set foot outside Wales to be driven to this place. I only know what I've heard, but from the stories Leo tells about his world-wide travels, I guess your Jack will be something of an expert when it comes to getting through Customs.'

Visitors were anxiously looking at their watches and Amy knew from past experience that it would not be long before the buzzer sounded and the visiting session would come to an abrupt end.

'Don't know when my next visit will be,' she told her father. 'With family matters now sorted I intend to have a bit – or make that a lot – of fun, so no need for you to worry about me.'

Her father looked at her as she rose at the sound of the buzzer and made her way to the door. They never hugged or kissed or hung on to each other, as did so many of the others at the end of a visiting session, but as Bob watched Amy leave he had a sense of foreboding, and wondered if he would ever again see the only person he had even come close to really loving.

Without looking back, Amy walked away from the prison and was standing outside before Jack caught up with her and slapped her on the bum. 'Anyone would think you had a plane to catch,' he laughed, and it was clear that the meeting with his father had put him in high spirits and he was ready for some fun. Amy caught his mood, and the two of them virtually ran to the car. Twenty minutes later they were pulling into the multi-storey car park adjacent to a large retail centre just outside Bristol.

Jack told her that they must get stuff for the beach, and said his mate's place came with its own pool, but instead of relishing the prospect, Amy's spirits sank. She didn't do beaches, they didn't really suit her image, and she couldn't remember when the sun had last seen any parts of her body beyond her face, legs, and arms, and only these if it were strong enough to get through tattoos and make-up. Another thing was that she had never learned how to swim.

'I didn't know we were going to stay with someone you know,' Amy said warily. 'I thought it was just going to be the two of us.'

'What? Shacked up in some bloody Spanish hotel, with millions of off-their-heads Brits, when we can be at Bruno's where it's non-stop party time? We might be on our own, but more often there is a full house, so it's find a bed or share a bed, whatever takes your fancy – and there's usually plenty to fancy.'

Amy was now struggling to show any signs of enjoying the shopping trip, even though both their arms were loaded up with bags and packages, and she had in the space of an hour acquired more new clothes than she could remember having in the whole of her life.

'Better get us each one of those pull-along things to stick all this stuff in when we get on the plane,' said Jack as he reached in his pocket for his mobile phone almost before it had started ringing, and as if he was expecting a call at that very moment.

Jack never said hello or spoke his name when answering his phone, always waiting for the caller to identify themselves before saying anything at all. His father had taught him well, and as Jack never had casual phone calls from friends, Amy suspected that this call would have something to do with the family business. And she was right.

Putting all his purchases on the floor, Jack reached into one of the pockets of his combat-style trousers and pulled out yet another stash of twenty-pound notes. He handed it to Amy. 'Got a job to do for the old man, but it won't take long so you just get what else we need while I sort out the business. Give me your stuff as well and I'll take it back to the car.'

Amy handed over her shopping, holding on to two of the bags saying she couldn't bear to be parted from the boots and leather jacket she had chosen, but she willingly giving over the bikinis and scanty underwear that had been chosen for her by Jack. This bundle of notes held a hell of a lot more than the one she had counted on the train. She said nothing and tried to stuff it into the pocket of her jeans, but they were already gripping her body too tightly to accept anything else.

Jack shook his head. 'You bought one of those arse-bags,' he reminded her. 'Why don't you fucking well use it, unless you feel like spilling twenties all over the bastard place.' For some reason she didn't understand, she was afraid that Jack would take it back off her if it wasn't secured, but she needn't have worried because Jack was not really with her now.

She looked at him as he took the parcels from her, and saw in his eyes an intensely ugly expression. She wondered what job he was about to do for his father. The jobs obviously paid well, as Amy counted at least ten pockets in those combat trousers and all but one looked to contain a similar wad of money as the one he had just handed over.

Jack turned his back on Amy and marched off in the direction of the car park. She was still staring after him when a few minutes later her attention was caught by a small boy who, from behind his mother's back, was grinning and pointing in her direction. Amy made a face and a most un-ladylike gesture that, although not fully understood, left the boy in no doubt that she was not someone to be laughed at.

'Cheeky little sod,' muttered Amy, but in a way she had been relieved by the distraction of the child, and it had reinforced her opinion that people in general were just a load of crap. The people she had known through being fostered, the social workers, the so-called friends she had made, were all crap. Jack and his family and the people in Spain would be no different, she knew that, but for now she needed Jack, and with everything that was happening she was aware that it would be hours, not days, before she needed some chemical help – and he could provide that by the bucket load.

Strange how in a very busy shopping area crammed with people you can suddenly be quite alone – just by bolting the door of a toilet cubicle. Amy used the loo and then, fully

121

dressed, sat on the seat and counted her money over and over, until she finally got it into her head that this was just a few twenties short of £2000. Mega shopping or what!

Chapter Nine

Arriving at Goleudy just before eight o'clock on Monday morning, Martin's spirits were raised as he spotted the shining, newly bobbed hair of Shelley Edwards, who was standing alongside the reception desk. Just as quickly, his spirits were lowered, as he realised that the person she was welcoming was none other than the Chief Constable, who cut an imposing figure in full uniform, adorned by the medal which everyone knew had been acquired for her extreme bravery above and beyond the call of duty.

Martin remembered Shelley telling him that the big boss was giving the opening talk at her seminar, but until now it had slipped his mind – not surprising given the nature of the weekend he had just endured. He wished he had remembered, as he would have taken the back stairs, knowing that now a meeting was inevitable, and that Chief Constable Barnes would know all about the Mark Wilson murder and would expect a concise report there and then.

Both women turned as Martin approached them, and after the usual professional pleasantries the senior officer wasted no time in asking if there was any progress in the latest murder enquiry.

'We have already had to deal with representatives of the gay community in Cardiff, as the press seem to be making a real issue of the fact that Mark Wilson was gay, but I get a feeling from your reports so far that you are not convinced there is a connection?' Chief Constable Barnes was not as tall as Martin but nevertheless seemed to be able to look him straight in the eye. And she would not expect anything other than a straight answer to her question.

'No, ma'am,' responded Martin. 'The victim had from time to time taken part in demonstrations related to the rights of gays and lesbians, but generally he seems to have viewed his sexuality as a purely private matter, and most people wouldn't have even been aware of it.'

'Well, DCI Phelps, it's unlikely to have been an intruder, is it? Nothing was taken from the house and from what I understand you haven't found a murder weapon or any credible witnesses and so de facto no possible suspects. No need to remind you that the first few days following a murder are crucial and so we won't hold you up any longer, but I am here until lunchtime, and I'll touch base before I leave, for an update.'

As the two women walked away in the direction of the stairs, Shelley looked over her shoulder towards Martin and raised her eyebrows in apology. The chance meeting of Martin and his superior officer had not been her fault, but she was sorry that it had led to additional pressure on him. It hadn't done her intended positive start to her well-arranged day much good either.

Coffee was now absolutely essential, and Martin grabbed one of the strong black variety and took it straight to his office. Was the woman really expecting him to come up with the whys and wherefores of this murder by lunchtime? Not a hope in hell, unless some psychopath walked through the front door with a set of five knives all fitting the crime and the desire to make a full confession!

No, it wasn't going to be that easy, and Martin sat at his desk and faced several piles of papers, which included the full details of the post-mortem and several toxicology reports. He was about to plough his way through the reports when the door opened and DS Pryor came in with yet another pile.

'Did you know the Chief Constable is here?' enquired Matt.

'Everyone is walking on eggshells, it's quite funny really.'

'Not funny at all,' Martin said. 'The woman is expecting an "update" on the case by the time she leaves at lunchtime. More like she expects to hear that we've solved it, made an arrest, and given her the chance to tick off one of her monthly statistics. Any chance?'

Matt shrugged his shoulders. 'The Turkish neighbour was our only potential suspect, and even to start with that was unlikely, but now we know that all his movements at the time of the murder can be accounted for we've have crossed him off the list. Having said that, there's not much of a list, and top of the column of people we most want to question is Mark's sister Amy – but so far we've not located an address for her.'

Martin shook his head. 'Nothing's really adding up, and I keep going back to the issue of a motive but not coming up with anything that makes any sense – talk me through the usual things.'

Matt drew up a chair opposite his boss and stared past him towards the window. 'Top of my list would have to be that someone really hated the victim, and that means we're looking for someone who knew him well. So we need to systematically trawl through his family, friends, and work colleagues. He was employed by a design company and I'll be going there at about 9.30, to speak to absolutely everyone who works there and getting details of their whereabouts on Saturday afternoon and evening. Anyone who is unable to provide a water-tight alibi will be brought here for further questioning and fingerprinting.'

'As for friends, we have already interviewed the three women he seems to have known for years. Suzanne is the only one with a definite alibi, as she was with her daughter and they were shopping. It was easy enough to check that out and put her in the clear.'

'Paula and Anne claim they were at their respective homes all of Saturday afternoon and Anne has given her boyfriend as her witness but we have yet to catch up with him as the mobile number she gave us just keeps going to answerphone.'

'Paula has no one who can confirm her whereabouts, as she

claims to have spent all day Saturday just pottering around her flat. We were there last evening checking with her neighbours – that was an experience in itself.' Matt continued. 'There are three other flats in the house, but all the residents were in the one on the top floor and not one of them was capable of stringing a few sentences together, so it's unlikely that they even knew where they were themselves on Saturday. They should have been rudely awakened this morning, as DC Lewis and DC Challinger were there at eight o'clock to interview all of them.'

Matt hesitated and looked at Martin. 'Guv, when I think back at that kitchen, I find it impossible to come to terms with the thought that such a vicious killing could have been done by a woman.'

Martin nodded seemingly in agreement. 'We are trying to focus on motive and so far we have considered hatred. We've got as far as needing to rule out the people he worked with, and his friends, but on the finding his friends front we don't seem to have got very far. There must have been other groups of friends – did he belong to a fitness club, or any other sort of club? We need to go through his house from top to bottom.'

Matt nodded. 'I agree, and that has been done, but there are no signs of any membership cards, and in fact very little paperwork at all, which leads us to believe that Mark made most of his transactions online. The good news is that Charlie is back from her weekend, and even if she did have an excess of Guinness she's showing no signs of it now.'

'I got here at about half seven and she was already set up with Mark's computer and other bits and pieces and was well in to unveiling its secrets, with Alex filling her in on the details of the crime. I suspect that by lunchtime Charlie will be able to tell us everything we need to know about our victim's activities.'

'Brilliant,' said Martin. 'If anyone will uncover everything we need to know it'll be Charlie, I hope we can hang on to her but she's being seriously headhunted.'

'Hang onto Alex, then,' winked Matt. 'Sometimes an incentive is, surprisingly, above and beyond the monthly pay cheque.'

Martin didn't respond to this piece of office gossip from his DS and rose from his chair, suggesting that they both go to Incident Room One to continue their deliberations.

When they got there, Martin recapped. 'The next thing for you and the team to do is to come up with a list of everyone that Mark knew, and that must include everyone he knew as a result of normal face-to-face contact, as well as anyone he knew through social networking. I know you're already working on that, but we need some deadlines, so let's say that by lunchtime we have all the relevant names displayed on that wall there.

'Keeping with the hate motive, let's think about why it is possible to hate someone you don't even know. People have been murdered because they have red hair, or because they support a particular football team, and certainly because they are of a different religion – or because they're known to be gay.

'Does anything like that fit into this type of killing? I don't think so. That sort of obsessive killer is more likely to randomly pick a target, and much less likely to go into the home of his victim. No, I keep coming back to the view that the murderer is someone who knew Mark. Someone who had a particular reason to hate him, someone with a hatred that was not as a result of a one-off incident, but more likely one fuelled by years of jealousy or anger.

'Yes, I'm more than ever convinced that this killing is a hate killing of some sort. But that's just my gut feeling so let's think about all the other motives for killing if only to rule them out.'

They considered a fight that had got out of hand, but there was no evidence of a brawl; burglary, but nothing had been taken; self-defence, but who would have five different knives handy, just to ward off a possible attack from Mark? Finally, after exhausting all the possibilities that they could think of, Martin went to the whiteboard and wrote across the space he had left in the middle.

MOTIVE – HATE OR JEALOUSY OR BOTH
VICTIM KNEW HIS KILLER.

It was a gamble to focus the minds of his team in one direction at this early stage of the investigation, but it would speed up the process if he was right, and all his instinct built on experience told him he was.

'What have we learned about Mark's early life and the years he spent in care? Were there any major upsets with any of the foster parents or their families?'

'Nothing of note that hasn't been checked out,' replied Matt, as he thumbed through one of the folders full of Social Services speak. He tried to consider what could be behind reports that made such comments as 'the family think Mark would do better in a smaller family' or 'Mark would benefit from being with older children', or even 'Mark is a lovely boy but we are not sure we are able to help him'.

There were pages and pages of reports, not surprising for a boy who had spent most of his childhood being looked after by a succession of strangers, but only one serious incident. It was the only mention of issues concerning Mark's sexual orientation, and found in a report where one foster-father, Peter Garfield, had accused Mark of turning his 'normal' sixteen-year-old son into a 'queer', even though Mark was just nine years old at the time.

Matt read the details of that incident aloud. It seemed to have been quietly dealt with at the time, but there was writing in the margin of the report that had been added some years later and while Mark was still in care. It gave the name and telephone number of a CID officer, who had interviewed Mark in connection with the murder of a twenty-one-year-old man in an area of Cardiff known to be a gay pick-up point.

The young man's father, who was subsequently convicted of the crime, had initially accused Mark of the killing, but the young teenager was completely innocent except perhaps in some twisted way in the mind of the victim's father – one Peter Garfield.

'Before you ask,' Matt pre-empted his boss, 'we considered the possibility of Garfield harbouring a grudge while he was doing his time, and then taking his revenge on Mark, but obviously the timing is all wrong, and Garfield would be over eighty by now – if he was still alive. DC Davies checked him out and discovered that he only did six weeks of his sentence, before being transferred to a mental health unit and committing suicide shortly after.'

The doors to the room opened automatically in response to the button outside being pressed, and the familiar hum of Charlie's wheelchair announced her arrival.

'You look far too lively for someone who has just spent a weekend sampling the hospitality of our Irish cousins,' commented Martin. 'How did it go?'

'Least said about that, the better,' was the reply. 'I'm quickly coming to the conclusion that I prefer wakes to weddings. Thought you would like to see what we've picked up from that poor man's computer – I've transferred anything of interest so we can look at it all from here.'

Years of experience allowed Charlie to manoeuvre her wheelchair around chairs and trailing wires to settle herself in front of one of the screens. In a matter of seconds, images from Mark's computer were being flashed up for her colleagues to view.

'Simple stuff first,' suggested Charlie. 'Here, we have Mark's electronic address book – it's quite a cute little programme and he has obviously spent hours configuring it to remind him of people's birthdays and anniversaries. My interest was sparked not by the names we can see here, but by the names that have been deleted. Most people think that if you permanently delete data from your PC trash bin, it's gone for ever, but not so, and here are the details of four people deleted this year.

'As you can see, they are all men, and unlike his other contacts where there is quite a good profile for each one, on these we only have a first name and a telephone number. We haven't checked out the numbers yet, as we wanted to run it past you first.

'As well as individual people he knew personally, we have the usual contacts such as builders and decorators, the doctors' surgery, dentist, and the phone numbers for seven clubs of one sort or another.

'Three of those are health and fitness type venues, and it looks as if Mark was a member of two of them, according to what we have found in the way of regular direct debit payments.'

'My curiosity got the better of me when I saw the other four numbers, and, as I suspected, they are all matchmaker type agencies and claim to be able to find one's perfect partner, either for a one-night stand or for life-long commitment. Obviously, I only made a general enquiry when I phoned the numbers, so I don't know if Mark has used all the agencies, but there is evidence of some payments to one of them, albeit on an ad hoc basis, and nothing for the last four months.'

'Any other regular payments?' asked Martin.

'Trust you to steal my thunder, DCI Phelps.' Charlie pretended to pout. 'I was just coming to that, and I have to admit it's never been easier to investigate anyone's bank transactions. Mark did everything online which is why are no paper records anywhere when it comes to the usual household bills. However, when he took out cash from the hole in the wall, just about every penny of it is accounted for. He kept receipts for everything and even made a note of the odd change he put into the tin of a street charity collector.

'Now me, I have difficulty in remembering what the hell I do with hundreds of pounds of my salary every month! Judging by the dates of the receipts we found, I suspect that Mark did a monthly trawl of what he had spent, and probably checked things against his bank statements before destroying them. So, we have a brilliant trail of all Mark's financial activity, except that for the past two months on the first day of each month Mark has withdrawn a thousand pounds in cash and there is no record whatsoever for it.'

Charlie sat back in her wheelchair and waited for the obvious reaction, and DS Pryor did not disappoint.

'Blackmail!' He could barely contain his excitement. 'It's got to be blackmail, and maybe he was slaughtered when he refused to pay up for the third time. Makes sense, and he certainly wouldn't want to make a record of those transactions, would he? What do you think, boss?'

Martin was trying to think of any other reasons for withdrawing such a large amount of money on a precise date each month, but each possibility begged the question of why Mark wouldn't account for it in his meticulous records.

He gave some orders. 'Matt, I want you to get hold of the four men on Mark's deleted contacts list, bring them in to help with our enquiries, and then pay a visit to the two gyms that he had membership of, and the agencies he might have used for meeting people. I want to come with you when you visit the one we know he used, and although it might just be a coincidence, there could be a link between the fact that he has not used them for a couple of months, and that it's over the same period that he has needed to withdraw this level of cash with no explanation.'

'OK.' Matt looked purposeful as he walked towards the door. 'I'll keep you informed of our progress – where will you be?'

'Speaking to Sandy and Norman Harding,' replied Martin. 'They should be able to fill us in with some more details about Mark, and I'm very keen to see if they can offer us anything, such as possible changes in his behaviour during the past few months. I should be back here by two o'clock, and then I think we need to get everyone together for a briefing.'

Martin's thoughts were already on the meeting he must now have with Sandy and Norman Harding and his experience reminded him that it was likely, in the process of grieving, that their initial shock would now be turning to anger. Well, he couldn't argue with that – they had every reason to be angry and he would have to be prepared to be the butt of their anger unless they could help him to point them all in a different direction.

Charlie had chosen to remain in the incident room, and was scrolling down numbers and tables across the computer screen at a rate of knots, making her beloved technology dance to her tune. She looked up as she became aware that Martin was watching her, and grinned as she said, 'Better get a move on, or this morning's seminar will be over and you'll be blessed with meeting the wicked witch of the north.'

By rights, Martin should have taken her to task for her unprofessional comment about the Chief Constable, but instead he practically ran to the back stairs to avoid a meeting that could potentially be even more demoralising than the one he was hurrying to.

The journey to the Hardings' home was uneventful, but as he turned the corner to approach their house his heart sank at the sight of upwards of twenty men and women of the press waiting just outside the house, and rushing towards his car as he slowed down to turn into the drive.

Chapter Ten

Matt walked through the doors of a rather imposing health club, and decided on first impressions that this was not a gym for the seriously minded fitness addict, but more a fashion statement for people who wanted to drop details of their membership into the conversation over dinner. He thought of the gym he frequented, which was nothing more than a few rowing machines, exercise bikes, and lots of weights, and not a trace of Lycra – but then he wasn't paying the sort of money needed for membership of this setup.

It was always interesting to watch people's reactions, and as both he and DC Matthews were in plain clothes they were greeted with the full flash of perfect white teeth from the bronzed, blond receptionist. At that point they were probably seen as a potential money stream, and two victims to sign up at the same time was something not to be missed.

'How can we help you gentlemen?' was the greeting. 'If you are looking for a place to realise your fitness potential and meet like-minded people who are achieving that level of perfection, you have come to the right place. Personal trainers are something we highly recommend and we will ensure that for a small extra fee you are placed with a trainer who totally meets your needs – after all we can't really put a price on that feeling of well-being that comes with being truly fit, can we?'

Matt relished watching the smile disappear and then the well-rehearsed greeting come to a faltering halt as he held up his warrant card and introduced himself and DC Matthews in the most officious voice he could muster.

'I am not allowed to speak to the police or the press and I don't know if our manager is here.' The receptionist's voice had changed from the assumed English public school variety to a distinctively Cardiff accent and Matt had difficulty in concealing his amusement as he replied.

'I suggest you find out if he or she is here as we need a word and now would be a good time.'

'It's Mr Wilson, and if he is here he will be working out so I will have to go and tell him you want him as we don't have phones in the place where members do their exercises – but I'm not supposed to leave the reception desk.'

Matt responded. 'We promise not to frighten off any would-be members and your reception desk will be safe in our hands, but alternatively we are happy to find Mr Wilson for ourselves if you point us in the right direction.'

This suggestion was obviously not to her liking, and the young woman, who looked the part but in Matt's mind probably did no exercise herself – other than the bedroom variety – got quickly to her feet and hurried towards a door at the back of the reception area.

DC Matthews was poking around the so called 'meet and greet section', where there was ice-cold water on offer seemingly free of charge, but there was also a selection of liquid healthy options, the prices of which more than offset any layout on the water front.

'Good God!' he exclaimed. 'You could feed a family of four for a week on what they charge for this stuff, and adding it all up I wouldn't think there would be much change from my salary if I was a member here.' He had picked up a menu that itemised the cost of the speciality drinks and post-exercise meals that, according to the blurb, were essential in order to obtain maximum benefit from the membership experience.

'Probably not far off the mark,' replied Matt. 'However we are here as part of a murder investigation, not to do the management for their extortionate prices and to be honest I think anyone who is conned into paying them is not to be pitied, as they must have more money than sense.'

The response from DC Matthews was lost as the door through which the secretary had disappeared opened inwards to reveal Mr Wilson in all his sweating glory.

It wasn't often that Matt was made to look small, but the size of this figure would have dwarfed most men, and the fact that he was red in the face from recent exercise seemed to emphasise his physique. He also looked far from pleased at having his workout disturbed by policemen, even though thankfully for his business they were not in uniform.

Matt once again displayed his warrant card and went through the usual introductions. He tried to assess the reaction of Mr Wilson to their presence – he was obviously angry at being disturbed, but was it more than that?

'So what's this all about?' The voice that came from the manager was not what had been expected, being more like contralto than tenor, and certainly not reaching anywhere near the depth of baritone. It was not just that the tone was higher than expected, it was also as if the words were being forced out, and it was a voice that once heard would always be remembered.

'We are investigating the recent murder of Mark Wilson. You will probably have heard or read about it, and we have discovered that he was a member of this club and would like some information about his pattern of usage. It would also be helpful if you could tell us if he was particularly friendly with any other members or perhaps members of staff.'

'Any member of my staff who had taken up a special friendship with Mark Wilson would have been out on their ear and if I had had my way he would never have been a member here in the first place – there are clubs that cater for his sort, we are not one of them.' These words were forced out and so much so that Matt almost felt the need to duck out of their way.

'What sort is that exactly, sir?' asked Matt pointedly.

'Well, he was gay, wasn't he, and our members are not in to that sort of thing. We had loads of complaints and lost a number of good accounts when he joined up, and I got it in the neck from the company for losing business.'

'How did your members know Mark Wilson was gay – was it tattooed on his forehead?' Matt could feel his temper rising, and it was not just what the manager said but the venom behind the words that was making Matt's blood boil.

'I sussed him out straight away. And it didn't help, him having the same surname as me, and having a few members of staff who are no longer with us suggesting we could be related. Can you imagine me being related to that?'

The receptionist who had returned with her boss suddenly spoke up with more courage than Matt would have given her credit for. 'He was a really nice man, and always spoke to me, not like some of the members here, especially the women who look down their noses and think I'm their personal servant.'

'It's your job to be their personal servant, you stupid bitch, what do you think we pay you for?' The words of this living Mr Wilson stung as they were spat out, causing the young woman's courage to desert her and her eyes to fill with tears as she walked away from the men.

Matt guessed he would not find her working there if they had cause to return and indicated to DC Matthews that he should track her down and speak to her. She needed to be told that contrary to the instructions of her boss, she was able to speak to the police.

Cutting to the chase, Matt asked Mr Wilson where he was on the afternoon and evening of the previous Saturday, and in what seemed like a totally rehearsed response he claimed to have been in the health club until lunch time, and then in the pub, where he met two mates and they all had a curry and more than enough lager. After that, he told Matt, he had gone to his sister's house and crashed out on her sofa, not waking up until after six o'clock when her latest boyfriend had arrived and started 'groping at her'.

So this giant of a man, who was obviously homophobic, was not particularly enamoured with heterosexual relationships either.

Matt couldn't wait to get away, and after taking the details of Mr Wilson's alibis, which were conveniently stored on his mobile phone, he was relieved to see DC Matthews coming towards him and they left together.

'What a nasty piece of work,' said Matthews as they approached Matt's car. 'Definitely someone with the strength to slice through bone and muscle without breaking into a sweat, and there is no love or even any tolerance for anyone who doesn't fit into his idea of what a man should be.'

'Yes, he certainly has the physical strength. And there is a mountain of hatred locked up in that imposing frame, but I suspect that he may be a bit of a wimp, like bullies often are. And he is a bully, judging from his behaviour towards that receptionist.'

'No worries of further bullying on that front, sir,' said DC Matthews. 'The secretary, Tina Chivers, gave me quite a bit of information about Mark's pattern of membership at the club before she left through the back door. I told her she should gang up with other ex-receptionists and do that bastard for sexual harassment and constructive dismissal.'

'Trust we know where to get hold of her?' asked Matt.

'No, boss, I let her go without getting any contact details – what do you think I am, a rookie?'

''Course not, I was just thinking aloud. Did she have anything else of interest to say about her ex-boss?'

'Not a lot, but apparently in front of the members he's really charming. They all like him and feel protected by his sheer physical size, especially the women, but he never seems to take advantage of the members, it's just the female staff he believes he has the right to play with. Apparently, quite a lot of the personal trainers have flings with the female members, but not Mr Wilson.'

'Interesting,' muttered Matt.

'He obviously has witnesses to his whereabouts on Saturday, but DCI Phelps will be more concerned with us checking independent witnesses at the pub, and neighbours who may have seen him at his sister's place, rather than believing the stories that may have been concocted with his friends and his sister. As always, one job leads to another.'

A similar thought was going through Martin Phelps's mind as he ran the gauntlet of the press, and felt a fleeting desire to scoop a few of them up on the bonnet of his car as they forced him to come almost to a complete stop before allowing him to move, inch by inch, into the Hardings' drive.

Even before he had opened the car door he saw their front door open. Helen Cook-Watts had been there for some time, and made it easy for him to ignore the shouts from the media, who were asking the usual questions about arrests, and making up their own statements regarding police incompetence, each one trying to outdo the others with their potentially headline-grabbing quips.

Martin raised an arm to acknowledge their presence, but to their obvious group annoyance did not respond to any of their comments and went straight towards Helen and into the hall.

Helen had obviously been waiting for him, not just because he had rung earlier to tell her he was on his way, but also because she wanted to tell him what had been happening at the house.

'I got here just after eight this morning after getting a phone call from Sandy. She was beside herself with worry because Norman had smashed a whole load of dishes and had subsequently locked himself in the downstairs cloakroom and refused to come out.

'He was out by the time I got here and Sandy had cleared up the broken china so everything appeared as normal. However he hasn't spoken a word all day and about an hour ago he went into the garage and came back with a large cardboard box and has been filling it with bits and pieces from all parts of the house.'

'What sort of bits and pieces?' asked Martin.

'Ornaments, a clock, items of personal jewellery, birthday cards, and even shaving soap and deodorant,' replied Helen.

She continued. 'None of it made any sense to me, nor to Sandy to begin with, but when he went upstairs and returned with a small bundle of cards that included some Father's Day cards Sandy realised that he was collecting and boxing up everything that had been given to him by Mark.'

'Maybe he just wants to have some contact with these things to help him come to terms with what's happened to his son,' suggested Martin.

'Exactly what I said to Sandy,' replied Helen. 'But about ten minutes ago he went back to the garage, and returned with a petrol can and started to pour petrol over the box. Because he had trouble opening the cap I managed to get it off him before he had done any real damage and Sandy rescued the box of matches so the situation was defused – but the poor man has flipped.'

'Ring his GP, now,' said Martin. 'I expected anger and recriminations to be the order of the day, but this is way outside my experience, and needs a different sort of professional help.'

Martin left Helen to make the phone call, and walked into the lounge, where Sandy and Norman were sitting on the sofa like a couple of bookends, not together as they had been before, but separate, each in their own personal world.

Sandy got to her feet as soon as she saw Martin, but Norman showed no sign he was even aware that anyone else had entered the room.

'I have just asked PC Cook-Watts to contact your GP as your husband may need something to help him cope with this – and what about you, how are you managing?'

'I've always been the strong one,' said Sandy. 'I can talk about Mark, and I have talked about him non-stop to Helen, who has been a lifesaver for me. If Norman could only talk he would find things easier. We've both found it difficult to sleep, but I must have gone off soundly around six o'clock this morning. I was woken by the sound of Norman smashing plates in the kitchen. That was bad enough, but then he locked himself in the toilet, and then the whole thing with Mark's presents and the petrol.'

Sandy sank back down on the sofa, and Martin pulled up a large footstool and sat on it so that he was facing her and at her eye level.

'If you could talk some more now, I would be very grateful,' he told her. 'The more I can get to know about your son, the better chance I have of putting the pieces together and catching whoever did this terrible thing. Did Mark know anyone who would want to cause him harm, anyone he has fallen out with recently, or anyone who may have had reason to hate him or be jealous of him?'

Sandy thought for a few minutes before answering. 'Yesterday, when Norman was talking still, we went through all of that and maybe we did too much of it – concentrating on all the negative aspects of Mark's life instead of all the joy he has brought into our lives.' She shrugged her shoulders and went on. 'There are certainly issues around his biological family and these were made known to us when we first fostered Mark, and they were discussed again during the process of adoption. We knew we were taking on someone who was part of an extremely dysfunctional family and whose childhood had been blighted by domestic violence, the death of his sister and then the father murdering his mother and her lover. We learned to love Mark even more because of all of this and because he had emerged from years of dubious fostering arrangements to be a thoughtful, sensitive man.'

Sandy swallowed hard and Martin waited for her to continue while thinking how lucky Mark had been to be adopted by this couple.

'To the best of my knowledge, Mark's father is still alive, and still in jail, but it's several years since we checked that out.'

'That is correct,' Martin told her. 'He's in prison in Bristol – did Mark ever express any desire to visit him?'

'It's something we asked him from time to time but he didn't want to see his father, although I sometimes got the feeling that it was more that Mark firmly believed that his father wouldn't want to see him. Mark was aware that his father blamed him for everything that had happened, and believed – and probably still believes – his son's homosexuality to be the root of all their problems. Do such people really exist?'

She directed her question at Martin not really expecting an

answer, and went on to finish what she had to say about Mark's family.

'Mark had two sisters, the one who was killed, and another one, Amy, who is presumably still alive; she's only a few years older than him. We also checked with Mark if he wanted to contact his sister, who like Mark spent most of her childhood in care, and around the time of his adoption he did say it might be nice to share some of his good fortune with her.

'So Norman hired a private detective who did manage to track her down, and came back to us with the news that she was a heroin addict with no desire whatsoever to kick the habit. He reported that she had spat in his face when he had mentioned her brother and made it absolutely clear that as far as she was concerned there was no brother, just a "worthless piece of shit", I believe it was, who had ruined the lives of the four people she cared about, namely her mother, her sister, her father, and herself.

'She also told him that if he dared to tell us where he had found her, she would get her dealer to plant drugs on Mark and then watch as his precious new family fell to pieces when he was picked up for possession. He told us that she was one of the most sick and twisted people he had ever had the misfortune to meet.

'We didn't tell Mark the outcome of the investigations, just told him the investigator had drawn a blank, and we then persuaded him into thinking that as she had gone to so much trouble to not be found then that must be her choice. I don't think from that day to this we have mentioned her name.'

Martin nodded. 'So to the best of your knowledge there has been no contact between Mark and any member of his family for at least the past twenty years.'

'More like thirty years – no, more than that!' said Sandy. 'After that one attempt to find his sister, we never had an inkling that he even thought about his family, and he constantly told us how lucky he was to have the best parents in the world – meaning Norman and I ...'

Sandy choked on these words and Martin could see the raw

grief in her face. Helen had re-joined them, and at Martin's signal she sat down next to Sandy and held her hand.

'Are you OK to continue?' asked Martin, and Sandy nodded.

'Yes, but I don't think there is anything else I can tell you about the family.'

'Did Mark tell you much about the time when he was in care?' asked Martin moving on.

Sandy managed a tiny smile that for a moment relaxed her mouth but made no impression on the misery in her eyes. 'Oh, there were stories, of course. Not all his experiences were bad, and we were always grateful to hear about a few of the short-term placements, and his memories of feeling part of a family for the one-off Christmases, and even a couple of brief holidays. Mark had the ability to focus his memories on these happy moments.

'We know from the meetings we had with his case worker when we first fostered him that there were more bad times than good, and we were told that it was almost certain he had been both physically and sexually abused over a number of years.

'Mark himself told us of one particular incident that had happened just a few years before he came to us. He was at the beginning of what everyone hoped would be a long-term fostering arrangement when the police turned up at the house to interview him in relation to a murder. As Mark was just in his early teens at the time, the woman of the house had been asked to sit in on the interview.

'Apparently, the boy who had been murdered was the son of a family that had fostered Mark about five years previously. At that time the son was about sixteen, and even though Mark was just nine years old it seems there was some attraction between the two boys.

'The father spotted his son's interest in the young boy, and reported to Social Services that the latest misfit they had landed on the family was turning his perfectly normal son into 'a woofter'. The reality of the situation was that although Mark was born gay, he was at the time too young to understand, and it was the son who was using Mark to experiment with his own

142

homosexual feelings.

'Through no fault of his own, Mark was moved on, but apparently the son came out on his eighteenth birthday and subsequently flaunted his sexuality by bringing home a string of one-night stands. It would appear that the father detested his son's activities, and for years the house was visited on a regular basis by the police as a result of neighbours constantly complaining about fights.

'Anyway, to cut a long story short, there was one night when the father had followed the son to a well-known gay pick-up point just outside the city, and stabbed him repeatedly with a kitchen knife.

'When picked up by the police, the father had accused Mark of killing his son, and although there was prima facie evidence that the father was the killer the police had to follow up on his accusations. We know all of this, not just from Mark, but also from his caseworker. She was keen to ensure that we knew as much as possible about Mark's past – I suppose so that we could not accuse them of withholding information if Mark had subsequently turned into a psychopath as a result of it all.'

Martin got up from his seat on the footstool and stretched his legs. 'We had picked up on that incident from Mark's Social Services record, but thanks for filling in the details that were omitted.'

'Shall I make us all a cup of coffee?' asked Helen. 'What about you, Norman? I know how to mix the blends you like, and I promise to give you your favourite mug.'

Almost as soon as she had said the words Helen regretted them, as she remembered that Norman's favourite mug was one shaped like a Welsh dragon, which had been given to him by Mark and was now somewhere in that box of rejected memorabilia.

She needn't have worried, though, as there was absolutely no reaction from Norman. She made her way to the kitchen anyway, suddenly realising how much this situation was demanding of her. When she had rung the surgery, Helen had been told that Norman's GP was doing house calls, but a return call had told her that the doctor knew about the situation and would be with them in about twenty minutes. That had been ten minutes ago and so Helen quickly made four mugs of coffee, thinking that DCI Phelps would want to finish talking to Sandy before the doctor arrived.

She carried the coffees into the lounge on a tray, and handed one each to Sandy and Martin before setting the tray down on a long sideboard, then moving one of the occasional tables near to Norman and placing his coffee within easy reach. Her actions were rewarded as Norman looked up at her and mouthed a silent thank you.

Sandy hadn't missed this first small sign of normal behaviour from her husband, and wanted to rush over and hold on to him but was worried that anything could send him back into himself. She pretended not to notice and continued her discussion with DCI Phelps.

'As I was saying,' she continued, 'soon after Mark came to us he went to Whitchurch High School, and it seemed to be the making of him. I like to think that he felt at home and safe there, because he had a comfortable home to come back to at the end of each day and, for the first time in his life, somewhere to bring his friends. He was very popular, and as we aren't that far from the school it was not uncommon for me to do lunch or tea for a dozen or more hungry teenagers. It was one of the best times of my life.'

As Sandy was speaking she was becoming more aware that her husband was listening and used the opportunity to inject some more positive memories into his mind.

'Norman used to pretend shock horror at the thought of our home being invaded most lunchtimes, but it was he who popped out to the shops in the mornings and came back loaded with goodies, and Mark loved him for it. After a while the numbers went down, but our usual, almost daily, visitors, were Paula and Suzanne. And Mark has remained friends with those two ever since. They are totally devastated and brought us that enormous bunch of lilies, they were Mark's favourite flower.'

'I thought there were three women in that group of friends?'

144

interrupted Martin.

'Not to begin with,' Sandy said. 'Anne and Mark met when he went to art college, and then they worked together for a while, but I suppose it was through visits here that they all got to know one another. Anne and Paula didn't hit it off at first, but I think that was because she felt a bit side-lined when Mark and Anne talked endlessly about art and design. They had an uncanny ability when given a particular project to sit down with a blank piece of paper and come up with almost identical ideas.

'On reflection, art and design was the only thing I ever remember them talking about, and Anne never seemed to participate in the other three's discussions about music, politics, families, and whatever – but then some people are just single-minded when it comes to something they love and are good at.'

Norman moved forward and took a sip of his coffee, and Sandy looked towards him and smiled, but didn't move. Her gut feeling was that her strategy was working, and her husband was coming back to her from that very dark place he had visited.

'Just to recap,' said Martin, taking his lead from Sandy and not directly involving Norman. 'We know there are issues surrounding Mark's biological family, and no love lost with any of them but Mark's father is in jail and your son had no contact with his sister. There are also a few incidents relating to the time that Mark was in care but the only serious one involves a young boy and his father, and both of them are no longer with us. No problems in school by the sound of things, so that brings us to people Mark knew through work or socialising, possibly clubs or other interest groups.'

To everyone's surprise Norman interrupted in a voice that was so normal it was quite shocking – it was as if nothing had happened with him and he had been part of the discussion all along. 'I taught Mark to play golf,' he volunteered. 'He joined the golf club but was never very good and I think he only persevered with his dreadful swing just to please me. There was never any trouble there and as far as I know Mark never made any enemies. Certainly nobody was jealous of his handicap!'

As if by some kind of mutual understanding, everyone

accepted his input and did nothing to indicate how worried they had been about him. Norman continued to reminisce about their short-lived golfing activities. Didn't he even remember his own actions of this morning? Could he have collected up all those things and attempted to set fire to them, and then forgotten about it almost immediately? Martin had seen grief play strange tricks on people but this was a new one on him and he was relieved that this was one problem he could hand over to Norman's GP – he had enough of his own to worry about, and for now he was just pleased to have extra input into his investigation.

'Were there any other clubs or any other people that Mark brought home?' he asked.

'Well, not exactly clubs, but Mark signed up to a number of things over the years, always wanting to learn something new. He did a one-year course in computing at UWIC, and several courses in different aspects of horticulture. And then there were the endless weekend and holiday-linked courses, usually associated with international food and cooking. Mark was an excellent cook, and the more complicated the recipe the better he liked it.'

Norman was on a roll now, as if the floodgates of his memory had been opened and the outpourings were outside his control. Martin did not want to inhibit what could be essential to Norman's recovery but needed to contain the conversation and get answers to some important questions.

'Any friendships develop from any of these activities?' Martin looked at Sandy, not wanting to lose her input as she was more focused and seemed to understand why DCI Phelps was asking these questions.

'No particular friendships,' she answered. 'Just a few casual relationships, and we met a number of people, both men and women, with whom Mark shared a common interest while he was doing the various courses. Nobody stands out in my memory and there was no trouble at that time.

'For a while Mark was involved with an organisation that promotes the rights of gay men and women, but I wouldn't say

146

he was a particularly active member and only got involved with it through Tony, who was the one partner Mark brought to our home. We had always told Mark that he was welcome to bring home anyone he was involved with, but there was never any relationship that lasted. As far as I recall, Tony and he were together for about three months, and we met him twice before it petered out and they amicably went their separate ways.'

'Did they stay in touch at all?' asked Martin.

'Not really,' said Sandy. 'I was with Mark about two years ago when we bumped into Tony as he was coming out of the HSBC in the centre of Cardiff. He was with his partner, whose name I can't remember, but whose Scottish accent was unforgettable! They told Mark that they had been through one of those civil partnership ceremonies and all three of them chattered away like old friends while I left them to sort out some payments. Afterwards Mark told me how pleased he was that Tony had found such a nice partner, and hoped they would both enjoy their new life in Scotland.'

Sandy had no contact number for Tony, but he would be easy enough to trace as each year there were only a small number of same-sex civil ceremonies recorded in Cardiff. From what Sandy had said, Martin didn't think Tony would be involved with the murder but he would still need to be officially ruled out.

Norman had been listening and suddenly interrupted. 'The only place we suspect there may have been trouble is at one of the health clubs Mark joined within the last year or so, and we only know that as a result of something Mark said to Paula when they were both here a few weeks ago.'

Martin pricked up his ears. 'What exactly did he say? Can you remember?'

'I caught a snippet of the conversation, where Mark told her that he wasn't going to be driven out of a place that suited his needs just because some gorilla was homophobic. He went on to say that he believed the guy was jealous as his steroid-enhanced body was already going to seed.

'Mark added that he had heard the manager say that it was

147

not normal for someone to be gay and at the same time look so macho – it confused everyone. I remember Paula laughed hysterically at that, and then asked Mark how this idiot had discovered that he was gay.'

Norman looked across at Sandy. 'That's when you came into the room and the conversation stopped, but I was anxious about what I had heard and asked Mark about it later. In his usual way of not wanting to worry me he told me that the man was just one of many bigots he had met during his lifetime and not someone for me to be concerned about – but I was left feeling uneasy at the time, and have thought about it several times since.'

'What about work?' Martin asked. 'Did he have any problems there?'

Sandy responded. 'Mark kept work and home very separate from the beginning and although he got on well there he was never ambitious, just content to do the job and come home. Of course, to begin with Anne worked in the same place as Mark but apparently they had such similar ideas on design that the boss decided he didn't need both of them and Anne left.'

'There was no problem over that, as Anne by her own admission has itchy feet, and history has proven that as she never really settled at any job and has apparently done a lot of freelance projects. According to Mark, most of what she called her "freelance projects" are more likely to have been periods of time on the dole, but he respected her privacy and didn't delve too deeply into that aspect of her life.

'I can't think of any problems with work, and since this has happened we have received numerous cards, flowers, and phone calls from the company. It's a pity someone has to die before people are able to tell them how much they are liked.'

A car was drawing into the drive, and as it pulled up alongside Martin's car Helen Cook-Watts got to her feet and made for the front door. She wanted to fill the GP in about the latest twist in Norman's state of mind before the doctor saw him and so she opened the door even before the bell sounded.

'Bloody hell, I'm glad I'm not famous! I would definitely be up for assault and battery if I had to face that lot on a regular basis.' The doctor, who was not much older than Helen, was referring to the press as she stretched out her hand and introduced herself.

Helen raised her eyebrows in response, and then quickly briefed Dr Kate Perry on what had happened, concluding with the thought that Norman may not even remember what he had done earlier and may be surprised that she had been called at all.

'Not to worry,' replied Dr Perry. 'Although Norman and Sandy aren't regular visitors to the surgery, we do know them fairly well, and I'll just say that this is a routine visit following their recent loss and take it from there.'

Helen instantly liked this level-headed young woman, and led her into the lounge where DCI Phelps was on his feet and thanking Sandy and Norman for their help. Dr Perry again held out her hand, this time in Martin's direction and after a brief greeting sat down between Sandy and Norman and immediately engaged them in conversation.

In the hallway, Martin asked Helen if there was anything she needed and requested she let him know the outcome of the doctor's visit.

'I believe I'm managing OK here, sir,' replied Helen. 'I think I'll go back in there now as they may say something to the doctor that could be of relevance to us.'

Martin opened the door to face the tireless onslaught of the media but allowed himself a brief smile – was he getting old, or were police constables and doctors just getting younger and much better looking? And were both professions being taken over by women? If so – bring it on!

Chapter Eleven

Jack was usually on a high when returning from a job for his father, knowing that not only were the jobs very well-paid, but that each time he did one his father's reputation went up a notch – and he lived to please his old man. His own standing amongst the big boys in the drugs world was increasing and they were starting to see him as the weapon of choice when particularly nasty messages needed to be given.

He pulled into the same parking space he had left earlier, expecting to see Amy wandering around the car park looking for him, but there was no sign of her.

Instead of the usual pumped-up feeling, Jack was agitated, as the job hadn't gone exactly to plan and he had ended up having to forsake one of the keepsakes he treasured from each of his successes. Never before had this happened, but he told himself it was no big deal, as there was nothing to link it to him and he was too clever to leave behind fingerprints or DNA – his father had taught him well.

It had been the first time he had left the murder weapon behind and it had also been the first time his target had been a woman. The stupid cow had thought he was chatting her up, and she had come on to him as he had suspected she would. It had been so easy to stick the long steel dagger in between her ribs and watch her body contort as the blade entered her heart and quickly stopped it beating.

Jack hadn't noticed her dog, and although there was no struggle or outward sign of violence the dog obviously sensed danger and started growling and barking fiercely and attracting attention. With no other option, Jack had to get away quickly, leaving his knife in situ. She had been the wife of one of Leo Thompson's fellow inmates and now her cheating days were well and truly over.

The job had been done, and the end result was what had been required, so the boys would be happy with that. But Jack knew he would be torn to pieces when his father found out the risks he had taken. They had already decided that Jack would not visit for the next couple of months, as there was a feeling that the cops were being fed information on a couple of fronts so best he keep away.

Jack hoped it wouldn't be too long before the prison leak was discovered. His mood lifted as he envisaged which of his treasures he would use on the next piece of shit who needed to be taught a lesson. Something really special would send out the right message to women who played away when their husbands were banged up.

He left the car and looked around, realising that the job that should have taken no more than ten minutes, plus just over an hour travelling time, had actually taken over two hours in total and they would now have to get a move on or miss the plane.

Where the fuck was she, and why wasn't she answering her mobile? He rushed around muttering to himself, and cursed the fact that she had some strange hold over him and he knew that for now he didn't want to dump her. But, hell, no bloody woman was going to make a fool of him.

She hadn't tried to call him, as he had checked his phone, but then he had told her that on no account was she to do so. At that time, with his mind fixed on the job he was about to do and the look of pure sin and evil in his eyes, she would have been left in no doubt that he meant it.

So where was the stupid bitch? They were already behind the schedule the airlines give for checking in, but being a seasoned flier Jack knew he could get there minutes before the checking finished and still make it. But that wasn't keeping a low profile, and last-minute activity seemed to attract the attention of airport officials.

'Pick up, you bitch. Pick up, you stupid bitch. Pick up, you stupid fucking bitch.' Jack bellowed at his phone, before he became aware that he was drawing attention to himself and this was not something he normally did. He had reached his current age and had committed some unbelievable acts of depravity without so much as a police caution or a point on his driving license. He was proud of this amazing achievement. It was what kept him invisible, and now wasn't the time to blot his copybook.

Pulling himself together, Jack headed back to his car and drove straight to the airport. If she was there she would have some explaining to do, and if not; well, that would be her loss. To override the feelings he had for her, Jack convinced himself that just lately she was starting to look her age, while he still had years of youth on his side. He would not be made a fool of, and driving into the airport while still alone in his car he yelled above the loud bass sounds of the stereo system. 'Sod her ... sod the stupid fucking bitch.'

Within ten minutes of Jack leaving her, Amy had become overwhelmed with cravings, not for the substitute drugs she had been swallowing in recent years but for the real thing. And why not? Cash wasn't a problem now that she had more than she ever had seen in her life, and her hands caressed the black leather bum bag she had strapped around her waist. It had been their first purchase that afternoon and as she looked down at it she expected it to be bulging with cash, but it surprised her to see that close on £2000 in assorted notes, mainly twenties, took up so little space.

Perhaps she had miscounted ... but no, she had done it at least half-a-dozen times, and each time got a total of one thousand nine hundred and forty pounds. And, after all, Jack had given it to her to spend as she wanted. But Jack would kill her if she ditched him ... She shuddered at the thought, knowing that he was more than capable.

Instead of bringing her to her senses, her fear of repercussions from Jack only served to heighten her cravings, and she knew they were past the point of no return and they would have to be satisfied.

She reasoned that Bristol would be no different to Cardiff, and at the edge of the retail park amongst the parked cars she would be almost certain to find someone who would give her what she wanted for a price. Even if they were personally unable to supply her they would know someone who could – that was often how it worked, and she now knew where she was headed.

Anticipation now raced through her mind, and she told herself that she would just get as much as she desperately needed to be in a better frame of mind to get on that plane with Jack. She wouldn't ditch him – that would be really stupid, as she realised that it would not only be her that would suffer, but her father, who would be punished in some unspeakable way.

She got to the edge of the car park and quickly spotted the sort of activity she was expecting. She justified what she was about to do by telling herself that Jack would get good value for his money. With her cravings satisfied she would show him the benefits of laying an older woman, and sexual experience was not something she lacked. After that, he would be more than willing to keep her supplied and to her troubled mind this seemed like a fairy-tale ending.

Less than ten minutes later she had found what she was looking for but had been forced to pay well over the odds for extras that included a rather dubious-looking syringe and a couple of needles. The signals she was giving out left her incredibly young supplier in no doubt that she was desperate and he milked the fact for all it was worth. Amy wondered what he would be like in a few years' time and hoped it would never be her misfortune to find out.

Back in exactly the same cubicle where she had previously counted her money Amy prepared and drew up almost a syringe full and as if she had never stopped injecting, braced her left arm against her body and clenched her fist to force her veins to the surface before inserting the needle.

By now she was shaking badly but her previous years of

154

practice made it easy for her to push in the murky fluid and she waited for the never-to-be-forgotten feeling as the gates of heaven opened …

No, this wasn't right! The only feeling she was getting was one of extreme nausea and almost instantly as the muscles of her stomach contracted a stream of projectile vomit hit the back of the toilet door.

'Bastards … bastards' she tried to get the words out, but instead a second lot of vomit followed the first. She started to imagine what she might have been given – the risks were always there, as every addict knew – but she gave up thinking about anything else as the pain suddenly gripped her.

Her hands could no longer hold on to anything, and everything that had been on her lap fell to the floor and mingled with what had previously been the contents of her stomach. She arched her back as cramps caused the muscles in her legs to go into spasm. Her boots skidded on the slippery floor, and as she slid forward one of her legs shot through the gap at the bottom of the cubicle door.

An elderly woman who was applying very red lipstick to her thin lips looked down at Amy's leg and then banged on the door of another cubicle to summon the help of her daughter.

The daughter, grumbling at the interruption, opened her door, accusing her mother of talking nonsense.

'Oh my God!' she stopped short in her accusations and pulled her mother towards her shouting towards the closed door of Amy's cubicle. 'Are you all right in there? Have you had an accident? Do you need any help?'

There was no reply and the younger woman made a half-hearted attempt to open the toilet door. She was almost relieved that it wouldn't open.

Several more women had now come in to use the facilities, and although some of them just went back out as fast as they could, there were two women who took control, with one ringing the number displayed above the washbasins and the other dialling 999. The first number was answered by the company with responsibility for providing the cleaners for the toilet block, and they promised to get an attendant there as soon as they could. The call to the emergency services provided information that there were paramedics close by and they would be directed to the incident immediately.

The four women stood wondering what to do next and considered looking over the top and into the closed cubicle by standing on one of the adjacent toilets but there wasn't an obvious volunteer. They were all wishing they had better bladder control and cursing their need for public conveniences when the cleaner arrived.

It was a routine visit, and she hadn't had a call from the company. She announced to everyone present, as she took out a bunch of keys, that it was no use anyone ringing that number as nobody in the company ever passed on messages. The other women looked at her, and were amazed by the fact that she seemed totally unfazed at the sight of one skinny leg protruding from under the door of one of the cubicles. If this was a familiar sight to her, then she should write her memoirs; maybe the Secret Diary of a Bristol Public Toilet Cleaner would be a bestseller!

However, speculation led to revulsion as she carefully opened the door, and everyone wished she hadn't.

'Is someone dead in there?' the elderly lady asked from her corner of the toilet block.

'Hell, I don't know,' said the cleaner. 'It's drugs, that's for sure, and the police …'

She was interrupted by the arrival of two male paramedics and with expert efficiency accompanied by lots of swearing they had Amy removed to a portable stretcher within minutes.

'Is she dead?' again the question from the same source.

One of the paramedics responded. 'No, but she is deeply unconscious and the sooner we get her to the BRI the better. The police will want to take a look and are on their way so please don't touch anything and don't let anyone else in here.'

The cleaner ushered everyone through the main door and from her uniform pocket she took out and unfolded an A4 sheet of card pinning it to the outside. The notice read FACILITIES

CLOSED FOR EMERGENCY CLEANING – PLEASE USE TOILETS AT THE FAR END OF THE CAR PARK. The notice was well-worn and had obviously been used frequently – it was the sort one would see attached to countless public amenities up and down the country, but who would guess the degree of human tragedy that could be behind it being posted?

Amy was, at this point, deeply unconscious, and so completely oblivious to being stretchered through the crowds of self-righteous shoppers who tutted and muttered their disapproval as she was carried past them. Had she been a little old man or a pregnant woman she would have had their sympathy, but there was nobody there today who could see past the external appearance of this strange-looking druggie and into the heart of a sad and abused woman.

At the A&E department of the Bristol Royal Infirmary, the paramedics handed her over, and mentioned to the receiving nurse that the bag strapped around her waist contained a large amount of money which would need to be checked in and witnessed by a couple of people. It also contained her mobile phone, and a passport that introduced her as one Amy Wilson.

'The police will be going to the place where we picked Amy up,' said the senior paramedic. 'There was evidence of drug usage at the scene, but I wouldn't like to guess at what she was using. This is one of the worse reactions I have ever seen. The police may well be aware of any bad batches that are on the street, and will undoubtedly be paying her a visit shortly. They may be able to tell you more –'

'Let's hope so,' interrupted the SHO who had joined them. 'Knowing what drugs she has injected will make all the difference to the speed at which we may be able to reverse the effects of the poison in her system.'

Their speculation and handover was interrupted as Amy stopped breathing, and with all the drama of a television soap opera the trolley was hurtled towards the Resuscitation Room where a team of real and very experienced professionals were waiting with defib. paddles at the ready and hoping to delay Amy's date with death.

On arrival at the airport Jack parked his car in the long-stay section, knowing that he would be using it again on Wednesday, when he would have to return to do yet another job for his father. That one would initially take him back to Cardiff and take his tally to three for that particular city. They had decided that Jack would do no more than three special jobs in any one city in case the police started to make links.

This afternoon's assignment had taken Bristol to that limit, and so with both Cardiff and Bristol soon off-limits he would have to look to Swindon or Reading, or even the Great Metropolis ...

Jack got a buzz from just thinking about his particular projects and remembered the unique details of each. Every one was different and every task undertaken in such a way as to send a particular message to the recipient of his cruel attention. Every successful job also served to raise his father's status and his father was now one of the top-dogs amongst his fellow inmates. Not surprising as none of the others could offer up a psychopathic son eager and able to sort out their problems on the outside.

He knew his way around the airport very well and went straight to the check in desk where there were still a number of people waiting to be booked onto the Malaga flight.

There was no sign of Amy, her time was running out, and as he held his boarding pass and made his way to the departure lounge he vowed to himself that as far as he was concerned her time had run out – she was history.

Chapter Twelve

As Martin drove back to base he reflected on the picture he had developed of Mark Wilson. If they had met, he would probably have liked the man, and he certainly admired him for making the most of his life after such a lousy start.

True, he had been dealt an ace when Norman and Sandy Harding came into his life, but Martin found himself believing that even without their influence and money Mark would have made it. And he definitely didn't deserve to have been killed, and so brutally.

He had barely got through the door of his office when Matt and Alex joined him. Alex looked smug and Matt had the look that anyone would have after a day of random visits to random people who may or may not be able to help with enquiries.

Martin deduced that the SOC team had come up with something interesting while his DS and their team had little to show from the drudgery of routine detective work. Still, as experience had shown over and over it was often this unsung element of their work that yielded the results.

He turned to face both of them and it suddenly hit him that since an early and bit of an apology for a breakfast he had not eaten that day and the only drink had been the coffee supplied by PC Cook-Watts.

'If you are about to tell me that the murderer has been apprehended and is languishing in one of our five-star cells, then please, go ahead, but anything short of that will have to wait until I have had something to eat. Join me if you want.'

Martin was already halfway down the first corridor and called the invitation back over his shoulder before the other two reacted and followed the boss on his mission to raise his blood sugar.

The clock on the wall above the serving hatch showed a quarter past four and lunches were well and truly over, leaving Martin with the choice of sandwiches yet again, or what was left of the soup of the day.

The latter, leek and ham soup, had most certainly been bubbling away in the pot-bellied electric cauldron since first lunches had started at twelve o'clock, for it looked well past its best. Nevertheless, he scooped out the last it, rescuing some crisp pieces of ham from the sides of the pot. Looking around for something to go with the soup, he was happy to find a piece of cheese and a baguette, and thinking this would do for now took his tray over to where Matt and Alex were already drinking their coffee.

They started to speak as he approached, but balancing his tray with one hand Martin held up the other to stop them. 'Just give me five minutes to eat this without any work talk and then I will be all ears. Meanwhile, talk amongst yourselves, or talk to me about anything, but, please, don't give me indigestion by talking about the case.'

Matt and Alex looked at one another, and then back at Martin, who had already devoured half the cheese and baguette, and was tucking into the soup as if he hadn't eaten for a month.

'So what's this, guv?' asked Matt. 'It can't be brunch, it's way too late in the day for that.'

'Is there a thingy for a combination of lunch and tea or lunch and dinner?' asked Alex.

'What do you mean, a thingy?' The two men were making small talk, and Martin was making short work of his meal, whatever name they found for it.

'Well, they call it something, don't they, when two words are mixed together in some way to make a word that is different but related. Like, we take the "br" from the beginning of the word breakfast and the "unch" from the end of lunch, and come up with brunch. I've just remembered – they call it a "portmanteau word". I heard it on one of those radio quizzes. It was a new one on me but some clever clogs even knew that it was first used by Lewis Carroll …'

'It's amazing,' interrupted Martin. 'No, I don't mean your never-ending fount of trivia. I am referring to the fact that this soup, despite what it may look like, is not just all right. It is truly delicious.'

He mopped up the remains and left his bowl looking as if it had just come out of the dishwasher. 'That's much better, I can think again – so come on, spill the beans.'

On the way from the staff cafe to Incident Room One the group of three turned into a crocodile. Doors were knocked and anyone who was available and involved with the case was invited to join an impromptu team session. Martin hoped that as they were now almost forty-eight hours into the investigation some pooling of ideas and brainstorming would give individual findings a better sense of common direction.

Already sitting at one of the tables and conscientiously writing some notes was Helen Cook-Watts, and Martin made the comment that he was surprised to see her there.

'That GP's visit was brilliant,' she told him. 'Wish I had a doctor like that – our lot don't even look you in the eye. They just shuffle their attention between their patients' notes wallets and their 'how to diagnose' computer programmes. Dr Perry was a breath of fresh air. She just asked a few questions about Mark's taste in music and about his design work and it was as if she had pressed a button releasing things they wanted to remember but were being held in by grief and anger.

'I think Norman will be OK now, and I'm not sure he even remembers his actions earlier, although Dr Perry has talked him through them. She said that rather than him discovering or remembering bit by bit what he had done with the things that especially reminded him of Mark, it would be better to confront his actions. In her view they didn't demonstrate any desire to burn away Mark's very existence, but showed that his love for his son was so strong he couldn't at that moment in time bear to see anything that reminded him of his loss.

'It seemed to work, and although I remember Sandy telling us that she was always the strong one, I saw a sea change in Norman and I suspect that from now on Sandy will be able to release her own feelings and lean on him a bit instead.

'Anyway, about three-quarters of an hour ago some friends turned up and after a few minutes of tears and the usual expressions of shock and condolences they were all off on a trip down memory lane, and I agreed with the GP that it was just the therapy they needed so we left them to it. I told them I would go back later and let them know what progress had been made from our end, so is it OK if I sit in on this session?'

'Of course,' replied Martin. 'Well done with the family liaison work, I know the Hardings are appreciating your support.'

Some twenty or so police officers and specialist support staff were now sitting or standing around and Martin began with a recap of the events of Saturday evening and then painstakingly went through the data he had previously written on the board.

'We have now got a complete report from the professor following his post-mortem examination and tests. Mark had no drugs in his system and there are no signs that he was hit on the head, so he was certainly conscious, at some point, when he was lying on that kitchen worktop.'

'We already know the order in which the limbs were severed but now we are told that this total act of butchery took less than five minutes. Prof. Moore has examined each of the amputation wounds in microscopic detail and has given us more definitive images of the knives that were used – so we now know exactly what we are looking for. Have we found anything?'

He looked towards Sgt Evans who was already shaking his head. 'Nothing, guv. We have searched the house, the garden, neighbouring gardens, and outhouses; in fact, every inch of the surrounding area, but nothing. The neighbours have without exception been very helpful, and it seems that Mark Wilson was liked by those who knew him, but in the main the information given was that he kept himself to himself.'

Martin turned to Matt, who had prepared a summary of what he and the other CID officers had managed to gather from their enquiries.

He began by saying that a total of sixty-one people had contacted the police as a result of the initial press conference and subsequent television coverage, although the majority just wanted to say that they had walked or driven past the house during that period of time but had seen or heard nothing.

'Timewasters,' muttered one of the PCs.

'Well, at least they came forward, and the number of people who saw nothing between half-past five and six lead us to believe that the crime was committed after six o'clock, and as we all know placing an accurate time on a murder can be vital – so not such timewasters after all.'

Martin looked from his DS to the constable who had made the comment. There was nothing he could put his finger on, but he had previously noticed some animosity between these two – well, hell, not everyone could like one another, but as long as it didn't interfere with the job they would just have to live with it. He nodded for Matt to continue.

'We got the usual, but thankfully not many, out-and-out crackpots, one claiming to have seen Daleks and Cybermen coming down the hill, and another telling us how he had seen the whole thing in a vision. The problem being that in his version of events, Mark is a blonde girl with a ponytail who is stoned to death by a vicar who is really the devil.'

The disgruntled constable rolled his eyes but couldn't resist a further comment. 'Well, if we have the devil and metal monsters amongst us, perhaps we should swap CID for Doctor Who.' A moment of much-needed laughter followed and then back to business as Matt went on.

'Of the potentially more credible witnesses, we have one middle-aged man who reports seeing a couple walking down towards the house at about ten past six. He had already passed the house and was going up the hill, and they were walking towards him, but he doesn't know if they went into the house and doesn't remember hearing anything like a gate opening.

'Three people were able to give information about cars parked at the time but we have checked them all out and they belong to local residents and have legitimate reasons for being there.

'Another man saw a couple walking up the hill, but this time on the opposite side of the road to the house, and he thinks this was at about 6.30, although it could have been a bit before that.'

Helen Cook-Watts asked if any of these men were able to provide descriptions of the couple and Matt answered.

'Yes, pretty good ones, especially with the man where both descriptions are virtually identical. But their recollections don't quite tally when it comes to the woman. Both men have worked separately with our artist, and as we speak she is putting together some images that might help. We would without a doubt like to speak to this couple, if only to eliminate them from the enquiries. They are not among the people who have come forward as being around at the time, so having a picture to circulate could be invaluable.'

Matt went on to describe the visits that he and DC Matthews had made to Mark's place of work, and to the health clubs he had frequented. ·

'If we are looking for someone that is homophobic, and who disliked or possibly even hated Mark Wilson, then the manager of one of our victim's health clubs comes straight to the top of our list of suspects. He seemed to be spinning us a yarn about his whereabouts on Saturday afternoon and evening, but fortunately for him we have spoken to independent witnesses who can place him where he says he was, so he's not in the frame.'

'Thanks, Matt. And now I know that Mr Griffiths here is bursting to fill us in on the results of recent SOC tests.' Martin nodded towards Alex, who eagerly took the floor.

'"Bursting" and "fill" couldn't be more apt, as it can't have escaped anyone's notice that our lab has been taken over by plastic sacks containing those countless fibres collected from the victim's lounge. As we know, his sofa was filled with very small soft particles of polyester fibre flock, and the first long

164

deep cut into the leather would have released scores of them and caused them to literally burst into the room.

'There were fifteen more cuts after that first one, and it seemed inconceivable to us that anyone in the room at the time would not have been covered with them. Prof. Moore has identified their presence in the hair and in the nasal cavities of the victim, and they wouldn't have missed whoever else was in the room at the time.'

'What's the first thing you do when there are small particles of anything floating around – look, some of you are even doing it now at the very thought of it! You're rubbing your eyes and your noses, and that's the natural reaction, as well as possibly using your hands to brush the stuff out of your hair.'

'So, amongst those bags of fibres, we were hoping to find anything that would give us the opportunity to do DNA tests. Through a boring and time-consuming process, we were able to isolate nine strands of hair, but to our disappointment it seemed that all of them belonged to Mark Wilson himself. A similar set of results came from a few pieces of mucous and skin that we were able to identify, but there were two exceptions and we have come up with two DNA results that don't fit the victim.'

'Unfortunately, we have fed the details of this DNA into the national database and there is no match, so either our killer is a first-timer or this is the first time he has been careless.'

Alex looked around at his audience, knowing that their hopes had been raised only to be dashed by this potentially case-cracking find having come to nothing.

'Not to worry, folks,' he suggested. 'When we get to finding a possible suspect, we will be able to match them with this DNA result and get a conviction.

'There is something else,' he added. 'You will remember I just said that the DNA from the nine strands of hair that were tested appeared to be from the victim but we are now certain that this is not the case. Five of them are very definitely from the head of Mark Wilson but the other four are from the head of another member of his family and it has to be from a brother or a sister.'

Martin interjected. 'How can you be sure of that?' he asked. 'Brothers and sisters don't share the same DNA, do they? I thought it was only identical twins that did.'

'No, they don't share the same DNA, but there is much more of a match than, say, between you and me, and there are some elements that are helpful in determining if DNA samples come from siblings.

'For example, mitochondrial DNA is passed from a mother to her children, and so all siblings of the same mother will have the same mitochondrial DNA. So you can see that at first we thought we were looking at nine strands of hair from the same person. The rest of our tests show around the expected 50% similarities and differences between the DNA we tested.

'So, to cut short what could be a long, though fascinating, lecture on the amazing world of DNA science, we have concluded that when the fibres of the sofa were released they found their way into the hair of Mark and one of his siblings. From the history of the family, we know there is only one living sibling, and that's his sister Amy.

'In addition we now have on file the DNA of another person who was present at that time and hope it won't be too long before we are able to match it against that of the murderer.'

'Excellent, and well done!' Martin looked genuinely pleased and he rubbed off some of his preliminary soundings from the whiteboard and created a new set of findings and possibilities.

'Let's concentrate on Mark's biological family,' he suggested. 'What do we know?' Answering his own question he went through a potted history.

'He started life with his mother and father and two older sisters. The eldest of the two sisters, Sarah Wilson, was killed during a domestic incident in 1975. She was eleven years old at the time. Her father, Bob, was convicted of manslaughter, but for some reason best known to the prison service was released under certain conditions seven years later.

'Immediately on his release he killed the lover of his now ex-wife, and the injuries he inflicted on her – Mark's mother, Joan – led to her death a short time later. He was caught, convicted, and sentenced, and is currently serving out that sentence at HM Bristol Prison.

'Apart from his father, whose whereabouts are easily confirmed, the only other member of his family still alive is his sister Amy, who is two years older than Mark – so putting her in her early forties.'

He looked at Matt, who did the sums and confirmed what Martin had thought.

'So, where the hell is she? Why haven't we had her here for questioning? She could be the key to this whole thing – what's the latest?'

Matt had expected these questions from his boss, and as he faced Martin and a room full of expectant faces he wished he had some more helpful information to impart.

'We have tracked her down through the benefits system, and it would appear that until two months ago she had a room in a house of multiple occupancy in Newport. However, we've checked it out, and she's no longer there. And the really surprising thing is that she hasn't claimed any of the money to which she is apparently entitled since the middle of March.'

'Someone must know where she's been since March,' said Martin. 'I was about to say that no one can disappear off the face of the earth but we all know there are some who seem to be able to do just that. Think, everybody. We have a woman, approaching middle age, apparently living alone, with no known job, and until recently claiming state benefits. What else do we know about her, Matt?'

'We know she was placed in care when her mother died and we know her mother died as a result of the horrific injuries inflicted by Amy's father. However, her social services records have a number of psychiatric assessments and she at no time blames her father for either the death of her sister or her mother – always laying the blame for her family's misfortunes at the door of her brother Mark. "If he had never been born …" seems to be a phrase she used constantly.

'We have also uncovered a history of drug abuse that had already started when she was in care, and obviously continued, as we found out that when she was about seventeen she almost died of a heroin overdose. That obviously didn't cure her addiction, as there are police records for petty crimes over the years, usually thefts to help fund her habit. She was in prison for a short time last year, and it seems the rehabilitation she underwent then was successful, as we have nothing on her since then. But prescription records show that she has been supported by regular supplies of methadone, which should have been reduced in strength over time – but the dose has never varied.

'The last lot she picked up was on Monday the first of March this year, and that's the same day she was last seen at the house in Newport.'

'OK,' Martin interrupted. 'Any suggestions on what's been going on with this woman for the past couple of months – after all those years of dependency she's not suddenly going to be able to do without, is she?'

Several suggestions came from all parts of the room.

'She could be dead.'

'Perhaps she's gone back to the real thing.'

'Could have just moved away – even gone abroad.'

'Maybe her luck has changed and the woman has found someone to help her with her drugs problem and generally look after her.'

This last comment came from a young PC who would have looked more at home in a dog collar than a police uniform, and who Martin feared may have chosen the wrong career. Martin's fears were reinforced by the jeers that followed the young man's input.

'Yeah, like Father Christmas.'

'When did Mother Teresa move to Newport, then?'

'OK, settle down.' DCI Phelps banged on the table and turned to DS Pryor. 'Presumably we have checked out records of deaths and flights.'

'There are no reports of her death,' replied Matt. 'Charlie has put her name on the computer to search against all passenger lists since the beginning of March, and so far she hasn't come up with anything. However there is evidence of her possible intention to leave the country, as on March 26th she renewed her passport.'

'So she must have applied for her passport either when she was still at the address we know or shortly after – what have they got on their records?' Martin waited for Matt's reply.

'They have the address in Newport and she has given her father as her next of kin. On the subject of her father the Prison Administrator in Bristol has confirmed that Amy has been a regular visitor ever since his term started. They referred to the forms that have to be completed by all visitors and gave us the information they have on her.

'To their total embarrassment their information is about two years out of date as the address is one she previously had in Cardiff, and according to Charlie's digging into mobile phone records the number they have was withdrawn in March 2008. They did say her father was sure to have her latest mobile phone number, and even if he refused to give it to them they would be able to figure it out from their outgoing calls records.

'Here's the really interesting thing, though. She apparently visited her father this afternoon, but that was before they had found out about their records being out of date and about our need to talk to her. Still, we now know she is still alive – or at least she was when she left the prison at three o'clock today.'

Martin looked around the room and realised that it was way past the shift finishing time for the majority of the officers, and that they had homes and families to go to. He drew the session to an end by thanking everyone for their input and encouraging them to continue throwing everything into solving this crime.

'I have a good sense that we are getting somewhere,' he concluded, and turning to Matt added, 'You and I will be crossing the bridge into Bristol in the morning.'

Chapter Thirteen

It was gone seven o'clock when Martin headed for the car park, and by then there were only a few cars he recognised. There was one in particular whose owner was just starting up the engine ...

As Martin approached, she spotted him, and the driver's side window electronically descended.

'I was tempted to call in on the way out to see if you fancied going for a drink, but then I thought with this recent case, which sounds horrific, you wouldn't want to hear me prattling on about the day I've had.'

Shelley's green eyes looked up at Martin and he thought, what the hell.

'A drink sounds like a good idea, but if you can manage it a meal sounds even better.' Martin took the plunge, knowing that the occasional casual drink had been the extent of their relationship so far. Somehow, a meal seemed more in the nature of an actual date. He then told himself that that was rubbish. They were just two people, who happened to work in the same building, needing something to eat and drink and to wind down after a long day.

'Well, I was just thinking about picking up some fish and chips on my way home so I need no persuasion – a meal would be great, where do you suggest?'

'Nothing too formal if that's OK, I don't feel like standing on ceremony at the moment – you choose!'

'OK. Well, what about one of the places in Mermaid Quay?

There's loads of choice there. Practically all the cuisines of the world on offer, as they say.'

'Sounds good,' replied Martin. 'No sense in taking two cars, we'll take mine and come back for yours later.'

Shelley killed her engine and followed Martin to the furthest end of the car park. He zapped the lock of the blue Alfa Romeo and she got in beside him.

'Great car,' she remarked. 'A bit beyond the wages they pay me, and especially with me basically being the breadwinner at home.'

The comment was made with good humour but it made Martin realise that he knew nothing about Shelley's life outside Goleudy. On reflection the total time they had spent together socially probably amounted to no more than a couple of hours, and their conversations had always been work-related.

'I was lucky,' replied Martin. 'Not lucky that a lovely old lady died, you know, but lucky that she had been my aunt and left me everything she had, including her cottage.'

'You must have had a fantastic relationship with her, and she must have loved you very much. Or maybe you were her only relation and she didn't fancy leaving everything to the cats' home!' The last remark was made in a teasing voice, as if Shelley had suddenly felt she may have jumped in too quickly with her comments about Martin's relationship with his aunt.

He was obviously not embarrassed by what she had said, and for the first time since his aunt's death he found himself telling someone about the good, no, the fantastic relationship they had shared.

'She was a great character,' he said. 'She called a spade a spade, and at times I thought she was a bit of a witch – she had such an uncanny knack of knowing what I was thinking. I owe her a lot and I don't think I would be doing this job if it wasn't for her. She taught me to look at things, not just see them, and those skills have helped with some of the more difficult cases of my career.'

'Sounds like you were really lucky, and I don't just mean the material things she left you.'

The journey from work to Mermaid Quay took just a few minutes, and they could have walked it. Martin knew however that if he had left his car outside the office, it would be assumed he was still inside and thus available to one and all. It wasn't a sure thing, but more than likely, that his work phone would remain silent if his subordinates and senior officers thought he had left for home.

This evening was cooler than it had been of late but not cool enough to prevent half the population wearing as little as legally possible in an attempt to show off their recently acquired summer skin colours, ranging from bright scarlet to deep mahogany. After all, thought Martin, we are in Wales. The recent spell of glorious weather could well be it for the rest of the summer, so making the most of it was the order of the day.

Shelley's first choice of the eating places was a Turkish restaurant with an excellent reputation for specialising in traditional sweets. How could Martin explain that his reason for not going there was the sight in his mind's eye of Mark Wilson's body strewn with similar Turkish delicacies he had made just before he was murdered?

He didn't explain, though; just said he fancied something a bit different, and asked how she felt about sushi.

'Only had it out once before,' she replied. 'I do quite often pick up some with the meal deal things they do at the supermarket – yes, OK, let's head for Tokyo!'

As they climbed the steps towards the Japanese restaurant they made quite a striking couple, and although Martin was over six feet tall Shelley only had to raise her eyes a tad to make contact. She was all of five feet ten inches herself, and had unhitched the long auburn bob that had been kept tamed by two large grips and taken off her lightweight jacket and tied it around her waist.

Martin still wore a shirt and a tie to the office, although he had noticed of late that more and more of the men at his grade were now wearing polo shirts or crew-neck sweaters and had abandoned the ties. He couldn't see himself ever joining them – and anyway, the shirts and ties he wore nowadays were so comfortable, being made of soft materials and with, thank heavens, not a hint of starch anywhere. This evening he had left his jacket and tie in the car, and with the top two buttons of his shirt open looked as relaxed and as casual as he was beginning to feel.

The restaurant was surprisingly not busy. Martin had been there twice before, both times much later in the evening when it would be impossible to get a table without booking in advance.

The waiters were attentive but discreet. 'The Japanese could certainly teach us a thing or two about service,' Shelley commented, as they were settled into a corner table for two and instantly provided with a glass jug of iced water and two tall glasses. 'You practically have to beg for a glass of water in some British-style restaurants; they only want to serve you with bottled water and charge the earth for it.'

After a few minutes of discussion with the waiter, they opted to start with a platter of mixed sushi, and then decided that as neither of them were experts they would opt for a selection from the teppanyaki hotplate. The wine waiter hovered nearby. Martin knew there was no way he could drink and drive, but it seemed a shame for neither of them to have a drink.

'Go ahead,' he said to Shelley. 'I was going to be taking you back to your car but I'm quite happy to drive you home instead. Your car should be safe parked in a police station.' Shelley needed little persuasion, and opted for a small glass of house rosé, but when Martin suggested she change her order to a large glass she readily agreed.

Although there were only about seven tables occupied, there was already a good atmosphere, created in the main by the showmanship of the chefs cooking freshly prepared food at two of the cooking stations.

As the couple ate the shaped and modelled sushi, their conversation inevitably returned to work-related matters.

'Hell, it's one big relief to get today over,' sighed Shelley. 'I went through the course appraisal forms before I left and wasn't able to pick out one negative comment, so that's brilliant.'

She took another large mouthful of the pale pink wine,

which looked pretty harmless but was certainly having the desired effect, and she relaxed further. 'Your illustrious Chief Constable got some really high scores and I must admit she was good, she got her points over without pulling any punches, but in spite of some pretty hard criticisms that she had to deliver she managed to keep the audience on board. Your turn next time, Detective Chief Inspector Phelps!'

Martin made a face, but was getting more and more concerned that when Shelley turned those deep emerald eyes on him he was likely to agree to almost anything.

The restaurant was now quite busy and the atmosphere, while generally mellow, was punctuated by the 'oohs' and 'aahs' of fascinated customers, as they watched the chefs expertly using the sizzling hotplate, and turning the raw materials of rice, fish, and marinated meat into beautifully presented oriental dishes.

Yes, this had been a good choice. Martin couldn't remember when he had enjoyed an evening more, and it was nothing short of a miracle that it should be happening just two days into the start of a murder enquiry.

There was no doubt that the reason for Martin's current frame of mind was sitting opposite him, and had been for the past two hours and as the evening wore on he found himself wishing he could capture it for a bit longer.

Although the desserts looked delicious, neither of them was tempted, and Martin chose to have a coffee while Shelley finished off what was by now her third large glass of wine.

Martin paid the bill, ignoring Shelley's suggestion that they should split it in half, especially as she had drunk half of it. And then, as if it was the most natural thing in the world, they walked hand in hand down the steps back to the edge of the Quay.

Instead of going straight back to the car they ambled around like a couple of tourists seeing the attractions of the Bay for the first time. Martin felt slightly intoxicated, although he knew for certain he hadn't touched a drop of alcohol. This woman was having some effect on him and it was hitting him like a bolt out of the blue.

The way Shelley looked at him was making his stomach flip, but why now? They had known each other for more than a year and he had never really thought of her as anything more than a colleague, although Alex had once told him she fancied the pants off him – though according to Alex, every available female did – but had he been right this time?

Even before they had got back to the car, they had exchanged their first kiss, and although it was anything but a passionate one it confirmed to Martin that whatever it was he was feeling was reciprocated. He told himself that it was not great timing to get started on a relationship at the start of a murder enquiry, but hell, he hadn't intended this, and although his head was saying stop now, his heart was offering a different viewpoint entirely.

Closing the car door, Martin leant towards Shelley and kissed her again, and this time as they were not in a public place there was no holding back. There were just the two of them and they took time to savour the experience. Martin took the plunge.

'I know a beautiful little cottage just near the coast where the brandy is warm and the bed is comfortable … but only if you want to – no pressure.'

'Well, it's an invitation I have been dreaming about for the last twelve months,' teased Shelley. 'So I'm hardly going to turn it down now.'

Martin looked at her as he started up the car.

'Why is it we don't see the good things when they are right there in front of us?' he asked.

Still in teasing mode, Shelley said, 'You tell me, DCI Phelps – as I said before, you're the detective.'

For a moment, Martin's mind left Shelley and conjured up an image of his Aunt Pat. He had never taken anyone back to Pat's cottage since he had moved in there, but he knew for certain that if she could have chosen someone for him it would have been someone like Shelley.

He put his foot on the accelerator and headed out of the city.

It wasn't a night of unbridled passion – it was better than that!

Yes, they had made love, but they had also talked and slept, and when Martin woke just after six to see the morning sun catching the burnt auburn of Shelley's hair on his pillow he closed his eyes again.

Now wasn't the time to panic, and he was surprised to realise that he didn't even feel the need to panic. The image that was still there when he opened his eyes made him feel warm and comfortable and he could easily have re-joined her in her obviously blissful sleep.

However, reality had cruelly invaded his mind and for the first time in more than eight hours his mind returned to work and he really woke up. The original plan had been to make an early start for Bristol but there were things he wanted to do before going, and so he had left a note for Matt to say they would leave as soon after nine as possible. Hopefully that would also enable them to miss the worst of the early heavy traffic.

Carefully he eased himself out of bed but needn't have worried about waking Shelley – she didn't move a muscle.

He had showered, dressed, and was in the kitchen making coffee and toast when he heard her moving about.

'There are some new toothbrushes in the blue basket on the shelf in the spare room, and the shower is all yours,' he called up the stairs.

She walked across the small landing, and as he saw her bare bum disappear into the bathroom it took all his willpower to concentrate on buttering the toast. Last night had been great, but this morning there was a serious job to be done and he owed it to Mark Wilson to keep his mind on that job.

Shelley came down less than ten minutes later, fully dressed in yesterday's slightly crumpled clothes and with her hair just towel-dried. If either of them had thought the morning would be difficult, they needn't have worried, as they fell into easy conversation.

'No, I don't have a hair dryer!' was Martin's response to her first question, and to the next, 'Yes, you can poke around all you like, as long as we are out of here within the next half-hour.'

'I love this house,' said Shelley looking into cupboards and opening doors. 'Your aunt had great taste – there's nothing frilly and fussy about it, just perfect decoration and furnishings, and all so in keeping with the overall character.'

Martin nodded in agreement, for apart from installing a dishwasher and a tumble dryer, the only other change he had made was to move out his aunt's three-quarter-size bed and replace it with the king-size one they had shared last night.

'Where does this door lead?' she asked, but without waiting for an answer she turned the key in the back door and stepped out into the garden. 'I think I have died and gone to heaven!' she exclaimed. 'This is my idea of a perfect cottage garden, but I must admit I never had you down as having green fingers.'

Martin had the grace to blush and owned up to the secret of his beautifully set out, freshly weeded piece of paradise. 'Nothing at all that I can take the credit for,' he told her. 'The gardens, both back and front, were laid out by my aunt and her best friend who lives next door, and who lovingly tends them along with her own. She says she does it because every shrub and flower reminds her of Pat and although that is probably true I think she is also concerned that I wouldn't have the time or the skills to keep it as it deserves to be kept.'

'I promise to be ready to go whenever you are,' said Shelley. 'But first I am going to sit and drink my coffee on that bench that's beckoning me over.'

True to her promise, Shelley was ready to leave twenty minutes later as Martin gathered up some papers and his car keys. After a quick look at the front garden that, with her mind on other things, she hadn't even noticed last night, Shelley climbed into the passenger seat and Martin drove off.

His usual routine of using the time between work and the office to think would have to be shelved for today, but he did need to re-focus on the case and so decided to use Shelley as a sounding board. 'You'll know something about the murder we are currently investigating,' he suggested. 'It's been well covered in the press and quite a bit on the radio and television.'

'More than that,' she said. 'The Chief Constable went down to Incident Room One to find you at lunchtime yesterday and took me with her. It's not uncommon for people to forget I'm not a member of the force, and I get to see and hear things that I probably shouldn't. The images were graphic, to say the least, and I'm amazed that the full details haven't come out, but I'm glad for the sake of the victim's family that they haven't.'

Martin gave an outline of Mark Wilson's two separate and very different families, and Shelley listened with interest as he looked for motives and opportunities in connection with all the people who had been interviewed. He put forward his own theory that the motive was hate or jealousy, and his conviction that the victim knew his killer.

'I'm no expert but that's the only thing that makes sense to me,' said Shelley. 'No one lets an unexpected stranger into their home; it's something we are constantly warned against. Perhaps some frail elderly people would be duped, but Mark was only in his forties, and with his background he would be quite streetwise.'

'We're having difficulty getting hold of his sister, and our planned visit to Bristol today is to visit his biological father at the prison.'

Shelley suddenly interrupted Martin. 'Do you mind dropping me off at my house? And that's a first right at the end of this road. I need a change of clothes and my father will want his pre-breakfast insulin jab, and that's down to me.'

Martin turned the car as directed and after another hundred yards or so drew up in front of one of the semi-detached houses. 'What about your car?' he asked.

'No problem, I don't need to be in work early as today is a review day for me, and as you can see I don't live far away, so a taxi is easy or I could even walk.'

She made to open the door and Martin held her arm, not wanting her to get out of the car without telling her how much he had enjoyed their time together and how much he hoped there would be more of the same.

She grinned, leaning over to kiss him firmly on the lips, and answered his unspoken questions with, 'Well, you know where I am now, both at work and at home, so no excuses, not even the ones about too much work!'

Within five minutes, Martin pulled into the car park of Goleudy, and although he was happy with the start of this unexpected relationship with Shelley he was relieved that she wasn't with him now. The gossip machine was brutal and if she had been seen getting out of his car they would have been easy targets. He wanted them to have time to get to know one another better before other people got involved and did their best, however well-meaningly, to mess things up.

Nevertheless he did cause a few raised eyebrows as he walked down the corridor towards his office humming 'Oh, what a beautiful morning.'

Matt had seen him come in and so would most certainly have seen his passenger had she still been with him and his DS would have greeted him not just with a large strong coffee, as he did now, but a great deal of leg-pulling.

Now completely focused on the day ahead, Martin read the reports that had been electronically transferred from the prison in Bristol, giving him answers to some of the questions he had posed about Bob Wilson's record inside.

The first prison sentence records were of a model prisoner who admitted his guilt and regretted his actions. However, even the contemporaneous reports questioned whether or not the contrition was genuine, and the notes in the margin added when he was readmitted after murdering his wife's lover highlighted that those initial doubts were justified.

The reports of the years following his second sentencing were of a very different nature and there were no regrets regarding his wife's death.

Time and time again, the records showed that he held his son responsible for everything bad that had happened to the family, and the latest entry, written at the time when Bob was told of his son's death showed the depth of the father's hatred. He was reported as having told the prison officer that he didn't have a son, but the waste of space that everyone was calling his was at long last making him happy and he hoped the piece of shit would rot in hell.

Matt knocked the door and asked whose car they were taking. On hearing the answer he dropped his own keys into the tray on Martin's desk and followed his boss to the car park. He was happy to get in to the passenger seat for a change, and settled down for a journey that would take close on an hour, during which he knew from past experience they would cover every detail of the case so far, and maybe even come up with some answers.

Chapter Fourteen

After authenticating their identities, DCI Phelps and DS Pryor were allowed through the barrier and into the staff and VIPs' area of the prison car park. They were met at the staff entrance by the acting prison governor, who had been in that position for nearly a year, as the usual governor was recovering from a serious car accident.

Acting Governor Mike Waverley welcomed them and led them to his office along a maze of corridors at the back of the administration block of the prison. There was no evidence of locked doors here, and the offices were surprisingly spacious and airy. Best of all, there was a freshly filtered jug of coffee waiting for them.

'Cardiff to Bristol can be a great run, just straight up the M4 – I should know, I do it every day, as I live in Cardiff.' Waverley was pouring the coffee as he spoke. 'But all it takes is one set of roadworks, or a bump, and you can be sitting in the car for hours – you obviously made good time.'

Martin nodded, but was keen to get the pleasantries out of the way and get on with the purpose of the visit. Mike sensed this and responded. 'You will have got all the background reports that we sent you on Wilson,' he said. 'It occurred to me that you may want to hear some of the off-the-record stuff, things that we can't substantiate but which will undoubtedly give you an insight into what the man is really like.'

'Thanks, we appreciate it,' said Martin, and the three men sat down at the round table in the middle of the office.

'I have only been in my current position for coming up to twelve months, but I was the deputy governor before that, and as such had a particular responsibility for long-term prisoners.'

'Are they segregated from those serving short-term sentences? And what about the violent and non-violent prisoners, are they kept apart?' asked Matt.

'It's something we have talked about for years, but with the numbers we have to cope with it's just not possible. So unfortunately, yes, they can be all locked up together. Violent prisoners get paired up with men who have no history of violence and hey-ho; as they say, behaviour breeds behaviour, and we incubate more violence.

'We have some pretty unsavoury characters here at the moment and we know they have contact with the lowest of the low, the really ugly side of criminal activity. Even though they are locked up we believe they are still able to exercise control over some undesirables on the outside and are the instigators of all sorts of crimes: drugs, beatings, and possibly even murders. But knowing and believing is not the same as having the evidence we need, as you will know better than I do.'

'Is Bob Wilson one of those prisoners?' asked DS Pryor.

'Well, that's the thing,' replied Mike. 'Until a few months ago I would have said he was not even in their league. His crimes were all about his own personal hate and anger – he was never a career criminal and had no links to drugs or any other category of criminology. He's just a nasty piece of work capable of sudden and violent anger; even since he's been back with us he's put two other prisoners in hospital with considerable injuries.'

'So has something happened in the past few months to make you change your views on him?' asked Martin.

'He's been cosying up to a prisoner called Leo Thompson, who I think quite honestly was born evil. His record reads like your worst possible nightmare. You will have heard the saying about killing one's grandmother for a few bob. Well, Thompson killed his son's grandmother, that is to say, his wife's mother, by battering her to death with the baseball bat she had given her grandson for his sixteenth birthday. The old woman had apparently forgotten to give him change from the money he had left to pay a bill.

'That's the crime he is doing time for now, but he has been in and out of prison all his life, mainly for convictions of robbery with violence, grievous bodily harm, and aggravated burglary. It's almost certain that he is one of a known gang of drug dealers, and was in the frame for the killing of two of them, but there was no evidence that would stand up in court. We believe he is still making a shedload of money from arrangements set up years ago, but despite the best efforts of our local CID nothing has been proven.'

Martin shook his head and wondered how many times the governor of Cardiff Prison had spoken of the thwarted best efforts of his local CID.

Mike Waverley continued. 'Bob Wilson and his cellmate – another one who killed a family member, it was his brother this time – are both thoroughly evil bastards, but Thompson is in a different league altogether, and in my experience prisoners only become friendly if one wants something from the other and the price is right.'

'And in this new-found friendship, what is that something likely to be?' asked Martin.

'We've tossed that around at our weekly warders' meetings,' was the reply. 'The only thing we have to link them is that a couple of months ago Bob Wilson's daughter Amy and Leo Thompson's son Jack were visiting their respective fathers on the same day and were seen leaving together. Since then, their visits have always coincided, and the word is that he is completely besotted with her but her feelings are cooler.'

'When are they next due to visit?' asked Martin.

Waverley had obviously been waiting for the question and as if he was expecting to be challenged gave the answer he had prepared earlier. 'They were actually here yesterday, but unfortunately it was before we knew of your interest. If we had known, we would most certainly have ensured we had up-to-date contact details before they left. The ones we have for Jack

Thompson are correct, but it appears that Amy Wilson's are out of date.'

'Yes, we've been told that, but if he is as smitten with the woman as your warders seem to think perhaps she's with him anyway. We could pay him a visit later and hopefully kill two birds with one stone.'

Mike Waverley got to his feet and the others followed his lead 'I've arranged for you to interview Wilson in one of the secure rooms that joins the visitors' block to the main wing of the prison,' he said. 'We have obviously told Wilson you're coming and made him aware of his rights in this matter. He has apparently made it known that he'll say nothing, so it's possible you'll have had a wasted journey, but let's give it a go.'

Martin and Matt followed behind, and it wasn't long before they were hearing the clanking of keys before the opening of every door and the same sound as the doors were locked behind them. Although Martin had made numerous visits to a variety of prisons during his police career, the sound of doors being locked in this way still sent a shiver down his spine.

A door just off the main corridor was unlocked, and the three men went into a good-sized room furnished only with a large oblong table and a perfectly arranged set of six chairs. Sitting on one of the chairs, with a warder standing behind him, was Bob Wilson, and the first thing Martin thought was that there was no doubt that this was Mark's father – there was a strong family resemblance, especially in the shape of the face, the mouth, and the lines of the nose.

Martin took the chair directly opposite Wilson, and as he did he realised that the chairs and table were so perfectly arranged because they were all fixed to the floor.

Waverley, who had chosen to stand next to the warder, made the necessary introductions.

Realising his words would not be welcome, Martin nevertheless started by offering his condolences to Wilson for the loss of his son. The reaction was not unexpected, as Wilson cleared his throat and spat on the floor. He would have repeated the action if the warder hadn't warned him of the possible repercussions if he did.

Ignoring the pantomime, Martin asked Wilson when he had last seen his son, but in reply all he got was a shrug of the shoulders as Wilson looked vacantly at some unseen spot on the ceiling.

Trying a different tactic, Martin asked him when he had last seen his daughter and the reaction was very different.

'You fucking well leave her out of this, she knows nothing, and you've got nothing on her, so leave it out.'

The words were spat out with such vehemence that everyone in the room was left in no doubt that here was a man capable of murder, although as far as the murder of his son was concerned his alibi was one hundred per cent watertight.

'No one is accusing your daughter of anything,' said Martin, calmly, though secretly he was a little unnerved. 'We would like to speak to her, if only to rule her out of our enquiries.'

The last half of the sentence brought a look of absolute disbelief and disgust to Wilson's face, and at first it looked as if he would not be able to resist responding but instead another shoulder shrug and a re-fixing of the eyes.

'We understand she has developed a relationship with the son of one of your fellow inmates. Do you think she is likely to have moved in with him?'

Bob Wilson didn't reply to Martin's question, not even giving a shoulder movement this time – and his eyes didn't leave their fixed point. Although there was no external reaction, the question had made Wilson think about something he had been deliberately avoiding. If his daughter had moved in with Jack he had good reason to fear for her future, if indeed she had one. He was aware of the sort of jobs Jack had been doing so proudly for his father and knew that sooner or later these crimes would be discovered, but even now the man was an unstable psychopath – and one who could be shacked up with his daughter …

But he kept his thoughts to himself as Martin persisted with this line of questioning. 'She isn't living at the address we got from the prison, or the one she went to after that, and for the last couple of months she has not been collecting any benefits, so you could say we are concerned for her welfare.'

'Well, unless she's one of the walking dead, you needn't trouble yourself on that score – she visited me yesterday – ask that lot.'

Wilson jerked his head towards the warder and the acting governor, before returning to his preferred posture, but the very fact that he had responded at all confirmed to Martin that his questions about Wilson's daughter were the only ones which were going to produce any results.

He continued. 'Are you happy with your daughter taking up with Leo Thompson's son, knowing as you must do the things the father is capable of? And as the saying goes, like father, like son?'

Wilson had obviously heard that saying before, and it wasn't the thought of Leo Thompson's son but his own that derailed him now. He stood up and headed for the door. 'That's not always the case. My so-called son was nothing like me, he should have been a girl, instead he was a fucking apology for a boy – I don't think he was even mine – now just get me the fuck out of here and back to my cell.'

Martin watched as the warder unlocked the door and he and another warder, who had been waiting outside, escorted Wilson back to what was ironically his place of safety. Wilson may have wanted to disown his son, but there was no doubt about paternity, and DNA testing if ever needed would only confirm what was easy to establish just by having seen both of them.

The interview provided as much as Martin would have expected, and on the way back to the governor's office he asked if the prison grapevine was saying anything more about Jack and Amy's relationship.

'The first day they were seen leaving together, there were odds-on bets amongst the prisoners that he would be "giving her one" before she got back to the station, and apparently Jack spoke to his father an hour after visiting the same day to settle the bet.'

The Governor anticipated Martin's next question. 'The

188

prisoners are allowed a quota of phone calls, but that one didn't come through any of our phone lines, it was via one of the mobiles we pick up at every unannounced cell search. Despite our best efforts, these mobiles get in and as the technology is constantly improving they are getting smaller and slimmer and easier to hide. We pick up a number during the routine search of visitors, and anyone found with one is denied further visiting permits. However, if the visitors are close relations they appeal on the grounds of infringement of their human rights, and they all cock a snook at us as their visiting permits are reissued.

'It's not easy and we have even dismissed staff in the past for bringing in phones in exchange for undeniably tempting large amounts of cash.'

'Do you think Wilson is happy with his daughter's choice of partner?' asked Martin.

'We know he liked the fact that it got him in with the biggest fish we have in our pond at the moment, namely Leo Thompson – Jack's father. He was a vicious devil when he was first sent down and has grown more evil over the years. During his time in here his reputation amongst our most notorious inmates has grown, and there are rumours that it is his son Jack who is behind this additional standing. Again there are rumours, nothing we can substantiate, that Jack is only too willing to do jobs for some of the prisoners and his father offers his services, sometimes for a fee, but often without charge, just to enhance his position.'

'What sort of jobs?' asked Matt.

'We don't know, and as I said, we have no evidence that these jobs even exist, as you must realise there is a lot of boasting and one-upmanship in here, as prisoners fight to be top dog. Our local force has nothing on Jack Thompson but we really believe that your quote of "like father, like son" is more than justified with those two.'

The Governor offered his two visitors more coffee and said he could rustle up a sandwich but Martin declined the offer.

'If you can give us the address you have for Jack Thompson, I think we will make the most of our time in Bristol and pay him a visit.'

'Yes we can give you Jack's address and although we are unable to give you Amy Wilson's latest address we can at least give you a really good photograph of her taken off our video footage from her visit yesterday.' Mike Waverley handed Martin a package of photographs saying he hoped they would be able to use the best ones in their efforts to track her down.

They took their leave with the usual expressions of thanks and headed out of the prison and towards Bristol city centre. They were actually heading for the St Paul's area of Bristol, but as neither Martin nor Matt knew Bristol they couldn't even guess at the type of house they were looking for.

With the benefit of a sat nav, they arrived at a street of medium-sized Victorian terraced houses lining both sides of the road. Outwardly it was a respectable-looking area, although on closer examination it looked as if the majority of the houses had been converted into flats and a couple were boarded up.

The street had definitely seen better days, and Martin felt sorry for the residents who were still struggling to stop the rot with their clean drives and well-kept gardens.

Number seventeen was towards the end of the terrace, and one of the better-presented properties, but once he had spotted the correct address Martin drove past and parked the car in the next street.

'Even though we aren't in uniform I think we must have COPPERS tattooed across our foreheads. And seeing us both get out of the car could forewarn Mr Thompson of our visit, so let's see if we can fade into the background a bit.'

Matt laughed, knowing exactly what his boss meant, but the thought the two of them fading into the background was a comical picture.

The door to No. 17 was dark blue and recently painted, and the brass knocker and key plate so beautifully polished it seemed a shame to touch it, but in the event that proved to be unnecessary as the door was suddenly opened.

To say the face that greeted them was worn out would be the understatement of the year. The woman standing in front of them, no more than five feet two inches tall, was thin almost to the point of emaciation, and if the number of wrinkles on a face was a method of determining age she had received more than one telegram from the Queen.

The voice, though, was years younger, as were her movements as she retreated back into her hall and spoke. 'Oh, I thought it was Jack. If I had known it was Jehovah's Witnesses I wouldn't have opened the door.'

Well, that was a new one, and out of the corner of his eye Martin saw Matt smirk, but he managed to keep a straight face himself and reassured her on one front before making things much worse. 'We are not Jehovah's Witnesses, madam; I am Detective Chief Inspector Phelps and this is my colleague Detective Sergeant Pryor. We are from the Cardiff CID and we were hoping to speak to Jack ...'

She jumped in. 'Jack's my son. What do you want with him? Anyway, he's not here, and I don't know where he is and I don't know when he will be back, so there's no point in you waiting.'

Martin could barely believe that this woman was Jack's mother, having thought her likely to be his grandmother. And then he remembered that at least one of Jack's grandmothers had been murdered by his father.

'Perhaps we could have a word with you,' suggested Martin. 'The person we are trying to trace is named Amy Wilson and we believe she may be a friend of your son.'

'So it's not Jack you are after?' Eileen Thompson enquired. 'He hasn't done anything wrong?'

'As I said, we are trying to contact a woman who may be a friend of your son and perhaps you could help us if you will spare a few minutes.'

Martin didn't think for one minute that they would be allowed over the threshold, but a miracle happened in the form of a nosy neighbour who had come out of the house next door. 'Have Social Services caught up with you at last?' he jibed. 'You can't keep claiming the old age for your mother, not since your old man bashed her head in.'

'Shut your effing mouth,' was the reply, and then turning to Martin she said. 'Better get inside before the whole street knows who you really are.'

So they'd moved from being Jehovah's Witnesses to being from the Social. Martin wasn't sure if that was promotion or demotion, but he was grateful to the neighbour and followed Jack's mother into her home. The front of the house had been well-presented, but the inside took the level of cleanliness to another plane, and the phrase you could eat off the floor sprung to Martin's mind.

Matt Pryor asked if they could sit down for a moment so that he could take some notes, and she pointed to a dining table and four chairs, presumably not wanting them to sit on her nicely plumped cushions. He thanked her, and then felt unable to continue without making a comment. 'Your son is lucky to have you to look after the house – it's a credit to you – I presume he does live here?'

'This is his home but he's away such a lot,' she replied.

Martin was looking around and left Matt to continue with the preliminaries when he heard his DS ask a question about what Jack did for a living.

'He's a clever boy,' she said. 'Always been able to find work and make good money but when I ask about his work, he gets annoyed so I just keep my mouth shut.'

'But he's away quite a lot?' continued Matt.

'Hang on,' she interrupted him. 'You said you wanted to find some woman, not ask questions about my Jack, so ask your questions about whoever she is and then get going.'

Martin took over the questions and asked Eileen if she knew of her son's relationship with Amy Wilson.

'Never heard of her,' was the short reply.

'Has he brought any lady friends home over the past couple of months?' continued Martin.

'Can't imagine Jack ever having something as grand as a lady friend,' she laughed. 'No one has been here with him for ages. He doesn't like to see the place messed up and girls these days seem to be a messy lot with their bags and shoes and make-up left all over the place.'

'Hasn't Jack got a room of his own he could take his friends to?' asked Martin.

'Yes, he's got the large front bedroom, has done since his father was put away, but it's locked, and nobody but him is allowed in there. I can't even clean the place and I can't imagine what state it will be in. Jack likes things to be just so, but has never washed a dish or picked up a duster in his life – that's my job. He puts some dirty washing in the basket in the bathroom but more often than not he goes out in one set of clothes and returns with some new gear he's bought and no sign of the stuff he went out in.'

Realising she was speaking too freely to the police she suddenly terminated the meeting.

'I've never heard of the girl and she's never been here. My son does live here, but he's not here now, and I don't know when he will be back, so there, you've had a wasted journey.'

'Maybe,' said Matt as he handed her a card. 'We will leave this phone number with you, and when your son returns we would be grateful to receive a call.'

They hadn't mentioned their earlier visit to one of her husband's fellow inmates and still didn't, but on the way out Martin asked her if she ever made prison visits, and got the full force of her pent-up anger.

'My bastard of a husband used me as a punchbag for years, and is in the nick because he murdered my mother, so take a frigging guess, *detective*!' She slammed the door behind them and Matt barely got his foot out in time.

Back in the car, Martin wasted no time in starting up the engine and heading down the quickest way he knew towards the M4. 'There must be a half-decent pub or café between here and the motorway,' he muttered. 'I'm absolutely starving – let's find some food and then head back to Cardiff.'

Chapter Fifteen

Within minutes of getting back to the office, Matt had circulated pictures of Amy Wilson and arrangements were put in place via the press officer for their broader distribution. The latter also arranged for a public appeal to be launched, asking for anyone who recognised Amy, or knew of her whereabouts, to come forward as a matter of urgency.

The team were hopeful of a good response, as they were not looking for some nondescript woman – this was someone who would stand out in a crowd and turn heads, even if only in a contemptuous way.

It was looking more and more as if the key to this case was Amy Wilson. Martin was certain that even if she had not been directly responsible for the murder, she would somehow be involved. They now knew from the evidence provided by Alex and his team that she had certainly been in Mark's lounge either at the time, or soon after, the sofa was slashed. Had she done that? Did the four seemingly deliberate cuts in each of the four separate parts of the sofa have any significance?

Mark had been in the room when his precious doona had been destroyed, and the evidence for this had come from his post-mortem examination when Prof. Moore had found particles of the white fibre in Mark's hair and in his nose and ears.

However, there were not many of the fibres on Mark's body, and they could easily have been missed if they had not been specifically looked for. Martin concluded from this that Mark must have been standing at the very edge of the room, possibly in the doorway, and possibly being forced to watch the whole twisted pantomime. Was that how it all started?

All the information the teams had gathered seemed to confirm that Mark had not seen his sister since he was a small boy, and probably wouldn't have recognised her if she suddenly turned up on his doorstep. The profile that had been constructed around Mark seemed to indicate that if she had unexpectedly re-entered his life he would have made her welcome and invited her into his home.

Is that how she gained access? Questions, questions, questions, and no real answers, just more and more speculation and downright guesswork.

After a few more hours of looking at every detail of the case Martin decided to call it a day and headed off home. He arrived at the cottage just in time to see his aunt's friend Nancy leaving his garden, opening her own garden gate and carrying with her a bag full of the flowers she had just dead-headed.

Nancy was in her seventies, but he had never seen her wear glasses and her hearing was in no way impaired; she knew Martin was arriving way before he pulled into their side road. Having heard the car, she turned as he approached the terrace and waved to him before walking up her path and going into her house.

Typical of Nancy, thought Martin, and although she would surely have seen Martin leave with Shelley that morning, there were no questions and as always no interference – she really was a perfect neighbour.

The memory of leaving the house with Shelley reminded him of how much he had enjoyed their time together, and he found himself thinking it would be great if she were there now to help him rustle up a meal. 'Wow,' he told himself, but it had surprised him to think he would even consider such a distraction when his mind would normally be on nothing but the case at such a critical point.

He forced his mind back to sorting out the immediate issue of satisfying his hunger, but on opening his fridge door he realised it was time he did some serious shopping. He considered popping to the corner shop, but he was well-known in the area and the locals would have seen him on the television. There would be the inevitable questions about the case – questions that given the sensitivity of his work he genuinely could not answer – but his refusal to do so wasn't always seen in that way.

Thankfully, the freezer was more helpful than the fridge, and he fished out three packages, with his main consideration being that their contents could be cooked from frozen. His aunt had been a stickler for eating properly, and although Martin could have used a tray and sat in front of the television he dutifully laid a place for himself at the table. He could see the television from there anyway, and placed the remote in preparation for flicking through the news channels in order to get the full coverage of the Amy Wilson appeal.

To his surprise, the smells of cooking coming from his oven were appetising and when, just as the evening news programmes were starting, he took from the microwave a cook-in-the-bag packet of broccoli, carrots, and beans, it all came together quite nicely.

He felt quite pleased with himself as he sat down to beef bourguignon, mini roast potatoes, and the vegetables, and his only regret was that the cans of cider he had earlier noticed in the fridge would have to stay there. It was unlikely that the television appeal would produce a result requiring immediate action, but it was possible, and could therefore mean a drive back to Cardiff or even further afield, so he couldn't risk having a drink.

The pictures that were already well-known to Martin were now being flashed across the television, and the first thing Martin thought was that the girl looked familiar – but then he had been looking at the photographs back at the office, so they were already ingrained on his memory.

One photograph, which was a good image of Amy's face and upper body, remained on the screen as the news presenter explained that the woman being shown was the missing sister of the man recently murdered in Cardiff and that the police wanted to interview her as part of their enquiries.

The pictures and coverage of the story were excellent, and Martin was grateful that Bristol Prison had been able to produce these – he felt quite confident they would get a good response. Because the last place Amy Wilson had been seen was outside the prison, the same images were being shown and a similar appeal was being made on the news channels in the South-west of England.

This was the frustrating part of the job, and Martin knew that even an appeal with such good visuals as this one had could end up just producing a string of red herrings, but it was their best shot so he just had to sit tight and wait for any sort of response.

Martin cleared the table, thinking that the best part of ready meals was the lack of washing up, and after depositing the plastic containers in the bin and rinsing one plate, knife and fork it was job done.

He had barely got back to the lounge when his phone rang and without having the chance to acknowledge his presence he heard the voice of an excited DS Pryor.

'Brilliant news, guv – the television appeal hadn't even finished when we got a call from a guy named Palash. He's a taxi driver in Newport, and remembers dropping Amy Wilson off at the train station yesterday morning.'

'Is he sure it was her?' asked Martin.

'Positive, guv,' came back the reply. 'She apparently gave him a tip out of all proportion to the fare, and bragged that there was plenty more where that came from.'

'That doesn't sound right – where would Amy Wilson have got the money for taxi fares, never mind over-the-top tipping?' Martin was sounding less confident about this possible lead.

Matt however was still convinced. 'That's what I thought initially, but what if she had made contact with her brother in recent months, and what if he was been giving her the money that is unaccounted for in his bank statements?'

'It's possible, and if she has visited Mark at his home it could account for her DNA being in his lounge, so she could have been there at any time, not necessarily at the time of his murder. But if his long-lost sister had suddenly turned up, surely Mark would have shared that news with his family and his friends? Have you actually spoken to the taxi driver?'

'No, and he wasn't the one who saw the appeal; it was his wife. Apparently Amy Wilson left such an impression on Palash that he told his wife, and she recognised the television images from the description he gave her – but before you start to worry, I can confirm that he has since been shown the images and is in no doubt the woman is the same one he picked up.'

'Have we got an address?' asked Martin.

'Yes, the call for the taxi was received by the company and they have a record of the time of the call, time of the taxi required, address of pick-up, and the name of the driver allocated to the job – they sound like quite an efficient bunch, actually.'

Before Martin had a chance to say anything, Matt played his ace card. 'They even know the name of the person requesting the taxi … someone by the name of Amy Wilson.'

'Took your time getting to that little gem,' Martin said, but he didn't begrudge his sergeant enjoying having the opportunity to use such a trump card. 'Anyway, well done, Matt. So we know for sure that Amy Wilson was taken from an address in Newport to the station yesterday morning, and we know her destination. How have you left it with the taxi driver?'

'I said it was more than likely you would want to interview him yourself, so he's back at the taxi office waiting to hear from us.'

Martin took the address and postcode from Matt and indicated that they should meet at the taxi office as soon as possible. 'Meanwhile, will you get the team checking out the address Amy Wilson gave the taxi company, and find out who owns the property and how long she has been there?'

'That's already being done,' said Matt. 'See you in a bit, guv.'

Martin locked up and walked down the path towards his car. Once inside, he tapped the postcode his sergeant had given him into his sat nav, as he didn't recognise the address of the taxi firm and didn't want to take an impromptu scenic tour of Newport.

In the event the journey was straightforward and Martin arrived only a few minutes behind DS Pryor, who was waiting outside the office and they went in together.

The office was busy, and two women were constantly taking names, addresses, and destinations, before passing jobs, which were each allocated a job number, to the most appropriate drivers. Matt was right – they did seem like an efficient company, although it was obvious that the women, at that moment, had at least one ear on the happenings inside the office.

Martin introduced himself and Matt, and was subsequently introduced to the office manager – and more importantly to Palash Chaudhry, who the manager was keen to describe as one of their best drivers.

Matt produced one of the photographs of Amy Wilson and Palash confirmed she was the woman he had picked up. A printout of the booking had been made and all the facts matched what had already been said.

Martin turned to questions relating to Amy's state of mind at the time of the pickup. 'How did she seem when you collected her?' he asked.

Palash Chaudhry smiled, showing some of the straightest, whitest teeth that Martin had ever seen. He replied, 'That's the thing with fares, what you see isn't always what you get. Some of the weirdos we pick up can be really nice and some of the posh people treat you like dirt.

'She certainly looked like a weirdo, with all that make-up and the black clothes, but she didn't say anything when she got in the cab, just nodded when I asked her to confirm we were going to the train station. I could see her in my mirror, she just couldn't keep still, but she didn't say anything to me during the journey and that took less than fifteen minutes.'

'What happened when you dropped her off?' asked Martin.

'She gave me a ten-pound note,' replied Palash. 'The fare

was only five pounds and twenty pence, so I started to get her change when she let out an unexpectedly loud laugh. I looked up and I'm not sure exactly what she said but it was something like, "Have a drink on me, there's plenty more where that one came from," – as I say, I can't remember her exact words, and then she went off heading in the direction of the station.'

'Was she carrying anything?' asked Matt. 'Like a suitcase or anything to suggest she was going away for a while.'

'No, she had absolutely no luggage – I didn't even notice a bag, she certainly wasn't carrying one, and I don't remember seeing one over her shoulder. I think she took the tenner out of her pocket. Sorry I can't be more helpful.'

Martin assured Palash that he had been most helpful, and after thanking him and the rest of the staff in the office for their response he and Matt left the offices.

The sergeant had done the background work before leaving Cardiff, and as they left the taxi base his phone rang and he indicated to Martin that the lettings company responsible for the address they had for Amy Wilson had been contacted, and an agent was already there waiting for them.

Unlike the reception at their previous venue, they were greeted, if you could call it greeted, by a middle-aged, sour-faced woman who could easily have been a founder member of the jobsworth society.

'I can only show you the outside of the flat we are currently renting to Ms Wilson,' she said sharply. 'She is up to date on her rent and there have been no complaints about our tenant, so we have no authorisation to enter her home without her say-so, or 24 hours' notice.'

Martin ignored the words and subjected the woman to his most disarming smile. 'I understand you are Ms Pope – I am Detective Chief Inspector Phelps and this is Detective Sergeant Pryor. We are grateful for the speed at which you have come forward to help, but for your information we are not here to action any complaints against your tenant – we are investigating a particularly callous murder.'

'I didn't know that,' came back the reply. 'Anyway, it makes no difference, because my boss says I can't let anyone into the flat, not even the police without a warrant.'

Charm having failed – may never have won at any time in this woman's life, Martin thought – he turned officious. 'We don't have time to argue the pros and cons of your tenant's rights. She is the sister of a man who was the victim of a horrendous murder in Cardiff last Saturday. We have appealed countrywide for her whereabouts and have arrived here – so keys, if you please, and round about now would be good.'

Reluctantly, and still muttering about getting into trouble with her boss, the woman led them to the building in front of them, turning right at the end of a short path to reveal a separate entrance to one of the ground floor flats. She purposefully rang the doorbell, and insisted that they at least wait to ensure that Ms Wilson was not inside and possibly not dressed for visitors.

Martin's patience was wearing thin, and after the second ring of the bell he demanded the keys and entered the flat, completely ignoring the woman's request that they should all stay together as this was company policy when entering the property of a tenant with a bona fide contract.

Her prattling stopped as they did in fact all walk into the kitchen together, and were hit by the smell of sour milk, countless cardboard trays of half-eaten pizza, and foil dishes with the remains of curry and other takeaway dishes.

'I didn't like the look of her when she came to look for a property and I told the boss she could be trouble, but he was persuaded by the fact she paid a full bond and three months' rent in advance. Just look at this awful mess, how can people live like this – in just a couple of months she's turned a beautiful flat into a slum.'

Martin looked around. It was true that the place looked like a tip, but a really good look showed that it had never been a palace, and that the quality of the fixtures and fittings were at the bottom end of poor.

The bathroom smelled mouldy and the black around the tiles and the edge of the window frame showed evidence of serious damp problems, which had clearly accumulated long before

Amy Wilson had moved in. In spite of it being a warm evening, the whole place felt cold, but in a strange way somehow sweaty, too.

'Not exactly a des res,' suggested Matt. 'She must have been pretty desperate to shell out good money in advance for this flea-pit.'

Ms Pope rose to the bait. 'I can assure you the place was in tip-top condition when Ms Wilson took up her tenancy.' She was about to continue defending her company when she saw Martin shaking his head. Did these people really believe their own advertising? Anyway he wasn't interested in the flat itself – only in what, if any, of Amy Wilson's personal belongings were still there.

On the bathroom windowsill were several boxes of hair dye, and more empty boxes in an overflowing bin next to the bath. The only other things in the bathroom were two large cheap towels, both in a heap on the floor, and an economy-size bottle of lotus flower shower gel.

Matt had moved into the bedroom, where there were clothes strewn across the bed and in piles on the floor, but there were also a few items hanging up in the wardrobe and he looked more carefully at these.

'Wouldn't have thought some of these clothes were Amy Wilson's style,' he called over his shoulder to his DCI. 'Almost all the gear on the bed and on the floor is either black or dark shades of red and purple, but there are trousers and tops in here in much lighter colours. Perhaps she was coming out of her gothic phase.'

Martin had by now opened every drawer and cupboard but found nothing of interest. In the kitchen area, on one of the makeshift working surfaces, he found a pile of papers, and although most were circulars for local fast food chains and supermarkets there were a few letters. Nothing addressed to Amy herself, though, as the letters that looked like council tax notices and utility bills were all directed to 'The Occupier', or to names that presumably belonged to previous tenants. At the bottom of the pile were several letters addressed to 'Andrew

Coles', and Ms Pope was able to confirm that he had been a previous tenant, but had been gone for more than a year.

It was impossible to say from the findings in the flat if Amy had intended to leave for good, or was planning to return, but it was now more than twenty-four hours since the prison visit – so where was she?

'Arrange for Alex and his lot to come here and see if there's anything they can find for us.' Martin's request was directed at Matt, but he saw Ms Pope prickle at the suggestion and finally put an end to her interference. 'We will be keeping the keys, Ms Pope, and please make it known that no one from your company should come here until our investigations are complete.'

He handed her his card, and suggested that if her boss had any problems with the arrangements he could ring the Chief Constable. 'We will be liaising with the local police, and an officer will remain near the flat for the foreseeable future in case Amy Wilson returns.'

A policeman parked outside one of their properties! Ms Pope looked as if her day couldn't get any worse, and she sloped off to her car, not relishing taking this news back to her pig of a manager.

Matt's phone vibrated and rang simultaneously demanding an immediate response. 'Yes, this is DS Pryor,' he confirmed, and for the next few minutes just listened, occasionally asking for more detail or acknowledging what was being said. It was clear from his manner that this call was important, and Martin waited impatiently for the conversation to end. He watched as Matt pressed the red 'end call' button on his mobile and looked up excitedly.

'She's in the Bristol Royal Infirmary!' he said. 'Apparently one of the ICU nurses saw her picture on the news and recognised her as a patient admitted yesterday with a drugs overdose. The nurse didn't ring the police directly, as she was concerned about the issue of patient confidentiality, but she did go straight to the hospital to get advice from the hospital administration.

'The Critical Care Manager notified the local police as soon as he was put in the picture and they passed the information to our lot.'

'OK, so it's off to Bristol for us! But no point in taking two cars.' Martin didn't have time to finish as Matt interrupted.

'No point in rushing there tonight. Amy Wilson is unconscious. It seems she was in a critical state when she was admitted, but her level of unconsciousness is getting lighter and they are now hopeful of a recovery though unsure of how complete that will be. They have promised to ring us as soon as there is a possibility of her coming round.'

'Blast!' said Martin. 'OK, well, let's both make our way home, and hope tomorrow brings the dawn of awakening for Amy Wilson – and for our case.'

Chapter Sixteen

Jack was back from Spain. This time he hadn't landed in Bristol airport, but had flown into Cardiff, and was in a foul mood. There were two reasons for his evil frame of mind, and he tussled with them both as he cleared airport security and headed for the taxi rank.

That bitch Amy hadn't returned any of his calls and he had come to the conclusion she had legged it with his cash. He couldn't get his head around this possibility, because surely she would visit her father again at some time and he could catch up with her. In any event she would know that messing with him would displease his father, who in turn would make life difficult for her father, Bob. She wouldn't risk that, so what did the stupid cow think she was doing?

Having a personal dilemma to cope with was a new one on Jack, and he knew he had to put it to one side and concentrate on the business he had to do.

He was livid at being railroaded into doing a job for his father without the benefit of his usual meticulous planning. At home were all the tools of his trade, but he was miles away and without what he needed and so he would have to buy some new stuff. The prospect didn't please him but the message from his father was emphatic and left Jack in no doubt that the job had to be done today.

It also didn't please him having no car at his disposal, and his already dark mood deepened as he got into the first available taxi. He needed to go fairly near the centre of Cardiff eventually, but first he had to go somewhere like a garden centre, where he knew from past experience that he could find the perfect murder weapon. Not that he thought of the jobs he did for his father as murder: they were perfectly justified terminations of lowlifes that had stepped outside the rules of their particular version of life.

He had already checked his iPhone and discovered there was a good-size garden centre probably no more than five or six miles from the airport and gave this destination to the driver.

About ten minutes later he was looking around the shrubs and seeds and mingling with the other Alan Titchmarsh lookalikes. Although there was no vestige of the Titchmarsh charm in Jack …

He was concerned that he would attract attention if he turned up at the checkout with just the buddy miner's axe that had caught his eye, and so he also picked up a pair of long-reach pruners and a curved blade saw. With the addition of some tree ties, safety glasses, and elbow-length gloves, he was satisfied that his purchases would add up to a picture of general tree maintenance, not the prelude to murder.

There were no questions at the checkout. He called another taxi and was given just a five-minute wait time.

That was just long enough for Jack to go into the cubicle in the men's toilets and leave behind everything but the buddy miner's axe, which he unwrapped and placed at the ready in his backpack. Someone would find the other things later and assume they had been left by mistake, but the store would have no way of linking them to him as he had used cash for their purchase.

He asked the taxi to drop him off about a mile from his eventual destination and he walked the rest of the way. His mind was now completely focused. He was starting to look forward to the task ahead and his footsteps quickened in anticipation.

A familiar shop came into view, and this time Jack made sure there were no have-a-go heroes on the premises before he entered. His target was standing in his usual place, watching over the till, and Jack wasted no time in lifting his new buddy and diagonally slicing into Ali Addula's neck. In the instant before the axe struck a look of recognition appeared in Addula's eyes, instantly replaced by one of absolute terror as he realised his fate.

For years Ali Addula had pocketed more than his fair share of the profit from the illegal tobacco and alcohol scam he fronted from the shop, and now it was payback time from the big boys. The police may never discover the motive for the killing, but other greedy shopkeepers would toe the line for years to come. Pleased with his work, Jack left the axe embedded into Addula's neck – it wasn't one of his treasures so he didn't need to retrieve it – and lowering his head walked out of the shop.

He needn't have worried about the possibility of being recognised, because the couple walking towards the shop were too engrossed in each other to notice him. He smirked as he thought of the sight that awaited them as they casually entered to buy some wine gums.

Martin had not had a good night's sleep, and facts were still going round and round in his head as he drove from home to Goleudy on Wednesday morning. There had apparently been hundreds of responses to the appeal for information regarding the whereabouts of Amy Wilson, and although they now knew that she was at the Bristol Royal Infirmary, there was still the need to process each of the responses.

Thankfully, the details of all that were not down to him, but he needed to ensure the responses were all handled properly and that all members of the public who responded were left feeling they had been of great help. This was important; maybe no longer for this current investigation, but certainly for future appeals.

Martin had been wandering around the cottage since about five o'clock, and though he hadn't felt like any breakfast, now he was feeling famished, so went straight to the staff café. When Matt Pryor found him he was tucking into bacon, scrambled eggs, and toast.

Matt grabbed a cup of coffee for himself and a refill for Martin and sat down before changing his mind and going back to get himself a couple of slices of toast.

'Not like you to eat breakfast here unless it's after an all-nighter,' said Matt.

'Didn't feel like anything earlier,' replied Martin. 'I have the feeling that today is going to be a bit of a stinker, so I'm charging the batteries in expectation.'

'Well there's no change in the situation at the BRI, but I know that Alex has been to the flat in Newport and gone through everything with a fine toothcomb. He says to meet him later if you want to catch up.'

'Yes, ask him to join us in Interview Room One at about eleven,' said Martin. 'I want to do some scribbling and you can get the updates from the things you've been chasing and then the three of us will get our heads together.'

Martin left the DS to finish his toast, made his way to the office, and shut the door. Peace and quiet was a rare commodity in the constantly moving atmosphere in Goleudy, but Martin was determined to have a couple of hours to gather his thoughts.

He did his usual trick of producing a blank sheet of paper and writing under the predetermined headings. It always worked for him, and he was amazed when there was a knock on the door and Matt came in. 'It's ten past eleven, guv, and I think Alex is waiting for us – do you want to change the time?'

'Hell no!' said Martin. 'Just didn't realise it was that late. I'll follow you down in a moment.'

Alex and Matt had their heads together looking at some pictures of Amy Wilson's flat when Martin joined them.

'I'm no expert when it comes to women's fashion,' confessed Alex. 'But this woman seems to be somewhat schizophrenic in her taste; the majority of her clothes are in this black and purple Gothy style, and then the rest are in what I would call 'cheap modern', and very, very different colour-wise: pale pink, peach, lavender. Not Gothic at all. She also has more than one hair dye colour, again with the main colour being black, but there are also boxes of blonde and copper dyes.'

'Nothing unusual about that,' Matt commented. 'As you know, I've got four sisters, and between them they must have done the whole rainbow. When I make comments about the possibility of their hair falling out I'm laughed at. Apparently the dyes they use nowadays are "kind to the hair" and it's even possible to change your colour completely a few times in one day.'

'Not something I need to consider,' laughed Alex pointing at his shiny shaven head.

'But what about the clothes, there are definitely two quite different styles – can we make anything of that?' asked Martin.

'Well, she wasn't getting any younger, so maybe she was trying to grow out of her black phase and take on middle age a bit more gracefully. The more normal clothes are obviously worn less frequently, and there are quite a number that have been bought but never worn.' Alex peered at some of the photographs of clothes where the price tags were still attached. 'And given that most of those tops have long sleeves, I wouldn't be surprised if they were bought to hide the track marks.'

Martin nodded. 'What puzzles me is where she was getting her money from. We know from the ever-friendly Ms Pope that she paid a bond and a few months' rent up front when she took on the flat. Even for a dump like that, you're looking at over a grand in total, and I don't think the Social Services are that generous, whatever the papers say.'

He paused, then continued. 'There are two places the money could have come from, and if she has been in touch with her brother and it's the money from his account she will have received two thousand pounds.

'However, we know she has become friendly with Jack Thompson, son of Leo Thompson, recently, and if it's really a case of "like father, like son", he could well be making big money out of drugs.'

'Wake up, Amy, we need to talk to you,' pleaded Matt. 'In

any event, shouldn't we be finding out exactly where Jack Thompson is and bringing him in for questioning?'

'In response to my request, the local CID have been to the Thompsons' home, and the mother is adamant that she doesn't know where her son is or even if he is ever coming home. It's difficult to justify, because the only thing we have on Jack Thompson is his relationship with Amy Wilson,' continued Martin. 'However, if he hasn't returned by tomorrow I will try to get a search warrant – I'm itching to see what he keeps in that locked bedroom of his. So tomorrow morning it's straight to the BRI, and even if she isn't conscious yet I would like to see the lady for myself – and then one way or another take a look behind that locked door.'

'Let's get an early lunch,' suggested Martin. 'I have promised to call in on Sandy and Norman Harding, as Helen Cook-Watts tells me they have been writing down anything they can think of that may be relevant and are now on their eleventh sheet of paper. God, I feel so sorry for them.'

Barely had the three men chosen their lunches and sat down when the door of the dining room opened, and Charlie glided in on her two wheels, closely followed by Shelley.

It was the first time since he had dropped her off on Tuesday morning that Martin had either seen or spoken to Shelley. He was delighted when, rather than singling him out, she had just joined the group with her usual friendly but professional manner. Why had he even thought their first meeting after spending the night together would be awkward? It was anything but, and, hell, he had to admit that she looked beautiful today.

Charlie and Alex were immediately teasing one another, and as DS Pryor looked towards him and winked, Martin knew that the rumour machine was up and running – and was spot on in this case.

The couple seemed suddenly aware that all eyes were on them, and Martin was amused to see Charlie blush. She looked at Alex, who shrugged his shoulders and grinned broadly. 'Go ahead and tell them if you must,' he said, in a voice slightly lower and softer than his normal pitch.

Charlie positively beamed, and to everyone's surprise started to open the top buttons of her blouse, but only to reveal a gold ring crowned with a star-shaped diamond suspended around her neck on a gold chain.

It was Alex who spoke. 'I popped the question before Charlie went on her weekend to Ireland, and I would have joined her there on Sunday to meet family and friends if this case hadn't made that trip impossible. We don't see any sense in hanging around, so the date for the wedding has been fixed, and it's Saturday 5th June at 2.30.'

'You two!' exclaimed Martin. 'Talk about dark horses. It seems I was the only one around here who didn't know you were an item – but I don't think anyone was expecting a wedding, and certainly not so soon.'

'Before you ask, no I'm not,' laughed Charlie, her hand tracing the outline of a pregnant abdomen. 'The wedding bit is really down to Alex. I would be happy for us just to live together, but it seems this party animal is a traditionalist at heart, and wants to settle down and raise his own rugby team – now, how many would that be exactly?'

'Well, congratulations, it's brilliant news, and I take it we are all invited to the wedding? Is it here or in the Emerald Isle?' asked Martin.

'It has to be in Ireland,' teased Alex. 'There isn't a boat big enough to bring the Walsh family over the water, not to mention the army of friends and neighbours. Anyway, you won't exactly need an invite to the wedding, as I was casting you in the role of best man – if you want the part, of course?'

'It would be an honour and a pleasure,' replied Martin, and was about to continue when he realised that their table had attracted the attention of everyone else in the dining room. Well, they hadn't exactly been discreet, and a young female constable set the ball rolling by coming across and drooling over the star-shaped diamond ring. Within minutes, everyone was around the table offering congratulations and the usual uninvited and unnecessary pre-marital advice. Everything from 'don't do it, you can always get a transfer', to 'places to go on

213

honeymoon', to 'where to get the best mortgages'. Even those with a string of failed marriages appeared to be in favour of the actual concept, or, if not, were keeping their real thoughts for another day.

Matt's demanding phone interrupted the moment, and not wishing to be a killjoy he went out of the room to take the call.

'Yes, this is DS Pryor.' He spoke loudly as there was still a lot of noise coming from the dining room.

'This is Sgt John Evans,' was the reply. 'I understand you are with DCI Phelps, and I know he would want to be immediately informed of the incident we have just been called to.'

'Go on,' urged Matt. 'Is it anything to do with the Mark Wilson case?'

'No,' came back the reply. 'It's to do with the last case the DCI headed – the one in which Daniel Philips was killed. Ten minutes ago we were called to what was initially thought to be another random stabbing in the same shop, but this time it's Ali Addula, the shopkeeper, who has been killed.'

'Bloody hell!' exclaimed Matt. 'I'll notify everyone right now, and the team will be with you within minutes – just hold the fort until we get there.'

The celebrations in the dining room came to a swift end as DS Pryor explained the content of his phone call and everyone involved did whatever they had to do before meeting up again less than fifteen minutes later at an all-too-familiar venue …

Chapter Seventeen

On the way to the tobacconist's shop, Martin speculated on this most recent murder. He simply did not believe it was a case of lightning striking twice in the same place. His gut feeling was that the first and second murders at the shop were in some way connected. But how exactly?

He tested his thoughts on Matt. 'The more I think about it, the more I'm convinced that Ali Addula was the target the first time, and that Daniel Philips got in the way, but I don't relish passing that piece of news to Elaine Philips. She believes her husband is a hero, having saved the life of a fine, upstanding family man. She will be devastated if we discover that the man he saved was the intended target of an organised killing, because as we know those hits aren't usually directed at pillars of the community – more likely criminals who have fallen out.'

'How much did we check the background of Mr Addula six months ago?'

'I can't imagine we would have thought there was much reason to check him out in the way you're suggesting,' answered Matt. 'At the time, we were considering him to be as much a victim as Mr Philips. There had been a spate of robberies at local corner shops, and we had no reason to think of it as anything other than another robbery that went wrong. I remember at the time that we all wished the money had been handed over without the dreadful consequences.'

Martin nodded. 'Yes, but did we fall into that awful trap of only seeing what we wanted to see? Were there details that could have pointed us in a different direction? The only thing I remember being surprised at was that the knife had been removed from the victim, which shows a more professional attitude. Forensics showed that Daniel Philips ran at the knife. Your average robber brandishing a knife as a threat would possibly have taken fright at that point and just run from the scene, leaving the knife behind. It takes a certain amount of sick courage to remove a knife that has just killed someone – and then we had the conflicting descriptions of the killer from Mr Addula.

'At the time his confusion was put down to shock and his was one of the most profound cases of shock I have witnessed. However what if the shock had been more to do with him knowing that he had been the target and that he could be targeted again at some point?'

'That's quite a lot of 'what ifs', guv,' pondered Matt. 'I'll ring the team and get them to dig into the background of Mr Addula, and to leave no stone unturned.' He got on to his mobile phone immediately, and even before they arrived at the scene of the crime there were people looking at every bank statement, both business and personal, that had ever belonged to Ali Addula. If he had more than one set of business accounts they would be discovered and if the stock in his shop didn't match the invoices on file this would be further investigated.

Martin was growing more certain by the minute that it wouldn't be a case of 'what you see is what you get' with this man, and it worried him.

The familiar police crime scene tape heralded their arrival and Sgt Evans acknowledged them as he lifted the tape to let them through. 'Nasty business, but at least there was only one weapon used this time, and it's still here – well, actually, it's still in the victim.'

Matt was about to say that there was only one weapon last time, when he realised that Sgt Evans wasn't talking about the last killing at the shop, but about the one he had most recently discovered in Penylan. The man must be feeling a bit shell-shocked, being the first professional on the scene of a monstrous murder twice in just a few days.

Sgt Evans' remained outside with his colleague while detectives Phelps and Pryor went in to witness the proprietor lying on the floor and very obviously dead. He must have been standing at the corner of the counter where the till was situated and been struck in the throat from left to right causing him to buckle at the knees and end up in a strange position with his legs partly caught up under his body. The axe was indeed still embedded in his neck, or more accurately in his right shoulder, and where he had bled out there was an almost perfect circle of congealed blood on the floor.

The head had lobbed forward in a grotesque way and Martin got the feeling that it was only the axe and some shoulder muscle that was keeping the head from falling off completely.

The shop door opened behind them and Alex and Prof. Moore came in and without further ado set to work undertaking the routine but vital task of picking over every piece of the crime scene.

'I'm getting a real sense of déjà vu,' indicated Alex as he dusted over surfaces that he and his team had previously worked on. 'How long is it since we were here for the previous murder?'

Matt answered. 'Mr Philips was killed here last October, and now the boss is thinking that the original killer was not out to rob the shop, but that Mr Addula was the target and Daniel Philips was in the wrong place at the wrong time.'

'So you think whoever killed Mr Philips came back today to finish the job he should have done then?' Alex asked Martin.

'I don't have any evidence, but I have a gut feeling that all is not what it seems here and I aim to get to the bottom of it. Look, there's nothing we can do here, so I have a few calls to make and will see you back at base as soon as you have finished.' Martin was heading for the door when Prof. Moore suggested he should wait a minute.

All eyes turned on the professor as he was kneeling behind the head of the body and with gloved hands was lifting out the axe.

Despite his advancing age, the professor's eyes were as sharp as pins and he had spotted something of interest. Calling for photographs of everything as he went along he carefully removed some clots of blood from the underside of the axe where the blunt part of the metal met the wooden handle to reveal a small sticky label. He carefully dabbed at the label to clear some of the staining caused by blood and looked up triumphantly.

'I can tell you this axe cost £22.50,' he proclaimed. 'More importantly, I can tell you that it was bought at The Vale Garden Centre, so maybe that should be your first call, DCI Phelps.'

Finding the label had been a brilliant piece of luck, and every case needed some of that. But Martin did not make the garden centre his first call instead he sent Matt. He had to visit a very important lady and tell her about this latest murder before she read about it in the press.

By four o'clock, everyone was back at Goleudy and settled in Interview Room Two for the first briefing of this new case. Martin's meeting with Elaine Philips had gone much as he would have anticipated and he had decided to share his theory with her knowing that his honesty would be appreciated – and it was. She was one of the nicest people Martin had ever met, and he grouped her with Sandy and Norman Harding in that, thinking, what kind of bastards had the right to ruin the lives of such good people?

The couple that had walked into the shop just after the murder had been interviewed, but were unable to offer much help other than an exact time. Yes, there had been a man walking out of the shop as they approached, but they were unable to remember anything about him – not even if he was tall or short, black or white, fat or thin. The only memory the woman had was of the backpack he carried, and that because it was exactly the same as the one her brother had. She described it as being dark brown, almost black, with the main pocket being a plum colour.

She particularly remembered this because she had told her brother the two colours did not go together, and that he had no taste whatsoever. It was clear she had spotted the same rucksack as her brother's, but she was describing her knowledge of this, not the killer.

Martin gave the meeting a brief outline of the murder scene, and when he got to the discovery of the price label on the axe he handed over to Matt Pryor for an update on his visit to the garden centre.

'The members of staff were all very cooperative,' began Matt. 'They certainly remember selling the axe to a man, probably in his thirties, quite tall and well-built. There is a CCTV camera over the till area, and the relevant footage is with our IT people at the moment.

'The staff thought nothing of the man purchasing the axe, as along with it he bought some other things all related to tree care. About ten minutes after he left, another customer came to the till with a bag containing all the items our man had bought – minus the axe. And the bag had been found in the gents' toilet. Of course, they just thought he had left it there by mistake, and were expecting him to come back for it so kept it behind the counter. We have it here and SOC staff are looking at it, but don't hold your breath. The cashier remembers the man was wearing gloves, and although she thought it was strange on such a warm day, she said it was no different to people wearing shorts in the middle of winter!

'They have CCTV at the entrance, and their manager ran through the tapes around the time of the purchase and bingo – we have shots of our killer getting into a City Co. Taxi.'

'Fantastic,' shouted Martin.

Matt continued with his findings. 'Our people have spoken to the taxi firm, and they are able to confirm that a pick-up from the garden centre was dropped off less than a mile from the murder scene. Timings all match up, so we have a pretty good record of his movements prior to the crime.'

'This really is good stuff,' Martin chipped in. 'Can we see the CCTV from the area after the killing? We know from last time that the cameras from the actual shop are unlikely to contain any tapes but there are others and as I understand it we have collected whatever we have been able to find from within a mile radius.'

'Hats off to our IT people,' said Matt. 'They tell me that after spending the last couple of hours on this we now have a good picture of our killer's movements and I can talk you through them.'

'These first images are those taken from the pay point at the garden centre and show a man, probably about five feet ten and quite well-built. Either by luck or by judgement, he kept his face away from the camera. This is also the case when he was caught on camera getting into the taxi. He was either lucky or well-drilled in the art of dodging the lens.'

'Take particular note,' Matt pointed out. 'As he gets into the taxi he isn't carrying any bags, suggesting that when he dumped the rest of his purchases in the toilet he put the axe, or hatchet as the Vale Garden Centre calls it, into his backpack. He has now pulled up the hood of a dark blue cotton jacket, and this is how we see him in all the films we have been able to acquire from the cameras in the vicinity of the shop – both before and just after the time of the murder.'

'Do we know where he went?' asked one impatient officer.

'He seems to disappear somewhere between the shop and the railway station, and we are still looking through dozens of tapes – but there is something else before that,' said Matt.

'If you look at these pictures they show our killer in the same clothes as we previously noted, but look at these – there's a gap of fourteen minutes and he's still in the same clothes, but carrying a bag. It looks like a bag from a clothes shop, but it's not the shop logo on the bag, it's a Nike carrier bag. It looks to me as if he's bought a new set of clothes.'

'This next set of images show him just four minutes later, and no prizes for noting that he no longer has the carrier bag but is wearing a full new set of clothes – even down to a change of shoes. He's now wearing a dark grey hoodie but the backpack is the same and we are certain these last images are still of our killer.'

Prof. Moore, who had been watching, carefully interjected. 'Contrary to what most people would expect, it is unlikely from what I have so far gleaned from the body that our killer would have been covered with blood. In fact, the probable cause of death will be that the windpipe was sliced open and no air could enter his lungs, followed of course by critical haemorrhage, not to mention an obvious degree of shock. I will be able to give a more accurate summary after the post-mortem examination.'

'So the killer may have wanted a new set of clothes just in case there had been some blood splatter, or it may be part of a ritual that some serial killers need to complete the act,' Martin added.

'That's a rum thought,' said Matt. 'In any event, we have a sequence of images lasting for about ten minutes, during which time he appears to have bought some new clothes, carried them for a short distance in a carrier bag, and then changed into them. Presumably putting his old gear back in the carrier and dumping it.'

'Unless he put it in his backpack,' someone suggested.

'That's possible, but the team has looked carefully at pictures of the backpack during this period, and it looks to be totally undisturbed, with no sign of an extra package being added. Anyway if he has gone to the trouble of buying new clothes with the possible motive of hiding incriminating evidence, he would want to dump it, wouldn't he?'

'This is good work,' said Martin. 'We've been able to narrow down the time and the place of this activity, and it's well worth getting some officers out there immediately to see if they can come up with anything. We need to talk to clothes shop assistants and search toilets, garages, or whatever to see if we can find that carrier bag.'

He looked towards Sgt Evans, who confirmed that as many officers as possible would be detailed to the task, but adding his regrets that not one of the CCTV tapes had come up with an image of the killer's face. 'If my officers take a picture of a man in a hoodie and ask local shop keepers if they have seen this man they will be laughed at – I mean, fifty per cent of their customers will be in hoodies! Still, we'll do our best, and maybe something like the backpack will trigger memories.'

'We also have a pretty good idea of the clothes he bought,' Martin reminded the officer. 'That could be something the retailers will relate to. We also need to keep looking for CCTV cameras around the area of the last place he was seen – this man couldn't have just disappeared.'

'As well as concentrating on where he went, what about finding out where he came from? Assuming that it took him less than twenty minutes to buy his chosen murder weapon and dump the other things he bought as a legitimate cover for the axe, he would have been there no more than half an hour. Let's get the earlier CCTV footage from Vale Garden Centre and check it out.'

There was a general buzz of things happening and officers were moving off in all directions and generally getting a good feeling that through this meticulous routine police work they would get their man. Martin wished they had such good leads in connection with the Mark Wilson murder.

True, two out of three wouldn't be bad, but solving the three murders and bringing the killers to justice would be so much better. Was there a killer in the Wilson case – or were there killers? They couldn't be sure that the man they were currently pursuing was the same man who had killed Daniel Philips and as yet they were not sure if there had been more than one person responsible for the slaughter of Mark Wilson.

Most people had left the interview room when Matt's ever-demanding phone rang again, and he took a call that lasted just a few seconds. After thanking the caller he turned to his DCI.

'She's awake, guv, so I guess it's a journey back across the Severn Bridge for you and me!'

Chapter Eighteen

The journey to the Bristol Royal Infirmary was uneventful and they made good time, being frustrated only by the twenty minutes it took them to find a parking space when they got there.

They soon arrived at the Intensive Care Unit, where a rather gorgeous nurse with a surprising but unmistakable French accent told them that Amy had been transferred to an area known as the High Dependency Unit.

'She is out of any immediate physical danger and no longer needs us, but where her mind is, and what she will need to repair – that is another story.' In typical French fashion the nurse put equal stresses on all the syllables of each word, emphasising the last full syllable of the longer words. The result was pleasing to the ear, and Martin had the feeling that his DS would have been happy to stay indefinitely and forge a new Franco-Welsh connection. But they had work to do.

The HDU was close by, and it looked as if there were two separate areas, each with four beds and a central area where what looked like workstations housed computers and clinical monitors. As they entered one of the four-bedded areas a young man got up from his chair and came forward to meet them.

It was impossible to distinguish who was who, as every member of staff wore pale blue cotton trousers and loose-fitting tops. However as the man walked towards them they could very clearly see 'PAUL' embroidered in large bold letters on his uniform top.

He followed their gaze and he spoke. 'Yes, I'm Paul, one of the charge nurses, and you must be the detectives from Cardiff – Staff Nurse Lemaitre just phoned to say you were going to pay us a visit.'

Martin made the formal introductions, with the aid of his warrant card, and asked if it was possible for them to interview the patient, Amy Wilson.

Charge Nurse Paul looked towards the bed in the left-hand corner that was surrounded by curtains, and told them they would have to wait about ten minutes as some of the nurses were attending to Amy and she was proving to be a bit of a handful. 'Come into the staff room and have a cup of coffee,' suggested Paul. 'We've just discharged two of our patients and most of us are having a five-minute breather before the next two are transferred down from ICU. Your Amy has been giving us the runaround – screaming and talking non-stop since she became conscious – but we don't know how much sense she is making. Perhaps it'll mean more to you.'

The cramped staff room was shared with the staff of ICU, but Paul clearly knew his way around, and within a couple of minutes the three of them had mugs of half-decent coffee and a place to sit.

'Is there anything in particular that Amy's been saying?' asked Martin.

'Not really,' Paul replied between mouthfuls of coffee. 'At first it was just a string of foul language – and I mean foul language. We hear a lot of it here, as I'm sure you do in your line of work, but her language is amongst the juiciest I've heard in a long time.'

Martin reflected on what he knew about Amy's background, and was not surprised that she had picked up a few choice expletives during her lifetime.

'The main butt of her anger and verbal abuse seems to be someone called Mark, and sometimes it's aimed at a Jack, but we think she seems to be apologising to him, in a funny sort of way.'

Paul's pager summoned him and he got up, leaving his

coffee half-drunk. 'Story of my life,' he said. 'Our new patients are on the way so I need to get back. Just finish your coffee and by then it should be OK for you to interview Amy, and good luck with that.'

Paul left them with three members of staff, all of whom it was easy to recognise as, like Paul, they had their first names embroidered on their tops. Matt got into a conversation with, according to her embroidery, SARA. He discovered that this fashion of having whatever name the member of staff liked to be known as embroidered on the uniform top dated back to a patient satisfaction survey conducted by the hospital two years previously. Apparently before that, the staff had had a habit of forgetting their name badges, or sometimes they were torn off by patients or had to be taken off to avoid patient trauma. A patient had come up with the idea, and the staff liked it because it ensured that they had their own sets of uniform that were likely to fit.

Matt laughed. 'I can't see that working in the police force. Most of our officers don't even want the villains to know their official number, never mind being on first name terms.'

Coffee finished, the detectives made their way back to the HDU, where all the beds were full and the staff were now rushing around.

They were spotted returning and directed towards the bed earlier indicated to them, where the curtains were now drawn back to reveal a woman who only vaguely resembled the image they were expecting. She had been stripped of the black and white face paint, and the hair that had previously made such a statement had been brushed into a more conventional style.

The black nail polish had been removed and Martin remembered an ex-girlfriend of his, who was a nurse, telling him why they needed to remove nail polish from any unconscious patients – it was something to do with looking for signs of cyanosis, but that was as far as his memory took him.

Dressed in a hospital gown-type thing with longish sleeves, the tattoos on her arms were not visible, and she looked like the majority of other forty-something year olds, already sporting a number of wrinkles and some signs of prematurely relaxed facial muscles.

It was not until Martin's eyes rested directly on her eyes that he could see where her resemblance to most people's version of 'normal' disappeared completely. Her pupils were quite dilated, and darted to all corners of her eye sockets as if chasing some images only seen by her.

The arrival of two strange men at her bedside didn't in any way interrupt the performance she was watching through her mind's eye, and even after Martin had made the required formal introductions, nothing changed. She didn't say a word, seeming not to be aware of their presence and Martin feared they had made a wasted journey.

Suddenly, and with absolutely no warning, she let out a blood-curdling scream, causing her visitors to visibly jump but attracting only a momentary glance from the HDU staff, who had presumably heard it all before. The scream was followed by an outpouring of some of the same colourful language already described by the staff, and Matt muttered that there were a few obscenities that were even new to him.

Martin tried to engage Amy in conversation but it was impossible and he wondered if her mind would ever recover from what was happening to it.

As if to answer his unspoken question she suddenly sat up in bed and shouted loudly that she wanted to pee. This did produce a response from one of the nurses, who ushered the detectives away from the bed and quickly drew the curtains around it.

As they walked away from the bed, Paul passed them. 'She seems to know something about her basic bodily functions,' he said. 'Last time she said she wanted a pee, it was only minutes later that we were changing a soaking wet bed, so hopefully it will be better luck this time.'

Martin and Matt looked at one another, both thinking 'better them than me' but saying nothing.

Realising that any attempt to continue interviewing Amy Wilson was at present impossible, Martin walked towards the central workstation and spoke to Paul. 'Are there any records of what she had with her when she was admitted and do you know exactly where she was found?'

'Sorry,' said Paul. 'I assumed you would have been told about all of that – it was the talk of the unit at the time. She was picked up at one of the public toilets in a local shopping centre and according to the ambulance crew she had one of those travel bags around her waist. When the bag was removed, it was examined as they were looking for clues about the drugs she had taken, but what was found was one thousand seven hundred and seventeen pounds. I remember the exact figure because, as I say, everyone was talking about it.'

'There may have been other things with her, I don't know; the local police were involved and I believe they would have taken most of it away – but I'm not really sure.'

Matt indicated that the hospital administrator had only made them aware of Amy's admission but not of the circumstances surrounding it. Martin suggested to Matt that in order to clarify things, he should get on to the local police station immediately, and they could meet back at the car park when he had finished talking to Paul.

'Presumably she was unconscious on admission?' Martin asked.

Paul continued. 'Yes, and from what I can gather, lucky to be alive, although I wouldn't want to be inside her head just now. We get more than our share of people, usually kids much younger than she, who are the victims of the real bastards, that is to say the ones who supply them with their poison.

'Most of the time the suppliers don't even know themselves what they are handling, and the goods on offer can be anything from pure drugs, which give way above normally safe doses, to stuff that is cut with substances that are themselves toxic. The results are the bodies that are brought in here, either at or past death's door, for us to try and sort out – but for some it's the revolving door syndrome and we see the same faces over and over.'

Martin looked at the charge nurse and noted the intensity in his voice. Here was someone who cared passionately about his job and who, like Martin, knew about the misery in the lives of so many of the people their vocations regularly brought them in contact with.

'Are there any other names or places she has mentioned, or has she asked you to contact anyone for her?' asked Martin.

Paul shrugged and answered the second part of the question. 'She hasn't reached that level of rational thinking, and as far as names are concerned I can only remember Mark and Jack, but let's take a look at her notes.' He paused as he rummaged for them. 'OK – when she first regained consciousness, the ICU staff may have noted down things she said. We know her name and her date of birth from her passport, which was in the bag, but the section where it asks for two emergency contacts is apparently blank.'

As he spoke, Paul thumbed his way through the records that had been created since Amy was admitted and found what he was looking for. 'There are a few names here, two of which I have already mentioned, and she also called for her dad quite a bit. The other two names are Suzanne and Paula, but again these names were not used with affection, just attached to some vitriolic adjectives.'

Martin didn't need to make a note of the names, as they were already familiar to him, and he thanked Paul before heading off to the car park to find DS Pryor.

Matt had spoken to the local police, who had gathered up Amy's belongings after the ambulance had taken her to the BRI. 'They apparently looked at it as just another drugs overdose, and not high on their list of priorities. The two constables attending the call gathered up a couple of plastic shopping bags containing some new designer shoes and a leather jacket and that was about it.

'The syringes and the drugs packets were taken by the ambulance staff and the only other possession was a travel bag strapped around her waist. The amount of money found in the bag was exactly what the hospital had stated. They have since been in contact with the hospital, but have been told she is in no state to be interviewed at the present time. The cash and her passport are apparently in the hospital safe.'

'So, nothing we didn't already know,' replied Martin. 'I have got something that adds to the theory that Amy has been in contact with her brother recently. Amongst others that she has cursed since becoming conscious are Mark's friends Suzanne and Paula and the only way she could have known about them would have been if her brother had told her.'

'Yes, but there are three friends aren't there – what about Anne?'

'I wondered about that, but don't forget that at the time she was barely conscious and rambling. Anne is a name that could have been lost in a string of half-jointed sentences and a lot of bad language, so she could well have been denouncing them all.'

'Or Suzanne and Paula could be just two people she knows, and nothing at all to do with the friends of her brother,' muttered Matt.

'Not impossible, but my gut feeling is that it's too much of a coincidence, and the odds on Mark and his sister both knowing a Suzanne and a Paula are too high, really. What I can't get to grips with is that if Mark had started to see his sister, why keep it a secret from his new family and his three best friends? We need to talk to them again, and see if they are able with the benefit of hindsight to think of any way in which Mark and his sister could have been in contact.

'The person we really need to meet is Amy's boyfriend Jack. We left a number with his mother to contact us if he turned up, but we can't rely on that so we need to ask for some local co-operation and get a round-the-clock-watch on the house.'

'What about a television appeal? We have the photographs of him from the prison when he was with Amy, and appeals seem to have served us well in this enquiry.' Matt punched some numbers into his phone in response to the nod he got from Martin. 'Do you want to cover the Bristol and the South Wales area again?' he asked.

'Definitely,' said Martin. 'Jack Thompson may live in Bristol, but Mark was killed in Cardiff, and if Jack is our killer there may be a chance he'll be recognised in either place. We also need to show his picture to the two most reliable witnesses in Mark's road around the time of the killing. Nothing came of their time with our artist, but a photograph could produce a result.'

'Are we going to take another trip to Jack's house, or head back to Cardiff?' asked Matt.

'Well, at the moment, all the evidence we have to link Jack to the murder is circumstantial to say the least, and it won't get us a warrant to search his house and break down his bedroom door – much as I would like to do just that.

'The man has an unblemished record, not even a traffic offence, and the best we have to offer is that we would like to talk to him in case he is able to help with our enquiries. No, let's pull the local police and media in to help trace his whereabouts and head back home.'

Against all his better judgement, but in order to stop the constant grumbling of his sergeant's stomach, Martin pulled off the M4 and into the Magor service station. He warned Matt that this stop was going to be a maximum of ten minutes, so suggested he head for Burger King and grab something quick. Martin only wanted coffee, as his mind had gone into overdrive and he was struggling to fit together pieces that were on the face of it ridiculous but starting to form a picture in his head.

He recognised this phase of any investigation and had learnt not to block out any ideas that came to mind, no matter how disjointed. His problem this time was that with the responsibility for solving three murders, he was having trouble in separating some of the facts – and he had to do that, didn't he?

The place was heaving as a result of the pouring of masses of schoolchildren from the four coaches that had pulled in just behind them, and Martin could barely hear himself think. 'Hurry up.' He prodded Matt. 'Let's get out of here, and you can drive the rest of the way; I need to sort some stuff out in my head.'

Martin took a notebook and pen from the compartment

under the dashboard, and willed his brain to focus on two separate murder enquiries. He was lumping the killing of Daniel Philips and Ali Addula together, as he was sure that even if there was a different killer for each victim the two deaths were linked, and he now firmly believed that Addula had been the target from the start. So although there were two murders they were being treated as one enquiry.

The second enquiry was the murder of Mark Wilson. Martin was becoming more and more convinced that Jack Thompson was the murderer of Mark, and had been in some way aided and abetted by Amy Wilson.

All he had to do was prove it!

As they were on their way back to Cardiff Martin focused his attention on the latest murder and phoned through to the office to get an update on the investigations into Ali Addula's affairs. He was put through to Charlie, who had been given the task of interrogating the computer found in the backroom of Ali's shop.

She sounded excited as she spoke to Martin. 'What a can of worms we have here – more wheeling and dealing than Del Boy, and nowhere near as innocent. I have so far uncovered at least three threads of money and none of it through the normal channels. I would never have had Mr Addula labelled as a computer buff but this stuff is really impressive and he certainly knew how to move cash around. It looks to me as if he has for many years been supplied with contraband alcohol and tobacco of all types – taking an educated guess, about three-quarters of his stock would have been acquired in this way.

'It looks as if the additional income from that illegal source wasn't enough and he became greedy. Not all the money that appears to have been agreed by his suppliers has been handed over, and in recent years more and more of it has been going into one of Mr Addula's accounts.'

'So my guess is that he's upset someone, big time, and has paid the penalty for his insatiable appetite for money. Maybe the initial killing wasn't a robbery that went wrong but an innocent man protecting a criminal from the punishment that had been arranged for him.'

Martin laughed. 'I'll put you on the case, Detective Charlie,' he said. 'I've been thinking along those lines for a while, and your findings have certainly given me the motive I was missing.'

'Glad to be of service,' came back the reply. 'We'll be handing all this information over to Customs and Excise and the Revenue – it may help them track down his suppliers, and perhaps that's where you'll find his murderer. I'm going to put you through to Alex,' she finished. 'I think you'll be pleased to hear some of the results from the CCTV searches.'

The phone made some clicking noises as Charlie cut off their line and spoke to Alex, before reconnecting him on a new line to Martin.

'Hi,' said the distinctive deep voice. 'Come straight to Incident Room Two when you get here and I'll show you some treasures, but just to brighten up the last part of your journey I can confirm that the clothes dumped by our killer have been found. They'd been left in one of those industrial-type metal rubbish units, and it's thanks to the efforts of the officers searching the area that the bag was found.

'There isn't much in the way of blood, but there is enough to provide us with a profile and I'm sure that it will match the blood we have from Ali Addula.'

'There are also some new sightings on CCTV cameras with our killer in his new set of clothes seemingly heading towards the railway station, or maybe the bus terminus.'

'That's brilliant news,' said Martin. 'We'll be there in about ten minutes, so see you soon, and it's a giant pat on the back for everyone involved.'

Martin relayed the news to Matt, who responded by putting his foot down a little harder on the accelerator and cutting three minutes off their estimated time of arrival.

Chapter Nineteen

Jack had gone from not being happy to being in the blackest of all moods. He now knew why Amy wasn't answering his phone calls or responding to his text messages – the stupid cow must have used some of the money he had given her and gone off in search of a proper fix.

Her face was all over the local newspapers, along with the story that the sister of the gay man murdered in Cardiff had been found and was lying in a drug-induced coma at a Bristol hospital. He was not to know that this news was not the latest.

His main concern was how quickly she would be traced to him, as by now the authorities would know that she had left the prison with him on Monday afternoon. But why would they want to investigate her further? Surely they would just be treating her as a sad junkie and would have no reason to link her to the murder of her brother in Cardiff?

He wasn't convincing himself and his dark mood deepened.

He had not liked going back to the shop that afternoon, as it reminded him of a previous failure and Jack didn't do failures. Not only that, but today's job had not been prepared in Jack's preferred way, and he thought longingly of the more appropriate weapons he had at his disposal all neatly hanging behind the doors of his purpose built wardrobe.

Since he had been a small boy Jack had loved sharp knives, and as he grew older he looked for knives of all shapes and sizes and with an array of blades and teeth. His father indulged his son's passion and had built the wardrobe as a fourteenth birthday present.

Initially the wardrobe had housed only shiny new weapons, but now there was a much grimmer section behind the back wall. It was there that Jack had hung seven trophies so far, and he was now feeling evil as he thought of his last two trophies – they could have been numbers eight and nine and he had left both of them behind. He convinced himself that the latest one didn't matter as the axe had been a spur of the moment purchase and not one of his carefully selected tools.

But the job he had done for his father before going to Spain had been planned more carefully and Jack had chosen a long-bladed steel knife with images of fornication on the handle – appropriate, he had thought, for his target. That blade would have had pride of place in his wardrobe but for her fucking mongrel.

Only his father knew about the hours his son spent polishing those knives and fantasising about the job each one had to do, or more recently, had done.

It was some time after his father had been sent to prison that Jack's knives began to turn from tools to trophies. Each job he had used them for was for his father, and Jack felt no guilt or remorse for anything. After all, the jobs were only done on people who had grown too big for their boots, or who needed teaching a lesson, so there was nothing to feel sorry about.

Jack couldn't describe the feeling he got from actually killing someone, but it was addictive and he knew he would go on doing whatever jobs came his way for as long as he could. The only problem was that soon after each killing, he experienced the feeling of being suffocated, and he was now aware that the feeling was about to overtake him.

He needed to sit down and wait for this expected episode to pass, and although he didn't want to hang around and wanted to get home, he had no choice. His hands involuntarily smoothed the muscles in his throat, and he began doing what he had learned from experience helped him to breathe.

The first time this had happened his natural response had been to try taking in large amounts of air but his throat muscles seemed to reject this natural life essential element.

He remembered that initial feeling of total panic and how he had almost passed out as the agony of feeling suffocated overwhelmed him. But that was the first time and Jack was now an experienced killer and so within a few minutes of taking just short shallow breaths of air and massaging his upper chest he was able to manage the aftermath of killing and was very pleased with himself.

It hadn't taken him more than just a few jobs to reach this position, and he soon realised that, after each killing, he was getting this unexpected second adrenaline rush. And now that he could control it, he had started to enjoy it.

The experience cleared his mind and he made a few quick decisions. Amy was dumped, and he hoped she would not recover from the coma he had read about earlier, but in any event he would have nothing more to do with her. She had provided him with some really grown-up sex, and he knew she was the only person other than his father who he had ever had any feelings for, but he convinced himself that with the money he was now raking in from jobs women would be queuing up.

She had provided him with his best-ever job, and being able to use four of his precious tools and turn them into four trophies in one, or should he say four, foul swoops had been truly awesome. He had been a bit apprehensive about letting her use the long-bladed knife, as it was the first one he had bought himself, but he had enjoyed standing in the doorway with another knife in the ribs of her brother and watching her destroy that very expensive sofa. He had not displayed the knife she used with his other trophies, though, as it was not really one of the seven he had used to date.

She was crazy, he had to admit, but her actions had turned him on, and they had both enjoyed the misery and fear in Mark's eyes as he began to realise what was happening.

As she made four cuts into the first seat of the sofa she had screamed that there was one for each of the people whose lives he had destroyed. One was for her sister, one for her mother, one for her father, and one for her. They had planned things carefully beforehand, and she was supposed to stop there, but the unexpected release of the white fibres had made her giggle and she continued making four cuts in three other parts of the sofa, indicating each time the person to whom each cut was being offered.

She had suddenly turned her attention on Mark and demanded that he get his birth certificate and the certificate of his adoption. This hadn't been in their plans, and all Jack wanted to do was get on with his part of the action. However, Amy had become hysterical, and so with the knife still in his ribs Mark was forced to produce the papers, and then made to watch again in helpless disbelief as Amy set fire to them.

Jack remembered that there had been a slight movement from Mark and it had been enough to trigger the next part of the plan. He had pushed Mark towards the kitchen and got him to lie on the marble worktop. Mark didn't argue, as by now he was locked in a personal world of terror and was probably struggling to imagine why his sister hated him so much.

Had his sexuality really been such an issue for his family? As Jack had unwrapped the tools of his trade and forced Mark to watch in abject horror and disbelief he would certainly have known the answer to that question.

Now, sitting on a grass verge, Jack took psychopathic pleasure in remembering his part in this well-planned mental and physical assassination. He'd had his beloved tools ready, and had been able to look into the eyes of his victim as he had started his execution.

An axe with a longer-than-average cutting edge had been his first weapon of choice but as he had brought down the weapon Mark must have suddenly became aware that his right arm was the target and he had moved. However he had not moved quickly enough and with the blade cutting into his upper arm Mark had fainted. Jack had not quite achieved his objective, as the arm was still attached to the body, but another swift and a more accurate swipe had done the job.

As part of their planning, Amy had told Jack what she wanted him to do, and at this point he had called out 'one for your sister' and then with one of his favourite weapons, a small machete, he had taken off Mark's left arm and called out 'one for your mother.'

Amy had not moved from the lounge but Jack knew instinctively that she was listening and had picked up his third weapon – the Japanese curved double-edged blade set in a brown leather handle. It was a beauty, remembered Jack. He should have used the outer edge of the blade but he hadn't and so the tip of the blade had hit the marble worktop before the job was finished. A quick flip and the sharp outer blade had worked well, and Mark's left leg had fallen to the floor with Jack's call of 'one for your father'.

Anxious now to finish the job, Jack had selected as his last weapon something he had jokingly told Amy he could get his teeth into. He had shown her a stainless steel blade with razor-sharp fine edges: it was almost a cross between a knife and a saw, and Jack loved it. There had been little pressure needed as the saw had virtually glided through skin, muscle, and bone, and the right leg and the final limb had fallen to the floor with an even louder and triumphant shout from Jack of 'and one for you!'

Jack remembered how surprised Mark had been when they had arrived at his door. He had obviously just taken a shower and dressed, and was smelling of expensive cologne, but on recognising Amy he had let them in without question. Jack had barely recognised Amy himself that evening, but her amazingly different appearance had added to the fun. Mark's smile of welcome hadn't lasted long, and as soon as they were inside Jack had pulled a knife and Mark had been forced to watch as his visitors put on paper all-in-one suits of the type used to prevent cross contamination. They had come prepared and less than fifteen minutes later they left the house with the suits rolled into Amy's handbag, looking like any other couple out for a Saturday night.

It was because they looked so much like any other couple that the witness who had come forward was only able to give a vague description. Jack laughed as he thought that would never have been the case if Amy had been painted that night in her beloved Gothic image.

He allowed himself just a few more minutes of nostalgia rather than thinking about the job he had done earlier that day – one that he knew would never be ranked as one of his best. It had been botched first time round by a stupid customer taking him on, and although the knife for that man's killing hung in Jack's trophy cupboard it was not in Jack's top-ten list of trophies for jobs well done.

Were there ten to consider? Well, not quite yet, but there were lots of blades ready and waiting and he was sure there would be no shortage of punishments to hand out. He vowed never again to take on one of his father's requests without his usual detailed preparation – after all, that was a vital part of the pleasure of the performance for him.

Jack knew he had work to do, and had been considering a move from the family home for some time, but would have liked more time to plan. He would be linked to Amy, but he was sure there would be no evidence to put him in the frame for her brother's murder, and his mother would give him an alibi for last Saturday.

Still, he knew that as soon as the police got you on their radar, they were difficult to shake off. Most likely they would be asking him for a DNA sample to, as they put it, 'eliminate him from their enquiries', but that alone would mess up his years of careful planning to remain anonymous.

He had set up a few new contacts during his recent couple of days in Spain, and had been pleased to learn that skills of the type he was able to demonstrate were as much in demand on the Costa del Whatever as in the UK. Already there was a job lined up for him, and he had spent time combing the antique shops of the area and found an amazing Spanish Main Gauche short sword with a twenty-two inch blade – and something called a Taza that looked as if it could decapitate a giant.

He was excited by his finds, and couldn't wait to use them, but moving his existing treasures had to be his first priority.

He made some decisions and walked briskly towards Cardiff

Central Station. On the approach to the station he kindly helped an elderly lady with her luggage, and they walked into the ticket hall together. He waited just twenty minutes before getting the train to Bristol Temple Meads.

DS Pryor and DCI Phelps returned to Incident Room Two to find the team buoyant. They had found the bag with the killer's clothes and shoes, and already the items were undergoing stringent forensic examination.

The small amount of blood would most certainly have come from the victim, but there would surely be something left behind from the killer that would give them a DNA result. Everyone had their fingers crossed.

Charlie commented. 'The tapes we have managed to retrieve have shown him apparently going towards the main station, but we haven't picked up anything from the station itself. There are some lone men with backpacks, but none of them are our man and the majority of travellers are couples or family groups and he sure as hell wouldn't fit into one of those images.'

'Well, keep looking,' said Martin. 'Ask at the station, especially the ticket office. We may not have a clear facial image, but we do have a good idea of height and build, and that backpack has been identified once so let's see if it lets him down again.'

Martin desperately needed some personal thinking time, and being satisfied that everyone in the team was pulling out all the stops to find this man he shut himself in his office. He pulled from his pocket the scribbling he had been doing in the car and took from the drawer an A4 sheet of paper and began trying to make sense of what he had written.

More than an hour later he had two sheets of paper on his desk. The one sheet held details of what was known about the Philips/Addula case and a list of what had to be done next. The second sheet was a similar layout for the Mark Wilson murder.

Armed with the two sheets of paper, Martin returned to Incident Room Two and ran through his analysis with the team.

'Hopefully, when we apprehend this man, we'll have enough

to arrest him for the murder of Ali Addula, and as I am certain this is a return visit we should be able to move on the Daniel Philips murder. We have him at the scene today, have followed his movements since, and have picked up the clothes he was wearing at the time of the murder. All we need to do is find him!

'Go over the tapes in slow motion, especially those around the station, and let me know of any results from the interviews of station staff. We don't want him getting on a train to some unknown destination and slipping away from us. Time is of the essence.

'Finally on this one, we are waiting for the results from the examination of the clothes, so Matt, please chase those up, every five minutes if necessary.'

Martin left everyone with their work cut out and took his second sheet of paper to Interview Room One.

'Our problem with this case is the lack of evidence, with an almost sterile crime scene and no sign of the murder weapons.' Martin paused. 'At best, we have the DNA evidence of Mark Wilson's sister, but we don't know if she was there at the time of the murder or had been a visitor at her brother's house before that. We are certain that she could not have committed the murder, but she could have been an accomplice.'

'The other sample of DNA that has been processed is not identifiable from the national database, and will only be helpful to us when we have a suspect to match it against.

'The person we now most want to interview is Jack Thompson, but only on the basis of known association. We have nothing to suggest he was ever in Cardiff with Amy Wilson, and his mother told us he was with her last Saturday afternoon and evening, although I suspect she would give her beloved son an alibi for anything.

'We are getting no real sense from Amy Wilson, but I am bothered by her mention of Mark's friends Paula and Suzanne, and she may have mentioned Anne as well. It's too much of a coincidence for those names to have been plucked out of the air, or for her and her brother each to have a set of friends with the same name.

'We need to pay one or all of them a visit ASAP, or get them to come here – I would like to tease out the possibility that they could have met Mark's sister somewhere along the line.'

DC Davies responded. 'Paula Williams will be our best bet. She lives the nearest, and she saw more of Mark than the others as they sometimes had a weekday lunch together.'

'OK, see if you can bring her here and tell her I believe her help could be invaluable.' Martin looked away as DC Davies left the room and then he walked towards the whiteboard that had been a blank canvas just a few days ago.

Now it was a jumble of names, times, dates, relationships, possible motives, and more ifs, whys, and buts than hard evidence. He rubbed out everything that was not an absolute fact and was left with the name of the victim, the date, place and time of the killing, and the evidence that four different tools had been used to dismember the body.

He wrote down the names of the four people present when the police arrived on the scene, and a list of all the people who Mark knew and who had been interviewed. DS Pryor could check through the statements of each of them and re-check their alibis to ensure nothing had been missed.

Under the heading of 'forensic/post-mortem' evidence there was little to add. The order in which the limbs had been severed was noted, and the two DNA results – one now definitely directing them to Amy Wilson and the other not identifiable through available sources.

Martin put a sub heading of 'Lounge' and underneath it a brief description of the sofa and the almost complete destruction of the documents that a) proved Mark had ever existed, and b) that he had ever been wanted by Norman and Sandy Harding.

Martin's original note that Mark knew his killer and that the crime had been motivated by jealousy or hatred was the only thing Martin had left on the board that remained constant. Looking at the words again, he wrote the name 'Amy Wilson' alongside them, and under 'known associates' wrote 'Jack Thompson'.

241

His deliberations had been occupying him for about twenty minutes when DC Davies came back to tell him that Paula Williams had been contacted and should be with them very soon.

'Good,' replied Martin. 'I don't want her to think she is in any sort of trouble so we won't use one of the interview rooms. Ask Matt to come to my office with three cups of coffee and we will see her there.'

As predicted, Paula showed up less than five minutes later, arriving at Martin's office at the same time as DS Pryor. Martin moved to the table in the corner of his office and indicated that the two of them should join him there and thanked Paula for coming in so promptly.

Paula said she had seen the images of Mark's sister in the press and had been wondering if she had been found and if she was in any way connected with Mark's murder. Martin explained that the details of the investigation were not something he could share with her at this stage but that there was something she might be able to help them understand.

'Anything – I will do anything I can,' replied Paula.

'Well, what I can tell you is that Mark's sister Amy was admitted to the Bristol Royal Infirmary in an unconscious state following a drugs overdose. It is not certain how much permanent damage has been done to either her body or her mind, but we have visited her and she is now conscious.

'The reason we have asked for your help is that since she recovered consciousness there have been periods of uncontrollable anger, during which she has used every known obscenity to condemn Mark to hell and also to inflict the same fate on some of his friends. She definitely used your name and that of Suzanne, and we were wondering if at any time you had met her?'

Paula stared at Martin and took her time to answer. 'I looked hard at the images of Mark's sister in the newspaper and I had a feeling that I had met her, but the more I looked at her the more I realised that it was just that she reminded me of Mark – not feature by feature but more of an overall impression. To answer your question, I don't believe I have ever met her, and to be honest if Mark had ever been in the position to introduce his sister to us it is likely to have been with a fanfare.'

Martin got to his feet. 'I hear what you're saying,' he told Paula. 'Believe me, I have no reason to think you are not being totally honest, but there is just something that makes me think we shouldn't just leave it there. Perhaps if you could see Amy Wilson face to face it may trigger something. Would you be prepared to visit her with us?'

Matt looked at his boss, having not expected this turn of events, and was about to suggest setting something up for the following day when Martin continued. 'I plan on making my second visit to Bristol for today and leaving almost immediately, if that would be convenient.'

Paula looked a bit shell-shocked, but nodded in agreement. 'I don't know what good it will do, but I guess you know what you're doing and I'll do anything I can to help bring Mark's killer to justice.'

'We'll take my car,' said Martin, as the three of them walked towards the back of the building.

Matt would catch up with what Martin was planning as they drove for the second time in one day from Cardiff to Bristol. It was not something he relished doing, as he had made plans for the evening, but he knew from past experience that once his boss got the bit between his teeth there was no stopping him.

Chapter Twenty

Having missed the rush-hour traffic they made good time, and arrived at the hospital just before half-past seven. They had to walk quickly from the car to the building as the heavens had suddenly opened. It was the first rain after several weeks of prolonged sunshine and temperatures hitting more than the usual summer levels, and the air smelt like someone had dampened warm dust.

Paula spoke. 'Bang goes our summer, but at least the prospect of months of dull rainy weather, with the occasional risk of some hazy sunshine, will boost our foreign holiday bookings.' She had barely said a word during the journey and although she had listened to some of the conversation between the two detectives she hadn't really heard much of it. Her mind had been on her friend Mark, and she couldn't believe that only a few days ago she had set out for his home with high expectations of a fun evening.

Before receiving the call from DC Davies, she had been to lunch with Norman and Sandy and had been appalled by the wretched sadness in the house. They had been told they could go ahead with making arrangements for Mark's funeral, and asked her for her ideas on what songs he would want at the service.

As they had crossed the Severn Bridge and Paula noticed the rainclouds gathering, she remembered that Mark had often said that whatever the weather and whatever was happening, the one thing that kept him going was his music. It wouldn't be a particularly cool choice, but Paula wondered if 'Thank You For The Music' would fit the bill. She knew that Sandy loved Abba, and her son had loved music so it could be a song that would unite them – she would suggest it to them when she rang them later.

Matt caught her arm as she slipped slightly on the edge of the wet pavement, and she walked between the two men who knew the way to the HDU and seemed in a hurry to get there. Paula remarked that hospitals didn't smell like hospitals any more and suggested that with the shops and cafes dotted around one could be at an airport or such-like.

She was chattering away because she felt very nervous and the thought of coming face to face with Mark's sister was now hitting home. After all, Mark had been her best friend and this woman was one of his family, a family that had caused him most of the misery in his life. More than that, if the snippets of conversation she had picked up on the journey were true, his sister could have had some part to play in his murder …

She asked the men to slow down a bit, and they took it easy walking up the second flight of stairs. 'I need a couple of minutes to get my head around this,' she said.

'What about having a coffee first?' Matt suggested.

'No, on second thoughts, let's get it over with,' Paula replied, as they all entered the doors of the High Dependency Unit.

All the beds were occupied, the nurses and doctors looked to be at full stretch, and there was more equipment than ever in use. Charge Nurse Paul Dobbs caught their eye and indicated they should wait while he checked on the status of Amy Wilson, who was behind one of the two bed screens.

When he had checked, he came over to them and Martin introduced him to Paula. 'Not much change in Amy's mental condition,' he told them. 'She's still away with the fairies most of the time, although I hope the fairies have ear plugs as her language has not improved. We are getting more concerned about her physical health, as there appears to be more damage to her major organs than first thought. She could come out of this but we are getting more and more worried by this somewhat unexpected deterioration.'

'Is she fit to see us?' Martin asked, almost dreading a negative response.

'As fit as she is going to be,' Paul said, and they all walked towards Amy's bed.

Paul pulled back the curtains to reveal Amy lashing out at one of the nurses, who was attempting to adjust a line that was coming adrift from a vent going into the patient's arm. Amy looked up as the curtains opened and raised one eyebrow in the unusual way Martin had seen her do before. The effect was that the raised eyebrow sort of twitched involuntarily like a nervous tic – nothing of any significance just something she did.

The effect for Paula was anything but insignificant, and as she clutched Martin's arm he watched the colour drain from her face and her knees buckle as she headed towards a faint but somehow managed to stave it off.

'You all right?' He asked the usual senseless question of Paula but was also aware that the same question could be directed at Amy, who also looked shocked.

It was Amy who recovered first from their mutual shock and spoke. 'Bloody fucking Paula!' The words were spat out as Martin and Matt looked at one another in total confusion.

Paula whispered something that Martin didn't quite catch, but she repeated it louder as her legs steadied and she became a bit more certain of herself.

'Anne! It is Anne, isn't it? So why did they say you were Mark's sister, and what in the name of hell have you done to yourself?'

Barely giving her time to finish the question Amy shouted back. 'I'm not Anne, I'm not fucking Anne and I never was fucking Anne, but she was how I got close to Mark.

'I always knew how to find him and when he went to art college, well, that made it easy. I was good at art – much better than my freak of a brother – but I hated it almost as much as I hated you and soppy bloody Suzanne fawning over Mark's work and saying how good it was.

247

'When he was adopted by Mr and Mrs Too-much-fucking-money I hated all of you for making him out to be something special – he never was, he was always a fucking freak, from the minute he was born.

'He always thought me – his big sister – would come running to him at some time and that's why he fixed up his spare room – it was a glorified shrine for a pretty, pretty person who never existed – I hated it – I hated him. My father is all I have left thanks to your precious Mark and since my father was put away it's been my mission in life to get rid of Mark – I just didn't know how to do it.

'I needed money and the fucking idiot even provided me with that! It beggars belief. When "Anne" cried to him over the phone because she had got herself into debt, the moron offered to give her a thousand pounds a month until she got back on her feet. I made sure that money was used to finish him off.' She screamed and the whole ward froze at her last words. 'Imagine paying for your own murder!'

After this rapidly delivered outburst, liberally punctuated with obscenities, Amy suddenly and without any warning flung herself off the bed in Paula's direction, bringing medical equipment crashing down. Paula, transfixed with the shock of what she had just heard, was unable to move and would have been an easy target.

Fortunately, Amy didn't get very far, as demonstrating just why the hospital staff had cause to be so concerned about her physical condition, she collapsed in a heap on the floor.

But for Matt Pryor's intervention, Paula would have landed on top of her, as this time she did faint, albeit as a transient episode. Matt managed to get his arms under her shoulders and gently pulled her outside the curtained area. Her eyes had already reopened but she was obviously in a state of shock.

Charge Nurse Williams didn't have a clue what was going on, but understood well the effects of psychological trauma and helped Matt take Paula to the relatives' room.

Martin stayed behind the curtains and waited on one side while the HDU staff got Amy back to a place of physical safety.

All the time she continued pouring out the story of her sad life, that to Martin was very illuminating, but the hospital staff were more surprised this time by the lack of expletives than by anything else.

After a few minutes, much of what Amy was saying made little sense, and it became obvious that she was either drifting off to sleep or perhaps losing consciousness. He asked one of the nurses, who confirmed that Amy had been sedated but also that her underlying condition was deteriorating.

Martin left her bedside and joined Matt and Paula in the relatives' room, where they were both drinking the coffee that had been provided. Paula looked shell-shocked, but by now she had put together the pieces of the jigsaw and understood at least some of the saga that had unfolded.

'I just can't believe it, I really can't,' she told Martin, as he too accepted the coffee that was on offer. 'I mean, I've known Anne for years, twenty-odd years! And it was Mark who first introduced her to me and to Suzanne. She hadn't come from Whitchurch High School like the three of us, she met Mark at art college and then worked for the same graphic company as him – but she only lasted there a few months.'

'And you don't think Mark ever recognised her as his sister?' asked Matt, who had already heard Paula go over some of this.

'Absolutely not,' replied Paula quickly. 'He told me on many occasions that he would give the world to be reunited with his sister, so I'm certain he had no idea of Anne's real identity.' She turned her face towards Martin. 'Anyway, you met and interviewed Anne, and then you had the photographs of Amy – did you think they were one and the same person?'

'Not for one minute,' acknowledged Martin. 'Apart from their strikingly different appearances, there was nothing to take us down that road – I have to confess it never entered my head.'

'You hear about it, don't you? People leading double lives, and even having totally separate families with both being totally unaware of the existence of the other. If that is possible, then what Anne did was not that difficult. I'm sorry, but I can't get my head around having to think of her as Amy. Although I thought the four of us were close friends, if I think back now we weren't actually that close to Anne at all – well, me and Suzanne weren't, anyway. It's not as if we ever lived together, and we met up on a prearranged basis so she always had plenty of notice to change her appearance – and with work and everything even those catch-ups weren't that often these days. Do you think Mark found out the truth before he died?'

'I've been thinking about that,' Martin replied. 'I think it's likely that Amy turned up on his doorstep last Saturday night and he welcomed her as Anne into his home. We don't believe her to be responsible for the actual murder of her brother, but we know she had been in the lounge just before it and may well have destroyed his sofa and attempted to burn his documents. But she wouldn't have been alone.'

Paula shivered. 'It seems impossible that she would have known – caused – what had happened, and then just turned up on his doorstep with us a short time later and act all concerned. She must have really, really hated Mark, but she never showed any signs of it. How could she have just waited all these years … and who do you think actually did kill Mark?'

'We think we know,' said Martin. 'However, we need evidence to back up our theories – it would have been good if we could have formally interviewed Amy following your identification but that isn't going to be possible for the time being. We have to visit a house in Bristol but we also need to get you back to Cardiff.'

Paula came up with an unexpected solution to that problem. 'I have a cousin living about fifteen minutes away from here,' she said. 'I know I'd be welcome there, and to be honest I can't bear the thought of going back to my flat with all this going round in my head. Carole will come and pick me up if I ring her, and if you don't mind that's really what I'd like to do.'

Martin readily agreed, and told Paula that although she could offload her experience and tell her cousin what had happened she should not for the present say anything to either Suzanne or Mark's parents. 'We'll let you know the outcome of our planned investigations as soon as possible – then when everything is in the public domain you'll probably all have a lot of talking to do.'

Paula nodded, and made the phone call to her cousin who, as expected, said she was on her way. The nursing assistant who had provided the coffee agreed to stay with Paula until her cousin arrived and so the detectives made their way to the car, moving quickly as the rain was now coming down in sheets.

This time Martin did not park away from the house. He drove right up to it and parked behind the dark blue Vauxhall that he recognised as one of the Bristol police surveillance vehicles. The checks that had been done on Jack Thompson showed him to be the owner of a black BMW, but there was no such car in evidence.

Matt made their presence known to the driver of the blue car, who informed them that there had been no activity at the house since his arrival and that the best he had got from the lady of the house was her face at the window telling him to go away.

He added that as his brief had been limited to looking out for Jack Thompson he had decided to sit tight until receiving more information or new orders. He had one of the pictures distributed by Bristol Prison, but said that he had been involved when Jack's father Leo had been arrested, so he knew what his boy looked like.

All three men were aware that their conversation was being witnessed, by Jack's mother as her face was just visible in the downstairs window. At least two other faces could be counted in the windows of the adjoining houses – police activity at the Thompson household had been routine in the past, so maybe they had reason to expect some kind of show now.

Martin walked the short path in a couple of strides and rang the doorbell twice, not really expecting or getting any response. 'Mrs Thompson,' he shouted through the still-gleaming letterbox. 'You may remember me. I am Detective Inspector Phelps from the Cardiff CID and I need to talk to you some more about your son Jack.'

There was still no movement from inside the house and

Martin's patience was wearing thin. He continued. 'Look, we can do this the easy way with you opening the door, or we can break the door down – either way we will be coming in, so you have two minutes to decide which type of entrance we choose.'

It took less than a minute for Eileen Thompson to decide she wanted to preserve the appearance of her front door, and reluctantly she undid two bolts and released the lock to let them in. If she had looked old beyond her years before, she now looked older than even her mother would have ... if her mother had not been murdered by her husband.

Despite himself and the current situation, Martin felt a surge of sympathy towards the woman, but it quickly faded as she spoke. 'Don't know what you lot want back here – I told you, Jack's not here, and I don't know where he is, and that's all I have to say and you can't make me say any more, so there.'

'OK,' replied Martin. 'If you don't know where your son is, then you don't know where he is, and we understand that. But you in turn need to understand that it is of the utmost importance that we find him as soon as possible.'

'You lot never leave us alone,' she complained. 'Just because Jack's father is no bloody good it doesn't mean that my Jack is the same – he's a good boy, not the same as his father at all.'

'That may well be the case,' said Martin. 'We still need to speak to him, though, so if you know of anywhere he hangs out, or if there are any friends who may know where he is, then I urge you to tell us.'

The tone of Martin's voice left no doubt as to the seriousness of her son's position, but Eileen Thompson didn't respond to the question, instead asking a question of her own. 'What's he supposed to have done – robbed a bank or somethin'?'

'"Or something" would be more accurate,' said Martin. 'At this moment in time we can't prove that your son has done anything, but our investigations are regarding the brutal murder of a man in Cardiff last Saturday.'

At the mention of 'brutal murder', Eileen seemed to lose the full use of her legs, and just managed to get to a chair before collapsing. But then she seemed to go on automatic pilot as she spoke. 'Well that rules my Jack out, don't it – he was here all day last Saturday – with me – here with me, his mother.'

'Are you sure about that?' Matt questioned. 'He didn't go out all day or during the evening – not even for a couple of hours?'

'Don't you lot listen? I just told you he was here all the time so you'd better go and find someone else to stitch up for this – you're not getting my Jack.' Mrs Thompson's voice, that had been quivering, now held firm as she fervently defended her son and gave him the alibi neither officer wanted to hear.

'If you're sure there is nothing more you can tell us, then all we can do is to wait until your son turns up, and until that time I'm afraid our friend in the blue car out there is going to remain on your doorstop.' Walking towards the front door, Martin could not be sure if he really heard something or if it was just a gut feeling that made him whisper to Matt. 'Ask our friend in the blue Vauxhall to send for backup and then get back here pronto.'

Matt hurried to do as requested while Martin went through the routine of thanking Mrs Thompson for her help and encouraging her further co-operation. As soon as Martin saw his DS coming back up the path, he stepped behind Mrs Thompson and made his way up the stairs.

The reaction from Jack's mother was spontaneous, leaving Martin in no doubt that his suspicions were correct as she shouted in a voice triple its normal strength, 'Look out, Jack, they know you're up there!'

Three doors faced Martin at the top of the stairs, but only one had a lock as part of the furnishing and Martin stood outside that one waiting while Matt checked the other rooms.

'Nothing here, guv,' he confirmed. 'Just the same amazing level of tidiness and cleanliness we have seen everywhere else, the woman is a bloody fanatic.'

'This house is probably all she has in life,' said Martin. 'Except the son who is behind this door, and we're about to take that from her.'

Both men stared at the door. All their instincts told them to wait for the backup they had requested, but another thought had occurred to both of them and Matt expressed it. 'We will look a bit bloody stupid if he decides to top himself in there with us standing outside, guv, what do you think?'

'Well, the door is just your average internal door, but that lock will take some busting – how strong are you feeling?'

Needing no second bidding Matt thanked the gods for his rugby training and raised his leg so that his foot hit the lock full-on, followed by the not inconsiderable force of his body weight. In films and on the television, detectives always seem to use their shoulders to break down doors, but Matt's method was definitely more effective. Most of the lock gave way immediately, and with just another couple of strategically placed kicks they had gained entry to Jack's room.

If they had expected to encounter a murderer in self-destruct mode they could not have been more wrong, as they were met by a man more bent on killing someone else than himself.

Normally the man they were facing would have been just about a match for Martin alone, and under different circumstances Martin and Matt together would have taken him on easily. These were not normal circumstances and there were very good reasons why a two-detective tackle was not the chosen option.

Over the years, Martin had dealt with every class of criminal, ranging from rapists and arsonists to murderers and child molesters, and every other type between. However, he could never remember having been in such a vulnerable position as he was now, looking at a murderer with such a mixture of emotions in his eyes.

There was the hate and anger Martin had come to expect, but there was also something else that at first he didn't recognise. Then he realised it was uncertainty, and that was what scared him the most. Here was a man who could only function in line with a carefully prepared plan, one most likely thought out for him. This was not a situation he would have planned for and his uncertainty would make him unpredictable. And no one with a blade in each hand should be put in that position …

Surprised that his voice sounded so normal, Martin suggested that Jack put the knives down and not make things any worse for himself. That caused Jack some amusement, and he moved around with his back against the wall of the room, indicating that the two detectives should change places with him.

As he passed his beloved wardrobe, he could not resist one last look at the trophies hanging there in all their macabre glory. It was his fatal mistake, and in a flash Matt had moved forward and kicked the knife out of Jack's right hand, leaving Martin with the opportunity of tackling from the left. The move was a classic and would have been successful if Jack's mother hadn't followed them into the room. She was now close enough to Jack for him to grab her and press the knife he had managed to retain in his left hand to her throat.

Martin moved a step back and as he encouraged Matt to do the same he became aware that his DS was bleeding profusely. Jack must have managed to target something vital just before Matt's kick had disarmed him of the one knife. DCI Phelps went to take a step towards his colleague but Jack shouted. 'Stay where you are or I kill her. And don't for one moment think I won't just because she's my mother.'

Martin hadn't thought that for one moment – in fact he was sure that in order to get away Jack would have been prepared to kill all of them, and anyone else who stood in his way. He was seriously worried about Matt, who was now looking pale and standing in a pool of blood mainly surrounding his left leg. Where was their backup?

Even as he thought the question Martin heard the sirens as squad cars with the usual array of flashing lights screeched to a halt outside the house. Although the sound was music to Martin's ears, he saw that it brought more uncertainty that could result in more unpredictability from Jack.

Martin risked it. 'You have no chance of getting away, so why not let your mother go – she doesn't deserve this.'

'Judge now, are you?' shouted Jack. 'How do you know

what she deserves – me and my dad have had to put up with her moaning for years and years – would be good to shut her up and don't think I won't do it. Tell that lot not to think of climbing those stairs.'

Jack was referring to the uniformed officers who had entered the house and were opening doors downstairs.

Martin called out as he had been instructed to do. 'This is DCI Phelps speaking. We have a hostage situation up here so please stay where you are until I tell you something different. We also need a paramedic and an ambulance as my sergeant has been injured.'

'I said, tell them not to come up here,' bellowed Jack. 'Not to give them a list of what you want – it's what I want that's important.'

'And what do you want?' asked Martin with his eyes partly on Jack and partly on Jack's mother, who looked completely helpless as her son pulled her arms behind her back and kept his knife firmly at her throat.

But Eileen wasn't as helpless as she looked, for suddenly, and with no concern about her own safety, she lifted her knee and drove her foot into her son's leg. She was not strong and the movement would have done him no damage, but it had been totally unexpected and so caused him to slightly lose balance. Slightly was enough for Martin and he shouted. 'Get up here now!' as he launched a fully clenched fist into Jack's chest.

In the bedlam that ensued, Jack was disarmed and handcuffed by the backup team and Martin turned his attention to Matt. He was now half-sitting, half-lying on the floor and still losing far too much blood as he fought off falling into unconsciousness. Martin knelt down to see if he could find the source of the bleeding but before he could do anything two paramedics appeared and within minutes Matt had a pressure bandage in place with IV fluids being infused, and was being transported to the ambulance.

Martin looked around the room and saw with fascinated horror the extent to which the wardrobe had been purpose built to house an extensive weaponry. There were groups of gleaming blades in the main, but there was also a back section of assorted duller-looking weapons and he wondered what all that was about.

He didn't hesitate for more than a split second because he knew exactly where his priorities lay and he made his way quickly downstairs and into the ambulance with Matt. Jack was being taken into custody, still cursing his mother with every breath, and there was a kindly PC taking care of Mrs Thompson. The local SOC team would soon be there, and in the fullness of time Martin would get them to liaise with Alex but for now it was Matt who was his biggest concern. As they were driven back to the Bristol Royal Infirmary, Martin prayed as he had not done for a very long time. Matt had to pull through – those four sisters and twelve nieces would be lost without him – and so would Martin.

Chapter Twenty-one

'You're a fraud, a total fraud!' Martin confronted Matt who was relaxing on pillows just plumped up by one of the two nurses who had been helping him recover from the anaesthetic. 'I've been sitting out there for hours worried sick while you've been fraternising with the nursing staff.'

'Sorry, guv,' Matt grinned. 'I don't get many opportunities like this, so I'm making the most of it. But seriously, I have to admit I thought I was for the wooden overcoat back there, and I was worried I'd let you down big time.'

'Nothing could be further from the truth,' interrupted Martin, and he went on to explain what had happened at the house as Matt had limited memory of the events. 'Now, what did they say about your injury? I got some information but not the whole picture.'

'Well, when I kicked the knife out of Thompson's right hand it flew into the air and as my leg was moving back down the tip of the blade must have caught a big bleeder in my groin area.' Matt grinned again. 'Considering the area the knife was moving towards it could have been worse, in which case there would have been no point in me chatting up the nurses!

'Anyway, there's no permanent damage, and the blood vessel has been stitched and patched or whatever they do, and I have had six or seven pints of the red stuff so it's just a few days off and then back to work for me.'

Not for the first time in his life, Martin wished he was a woman, for one reason only. They were able to hug friends and family and even complete strangers with no one batting an eyelid. Martin wanted to hug Matt and embrace his sense of humour and optimism but grinned to himself as he imagined the look on his sergeant's face if he took that step.

Instead he just said. 'You gave me one hell of a fright back there, and I'm so glad you pulled through, but any more talk of getting back to work in a couple of days and you'll wish you hadn't. I understand we've arranged ambulance transport to get you back to Cardiff, but that's not until tomorrow, so I'm going to leave you with the knowledge that two of your sisters have just arrived with arms full of food and drink – I hope you're not nil by mouth!'

'No chance, I've been told that there are no gastro-intestinal complications and the anaesthetic hasn't made me sick so whatever goodies they have will be well taken care of as I feel like I haven't eaten for a week.'

'They're waiting impatiently for me to finish talking to you and before you ask – yes I will keep you up to speed on what's happening with the murder in Cardiff. From the information that's been fed to me it appears that things have got no further than when we left and there's nothing I can contribute to at the moment so I'm off home to get some sleep.'

Martin turned to leave and Matt made one last comment. 'Thanks Martin, I think I knew you were with me all the time. It was a good feeling and I really did appreciate it, so just wanted to tell you that.'

Again that 'I wish I was a woman' feeling came over Martin, but he just smiled and walked out, passing two anxious-looking women who would soon be giving Matt a generous helping of hugs.

Martin drove down the M4 and tried to orientate himself with time and space. Was it really 5 a.m. on a Thursday, and was it only four clear days since Mark Wilson had been murdered? He doubted if the news of Jack Thompson's arrest would have been in time for the early morning papers, but the radio and television news programmes would surely be running with it.

He refrained from putting on the car radio and instead concentrated on getting himself home and into bed before the day really woke up and shattered any chance of him getting some sleep.

Fighting an overwhelming urge to call earlier, Alex left it until almost half-past nine before ringing Martin. He almost regretted ringing then, as it was obvious from the time it took Martin to answer that he was still asleep.

'Sorry to wake you, mate,' said a far too-wide awake and enthusiastic Alex. 'I left it as long as I could, but there have been some amazing developments and I can't wait to share them with you.'

'Steady on.' Martin spoke in a voice that was deep and still heavy with sleep. 'Give me a minute to wake up, and then you can share all you like.'

'It's all a bit complicated,' replied Alex. 'It would be better if you were here to see some of the stuff we've put together. Oh, and the most important thing of all is that we've been in contact with Bristol Royal Infirmary and Matt is making a seemingly record-breaking recovery.'

'Yes, he was already doing well when I left him,' said Martin, now in a recognisable voice and well and truly awake. 'Look, Alex, I hadn't really intended sleeping this long, but nature kicked in and if you hadn't called I might have slept until tomorrow. Give me ten minutes to shower and grab a piece of toast and I'll be on my way, so see you about ten or just after.'

In less than ten minutes, Martin had showered, shaved, and dressed, and made himself sit down to eat some toast and honey and drink his coffee. Alex had sounded excited, and 'Brains' was not one to show that level of feeling without good reason. What could it be? Well, there was only one way to find out.

At a quarter past ten, as many of the team that were available were gathered in Interview Room One waiting for Martin's arrival. He got a round of applause as he walked in and then readily responded to all the questions of concern regarding DS Pryor. The local Bristol force had been in touch throughout the night and morning and apparently had described the actions of DCI Phelps and DS Pryor as nothing short of heroic.

Waving all that aside, Martin quickly briefed the gathering on what had happened when Paula Williams had seen Amy Wilson at the hospital, and outlined the events at the Thompsons' house. He then asked Alex to take centre stage and tell everyone the results of his communication with the SOC team in Bristol. Charlie got into position in front of the main computer and clicked through a number of programmes before indicating to Alex that she was ready whenever he was.

'Some of you have not been involved with the Mark Wilson murder, and will be wondering why I have asked you to join this briefing, but you will understand by the end.' Alex signalled to Charlie who projected the first of a set of images from the computer to the front screen.

'DCI Phelps will recognise this place,' he informed the meeting. 'It's a house in Bristol. More specifically, it's the bedroom of Jack Thompson. For the most part, it's like any other bedroom, but it had an extra-strong lock on the door and a wardrobe that would make the Chronicles of Narnia weep.

'According to Thompson's mother it was built by his father as a birthday present and kitted out to store his son's collection of blades from all over the world.' Images of the exterior and the interior of the wardrobe were then shown, and Martin was now able to have a good look at what he had briefly seen last night.

Alex continued. 'As you can see, the interior is divided into sections, mainly to separate the different types of blades. So, for example, he has stored all the dagger-type blades together, all the sword-type blades together, and so on. All of the blades hanging in these categories are spotless and shining, as if hours have been spent cleaning and polishing them.'

The screen showed image after image, all proving what Alex was saying, until the camera shots carefully rested on the back wall of the wardrobe. A close-up showed hinges on the back wall and the next shot demonstrated the back wall to be a false wall, usually hiding a very different selection of blades.

Martin went nearer the screen as the images of the newly exposed false interior showed a set of seven blades. These were not highly polished. All showed signs of being used in the most deadly way. Old bloodstains were present on all of them and even what looked like pieces of tissue and some strands of material.

Alex took them through each weapon, explaining how four of them at least, had been used. 'You will remember we were looking for four different weapons in connection with the murder of Mark Wilson, and I believe that the four you now see on the screen are those weapons. Prof. Moore told us that Mark's right arm had been hacked off with some kind of chopper and the top-right picture shows a hatchet with a longish cutting edge. The top left picture is of a small machete – exactly what we were looking for in connection with the amputation of Mark's left arm.'

The room was spellbound as Alex continued. 'Likewise we were looking for some sort of scythe for the removal of the left leg, and there on the bottom right of the screen we have a Japanese-style double-edged curved blade. Again, it fits the bill. And, finally, we knew that some type of saw was used on the right leg, and there it is – a fine-toothed, extremely sharp saw – more like a serrated knife, really.

'As well as matching the weapons, we are able to match the material from Mark's trousers to some pieces on the saw, and there is a lot of other blood and tissue that is currently being processed.

'We also believe that a knife hanging in this section of the wardrobe, but somewhat distant from the murder weapons, is the one used to destroy the sofa, and we are checking that out too.'

'Fantastic! Absolutely bloody fantastic!' Martin shouted. 'So we have all the evidence we need to secure the conviction of Jack Thompson for the murder of Mark Wilson, and to prove Amy Wilson conspired in her brother's murder.'

'Indisputable evidence,' replied Alex with a smile.

A second round of applause accompanied by a few

spontaneous cheers circled the room, and general conversation erupted. Martin let this continue for a few minutes before banging on the table and looking at Alex said 'Judging from the smug expression still on your face, I guess you haven't told us everything, Mr Griffiths.'

'No,' Alex teased. 'To paraphrase the song, I've saved the best till last.'

'What could be better than solving a murder?' asked PC Mullen.

'Solving two murders – or possibly three murders – or maybe even five or six murders.' Alex responded quickly and with obvious excitement.

Knowing beyond doubt that he was holding the whole room in the palm of his hand, he enjoyed every minute. He nodded to Charlie, who was obviously in the know too, and she projected some more images onto the screen.

'We have worked all night with our counterparts from Bristol and they have been brilliant. Look at the gallery of knives on the inside wall of the wardrobe,' he instructed the room. 'There are seven of them, and we believe that each one has been used to commit a murder. We can account for four of them in relation to the murder of Mark Wilson, but that still leaves us with three more.

'CID in Bristol has, over the past few months, been struggling with two unsolved murders and in both cases they have not discovered the murder weapon. Two of the remaining knives fit the pattern of execution in these cases, and overnight they have examined the knives and got additional forensic evidence that definitely matches two of the remaining knives to those crimes.

'They are also investigating the very recent murder of a woman who was the wife of a prisoner at Bristol Prison. In the case of her murder, the killer used a long, thin steel blade, and probably wouldn't have left it behind normally, but they think it is likely that the woman's dog attempted to defend its mistress.

'There is a gap on the new weapons side of Jack's wardrobe, and if that weapon had previously been hanging there it will be easy to prove. Apparently, some of the other prisoners are talking, and they are saying that Jack was available to his father Leo's inmates as the ultimate disposal machine – for a price!'

Without waiting for any reaction from his gripped audience, Alex went on to produce another rabbit from his hat.

'Finally, we have the seventh knife, and without any further theatricals I will just tell you that it positively matches the one we have been looking for since the killing of Daniel Philips.'

Martin stopped him there. 'That's incredible, and if it's true, then the man we have been tracking in Cardiff for the Ely murders is Jack Thompson!'

'Before you and DS Pryor went to Bristol yesterday, you set in motion the tracking of Jack Thompson from the time he left Bristol Prison. The team traced him to Bristol Airport, where he got a plane to Malaga. His return flight wasn't back to Bristol, though; in fact he landed at Cardiff airport yesterday.'

'From there we have CCTV evidence of him getting into a taxi, and interviews with the taxi company have led to the same garden centre from which we tracked the killer of Ali Addula – result or what?'

Martin slapped Alex on the back. 'What a team!' he shouted. 'What a team. Everyone here deserves a medal but the best I can do for the moment is to suggest that if anyone wants a coffee then the drinks are on me.'

The room cleared quickly, but very noisily, as everyone expressed their own opinions and commented on the evils of human nature. Charlie, Alex, and Martin remained, along with DC Davies who was standing in for Matt and who told the others the latest news about his DS.

'About half an hour ago DS Pryor was transferred safely to the University Hospital of Wales and is making an excellent recovery. Since he arrived there, he's phoned six times and my guess is that we will continue to get a call every five minutes or so until someone tells him what's going on.'

'That's a pretty fair guess,' laughed Martin. 'I promised to keep him informed of progress so that will be down to me – thank heavens he's been transferred and a visit won't mean another trip to Bristol. No offence, but I've seen enough of that city for a while.'

Martin turned to DC Davies. 'I'm just tidying things up in my mind, and no doubt the clothes Jack Thompson had on at his house can be traced to his purchases in Cardiff so can you make sure that we have that sorted. I'll spend all day tomorrow putting everything together and then be very pleased to hand the whole thing over to the Crown Prosecution Services. But for now I have three house calls to make, and then I'll be taking myself home.'

Martin chose to make his three calls alone, although he asked DC Davies to let the relevant people know he was coming. His first call was on Elaine Philips and it was the one he was most concerned about.

She invited him into her home and he was pleased to see her daughter there. Over a cup of tea, he told her that they had arrested a man for killing her husband. He went on to tell her that her husband's killer had been charged with the second murder at the shop, and with the murder last Saturday of Mark Wilson. Martin told her a bit more. 'In addition to that, the police in Bristol now have proof that the same man killed two other people in their area.'

'Why? But why? Is he crazy?' Mrs Philips had every reason to be shocked, and Martin felt he had to answer her questions as honestly as he could.

'To answer the second part of your question first – no, I don't believe he is crazy, in that I believe that he is totally aware of everything he has done, but there are those that will always put forward the mental health argument. As to why, we believe that most of his murders were pre-arranged, and may be revenge or punishment killings linked to his father and his father's associates. His father is serving life for murder in Bristol Prison, and the only murder that wasn't pre-arranged was that of your husband. We believe on that occasion it was Mr Addula who should have been killed – he was the original target – but your husband intervened.'

'From what you're saying, the people that this man killed,

with the exception of my Daniel and Mark Wilson, were all involved in some sort of criminal activity.' Martin nodded and Elaine Philips continued. 'So my kind and gentle husband, who was a wonderful father and a truly special man, was killed by what amounts to a paid assassin who was out to teach some villains a lesson?'

This was exactly why Martin had dreaded this meeting, as he knew from their past sessions that Mrs Philips had the knack of hitting the nail right on the head. He said nothing but took her hands and she allowed him to sit with her for a few minutes while the awful truth sank in.

It was her daughter Lucy who broke the silence. 'Look, Chief Inspector Phelps, I know I've have given you a hard time over the lack of progress about my father's murder, but my mother has found your support to be of enormous benefit. We thank you for coming here today. We had to find out the truth and it was best coming from you, so again thank you for that.

'My father taught us a lot, and even if he had realised that Ali Addula was not all he appeared to be he would still have intervened. We all know that – it was his selfless nature that made us all love him so much. Now that we know the truth, we can work it through as a family.'

She sat down next to her mother and took her hands from Martin's, allowing him to stand up and take his leave.

The image of the two women sobbing together would not go away as he drove towards his second visit and shortly afterwards pulled into the drive of the Hardings' home.

As arranged, Paula and Suzanne were there, as was Helen Cook-Watts, and it was she who opened the door. She had been fully briefed and told to answer as many questions as she could, and to allow Paula to tell Norman, Sandy, and Suzanne about her meeting with Amy Wilson.

'They can't take it in,' Helen said as she greeted DCI Phelps. 'It's hardly surprising, when the woman they knew as Anne, and had been friends with for years, turns out to be Mark's sister Amy. And although we know that she didn't actually murder her brother herself, they've all come to the conclusion that she set it up.'

'Given what Amy Wilson has said so far, they're almost certainly right,' said Martin as he followed her into the lounge. The first person he saw was Paula, and he asked her if she had recovered from her shock of recognising Amy as being Anne.

'It's not something I'll ever forget,' she told him. 'It was that twitch she did with her eyebrow that did it – we've all seen her do it a thousand times. I think I would have recognised her anyway but that was certainly the trigger.'

Sandy invited Martin to sit down and he did, remaining there for the next hour and a half while the four people who had been closest to Mark talked and talked and talked.

Hindsight is a wonderful thing, and between them they came up with lots of clues that Amy had given them over the years, and wondered that if they had been more observant they could have realised who she was. They were all aware that she was still a patient at the BRI and Sandy asked what would become of her.

'At present there's nothing for us to do, as she has been transferred back to the ICU and they are very concerned about her condition. If she recovers, she may be arrested for conspiracy to murder, but even that will depend on her mental health and that's a very big question.'

'The poor girl,' said Sandy, much to everyone's surprise, and an indignant Paula responded heatedly.

'You can't mean that, Sandy – she duped us for years, all the time hating us and wanting Mark dead. And you were always so good to her.'

'Yes, but to live your life like that! She must have been filled to the brim with jealousy and hatred. If only she could have let us know who she was from the beginning, perhaps we could have turned all that around and helped her build a more meaningful life.'

There it was again: that willingness to help others, and for a moment Martin returned to an image of Elaine Philips.

He took his leave of Mark's family and friends and suggested to Helen Cook-Watts that she stay for just a while longer and then head for home herself. 'You've done a great job with this family,' he told her, and was rewarded by a beaming smile as she closed the door behind him.

Grateful that the first two of his meetings were behind him, Martin headed for the hospital. He was pleased to be going to visit Matt Pryor – it could have been so different.

'At last, guv!' Matt complained. 'I thought I'd been forgotten, what's going on so that it's taken you all day to get here?'

'Shut up and just listen for once,' said Martin, as he pulled up a chair and went systematically through the investigation as it had unravelled that day. For once, Matt actually did just listen, and he didn't even ask any questions until Martin had finished.

'What a result,' he said finally. 'What a boost for the crime figures! Could be a gong in there somewhere for you, guv!' He grinned at Martin.

'Not for me,' replied his boss. 'But if they are giving them away for team efforts, then we should be in with a shout.'

Both men laughed, and then the conversation turned to Matt's injury, and then to rugby – and then to women. It seemed to normalise the world, and that's what the people who investigate such horrors need in order to keep themselves sane. Martin laughed as he heard how many female visitors had already been through the doors of Matt's side room. There was only one female visitor that Martin wanted to welcome – and he found himself hoping that her second visit to the cottage would be pretty soon …

Author Inspiration

I made Cardiff Bay the site of Goleudy, the base for DCI Phelps and his team. Cardiff Bay, pictured on the back cover, has many iconic buildings such as the Coal Exchange (the inspiration for Goleudy), the Pierhead Building, the Millennium Centre, and the world-famous Norwegian Church.

The building of Cardiff Docks in the 1830s, by the second Marquis of Bute, changed Cardiff for ever. In 1868 the Norwegian Church, founded by Herman Lunde of Oslo, was built on land donated by the marquis. The church provided the thousands of Norwegian sailors who visited the docks with a place where they could get spiritual and social care. It was funded by the Norwegian Seaman's Mission and soon became famous as a place where the seamen could relax in an atmosphere that reminded them of their own country.

As coal exports declined, so did the need for the church, and despite attempts by local worshippers to retain it, the costs were deemed too high and it was deconsecrated in 1974. It was a time when the whole of the docklands area had become a shadow of its former self, a time which lasted until plans for the redevelopment of Atlantic Wharf were finally agreed on. To avoid the destruction of the church during the regeneration of the area, the whole building was dismantled with care and a great deal of it put into storage.

The author Roald Dahl was born in Cardiff to Norwegian parents and was christened at the Norwegian Church. He became the first president of the Norwegian Church Preservation Trust and actively campaigned for the cause. By 1992 the church had been rebuilt, and was re-opened by Princess Martha Louise of Norway. The church recently underwent major refurbishment, and was established in 2011 as the Norwegian Church Arts Centre. Today, the striking white building stands proudly on Cardiff Bay's waterfront and once again attracts visitors from all over the world.

Wonny Lea

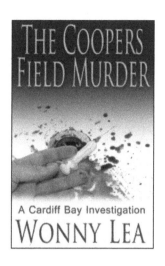

The first novel in this series, *Jack-Knifed*, saw the introduction of Detective Chief Inspector Martin Phelps, together with his sidekick, Detective Sergeant Matt Pryor, and their team, investigating a horrendous murder in Cardiff.

Now they are faced with a body found in Coopers Field, a Cardiff beauty spot – a naked body that has lain there so long it is almost unidentifiable. Pathology reports establish that the body is that of a woman – but who is she, and how did she die? Local nurse Sarah Thomas, a helpful passer-by when the body is found, soon finds that she has another unexpected death to deal with – at Parkland Nursing Home where she works. Colin James, one of her favourite residents at the home, dies suddenly – but the reactions of those closest to him are surprising. Was Colin's death due to natural causes – or is there something more sinister afoot at Parkland?

The Coopers Field Murder is the second in Wonny Lea's DCI Martin Phelps series, set in the thriving Welsh capital city of Cardiff.

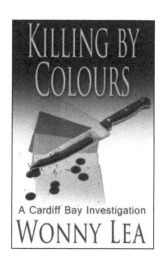

Killing by Colours, the third in the DCI Martin Phelps series, takes Martin in search of a serial killer who appears to have somewhat of a personal interest in the DCI himself.

When the body of the killer's first victim is discovered at a popular Cardiff leisure attraction, key elements of the murder link her death to a macabre colour-themed poem recently sent to DCI Phelps. As the body count rises, the killer teases the team by giving possible clues to the whereabouts of victims and the venues of potential murders, in the form of more poems. Are the killings random acts by a deranged individual, or is there something that links the victims to one another – and even to the DCI himself?

Meanwhile, Martin's sidekick, DS Matt Pryor, is worried about the safety of his boss. Are his fears warranted? Is Martin Phelps on the colour-coded list of potential victims – or is he just the sounding board for the killer's bizarre poetry?

MONEY CAN KILL

A Cardiff Bay Investigation

WONNY LEA

In *Money can Kill,* a school trip to the National History Museum of Wales at St Fagans ends early with the disappearance of a child. Is he just playing hide and seek – or is it the work of a criminal? Perhaps a kidnapper with designs on the boy's mother and her recently acquired millions?

DCI Martin Phelps and his team are back together just in time to take on the case – one that starts off as a possible kidnapping but soon descends into something even more sinister …

As the investigation exposes the complexities of family relationships, another long-standing mystery is solved – all while Martin and his colleagues anxiously await the results of a major police review that may result in them losing their jobs …

The DCI Martin Phelps Series

Wonny Lea

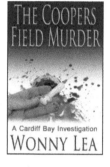

For more information about **Wonny Lea**

and other **Accent Press** titles

please visit

www.accentpress.co.uk